"What part of 'just be ready' sounded like 'run away'?" Karin yelled.

"Hey," Dave said. "If you'd let me in on your plans before you went charging out, I would have told you my gun was in the car."

"And there's a handy two-by-four next to the basement door, so don't aim those baby blues at me. You didn't have to leave me hanging!" Okay, maybe she wasn't being fair. She was the one who'd come out alone, preferring to handle things her way. But he *had* led the thugs here.

"You took care of them well enough."

She hadn't wanted to take care of them at all. Not like that. "They'll be back. So if you'll excuse me, I need to go think about that."

"You're kidding," he said with surprise. "You can't stay here and wait for them."

But she had nowhere else to go, not unless she pulled out one of her precious fake IDs.

Not unless she was willing to abandon what Ellen had died to give her.

Dear Reader,

I was one of those good little girls. Really. I thought if I told a lie, my young world would end, and that my existence depended on the Everlasting Goodness of Me. (It made sense at the time.) But the heroine of this book, Karin Sommers? Her growing-up years depended on just how well she could lie, deceive, playact and lead adults around by the nose.

You get the idea. If there were ever two people with more disparate personal foundations...

Okay, part of me is hoping that you won't notice that Karin is so real to me that I just referred to her as an actual person. But the rest of me hopes that in reading this book, you'll experience the same sense of discovery I did as I wrote it. The "Oh, wow, this is what it would be like..." experience. As well as the profound sense of pride in Karin as she discovers who she really is. And those con game details that I so gleefully worked up? Just don't tell my mom, okay?

Doranna

DORANNA DURGIN

Survival Instinct

Published by Silhouette Books

America's Publisher of Contemporary Romance

SILHOUETTE BOOKS

ISBN 0-373-51399-2

SURVIVAL INSTINCT

www.SilhouetteBombshell.com

Printed in U.S.A.

Books by Doranna Durgin

Silhouette Bombshell

Exception to the Rule #11
Checkmate #45
Beyond the Rules #59
Survival Instinct #85

*Hunter Agency stories

Silhouette Books

Femme Fatale
"Shaken and Stirred"

DORANNA DURGIN

spent her childhood filling notebooks first with stories and art, and then with novels. After obtaining a degree in wildlife illustration and environmental education, she spent a number of years deep in the Appalachian Mountains. When she emerged, it was as a writer who found herself irrevocably tied to the natural world and its creatures—and with a new touchstone to the rugged spirit that helped settle the area and which she instills in her characters.

Doranna's first fantasy novel received the 1995 Compton Crook/Stephen Tall award for the best first book in the fantasy, science fiction and horror genres; she now has fifteen novels of eclectic genres on the shelves. Most recently she's leaped gleefully into the world of action romance. When she's not writing, Doranna builds Web pages, wanders around outside with a camera and works with horses and dogs. There's a Lipizzan in her backyard, a mountain looming outside her office window, a pack of agility dogs romping in the house and a laptop sitting on her desk—and that's just the way she likes it. You can find a complete list of titles at www.doranna.net along with scoops about new projects, lots of silly photos and a link to her SFF Net newsgroup.

I made up some of the tech in this novel, but from the looks of things it'll be real by the time the book reaches the shelves.... But yes, there *is* a water tower on North Payne Street!

Thanks to:
The Things That Go Bang regulars
The Alexandria & Scotch Connection
Greg Davis, Associate Chief Medical Examiner,
Commonwealth of Kentucky

Chapter 1

Karin Sommers's Journal, March 12

Dear Ellen—
Happy birthday. I miss you terribly, and I'm sorry
you're dead.
    I wish it weren't my fault.

February 17, previous year

Karin Sommers twisted in the front seat of the Subaru
Outback, reaching for the bag of pretzels perched precariously
on the clothes crammed behind her. Every nook of the car held
the carefully chosen belongings she and her older sister, Ellen,
had extracted from Karin's small California apartment. Ex-

tracted, piled on and driven casually away as if it weren't the biggest breakout since the Birdman of Alcatraz.

But she wasn't looking at her things, and she wasn't really looking for the pretzels. She looked back at the dizzying curve of road disappearing into the darkness behind them. The sign for the Kentucky state line was already hidden behind a jut of construction-cut mountainside. The coal truck riding their bumper quickly lost ground as they hit this latest series of severe asphalt curlicues.

Have we made it yet?

"You'll get carsick if you keep that up." Ellen plied the wheel expertly, familiar with the abrupt and narrow Appalachian roads. "Besides, we're two-thirds of the way across the country. If dear old stepdad had a clue where you were, he'd have been breathing down our necks a long time ago."

Karin settled back into place, smoothing the seat-belt strap as she reached for the warm pop in the cup holder. Sleet rattled against the windshield, then eased into spattering rain. "We're not safe yet. If it occurs to him that you and I have been faking estrangement, he's going to come looking."

"He doesn't care about me," Ellen said calmly. "He'd never even consider I could have the nerve to help you break away."

Have we made it yet? Am I almost there?

But Karin had to grin at her sister—so alike in looks and close in age that they were often taken for twins, so dissimilar in temperament. They were still sisters at the core. They watched out for each other as they could, right up until the point Ellen had declared herself outta there and their stepfather Gregg Rumsey had declared himself glad to see her go.

And Karin had stayed behind with Rumsey, trapped by years of control and entanglement in scams and petty schemes and thievery—starting in her childhood, taking advantage of her steady nerve, cultivating and training her natural ability to lie, cry on cue and play her mark. She'd had no way to understand the unusual nature of her life. By the time she had understood the true consequences of her actions, by the time she'd realized she hadn't merely been playing games and skirting legalities at no real cost to anyone else, she had been irreparably tangled in her stepfather's activities. And when she'd wanted to quit anyway, he'd had plenty to hold over her head. *Quit,* he'd told her, *and you go straight to jail.*

And I can return the favor, she'd retorted—but had pretended to settle back into their routine. Unlike Rumsey, she hadn't been gathering incriminating evidence. She had no doubt he'd play the legal system as easily as he played his marks, and that she'd end up in jail while he went free.

Still, she'd always intended to leave. She'd contacted Ellen on the sly, made plans, skimmed Rumsey's takes and bided her time. She'd limited her involvement to the Robin Hood scams—steal from the rich, pay the bills, squirrel away some of the take. And that had been enough. It had worked. Until now, when Rumsey had finally crossed her admittedly flexible line by killing an elderly couple who'd caught on to his latest investment scam. Until she'd suddenly wondered if this was the first time.

Until she had wondered if she might one day be just as disposable.

And then she and shy, nervous Ellen had finally colluded on her departure. Her breakout.

The car swooped around another curve. On the other side of the guardrail, Pine Mountain plunged down to the Russell Fork in a drop steep enough to earn the area its nickname—

the Grand Canyon of the South. Under any other circumstances, it would be a place at which to stop and marvel and
snap endless touristy photos.

But there'd be no stopping just now. She and Ellen wouldn't
slow down until they reached the Blue Ridge area just west
of Roanoke. Ellen's new home after years in Alexandria.

Almost there.

Actually, another six or seven hours of driving to go. And
then she'd hide at Ellen's little farmhouse until she could
make her new life, using the money she'd taken from Rumsey.
Money she'd *earned.* She'd leave Karin Sommers behind and
become someone else. But still…she was so close. Seven
hours. Compared to the years it had taken to make the break,
compared to these past few weeks of heart-thumping stress…

Yeah. Almost there.

Karin laughed out loud, drawing Ellen's bemused gaze—
just for an instant, because in the darkness on these roads, no
one could dare more. "Just thinking about the look on his face
if he knew you'd helped me."

"Probably similar to the look he had when he first plugged
me into a scam and I threw up all over him," Ellen said drily.

Karin crunched into a pretzel bow. "I only wish I'd thought
of that. But no, I had to make it fun. A great big game."

"It wasn't your fault," Ellen said, unexpected fierceness in
her voice. "You're the one who got us through those years,
by playing his games." She slowed the car, flicking off the
brights as the sleet came down heavy in a sudden gust.

"Hey," Karin said, deliberately light in tone. "We should
thank the old bastard. If he hadn't taught me so well, I
wouldn't have been able to play *him* these past weeks."

Ellen snorted. "Don't give him any credit. If he hadn't

been jerking us around, you'd not only have finished high school, you'd have been grabbing all the drama club's juiciest parts. You're a natural."

"Tsk." Karin waved a pretzel in false admonition. "He 'saved my ass from jail' too many times to count. He told me so, after all, so it must be true—*look out!*"

Ellen spit a panicked expletive as a deer exploded into motion from the darkness. She hit the brakes, cranking the steering wheel as they spun over the narrow, slushy asphalt. The car slid sideways, its four-wheel drive futilely hunting a grip—and then gently bumped to a stop against the guardrail.

Karin glanced warily out her side window. A pitch black night couldn't stop her imagination from filling in the details of the steep drop to the river below. Damn good thing she was already sitting down; her knees were weak as water. She found Ellen sitting frozen, her hands clenched around the steering wheel so tightly they trembled. The windshield wipers slid across glass in a precise dance; the deer was long gone.

But we're okay.

When Ellen's shaky gaze connected with Karin's, a multi-hued gray so like her own, Karin deliberately looked over the side again and drawled most dramatically, "Cree-ap."

Ellen snorted, shaking herself free of her frozen fear. "That would *so* have sucked."

Karin looked down on the mess of pretzels and warm soda in her lap and lifted her hands away in disgust. "Cree—"

Neither of them had time to scream as the coal truck came rumbling around the curve and slammed into the back of the car.

Chapter 2

Karin Sommers's Journal, March 13

Dear Ellen,
I love this little dormer. I love the way it feels like a place where only you and I go. I love the way it looks out over the driveway and the yard, letting me watch from high shadows.

Things are so different here…I can see why you came here to think through your life. To make changes. I guess that's my job now, but my decisions still seem a long way off.

It's easier to think about the work. I just finished tilling a truckload of manure into the garden. Mostly I used the tiller, but you know…there's something fulfill-

ing about doing it by hand. Almost…meditative. I bet
you felt the same. Did you get blisters, too? And here I
thought I'd gotten hardened up over the past year. I fit
into your clothes, my hair's as long as yours, and I've
got your signature down pat. I even let my damned
eyebrows fill in. I'm not the woman Rumsey made of
me, not anymore.

I have to say he taught me one thing, though…how to
survive. You do what it takes, right? So here I am in the
middle of Blue Ridge country, learning to be a country
girl. And I'm damned good at it if I say so myself.

Ah, lookie here. Your dog is barking. I'm not expecting anyone (as if I ever *am*). And it's a city car, with a good-
looking city guy. You forget to tell me about someone?

I don't think he likes dogs. The door's open…no, I
really don't think he likes dogs. "Cautious" would be
kind. I'm not laughing, really!

Okay, yeah…I am.

He remembered her as a quiet woman, someone suited to the
solitude of these aged, rolling ridges north of Roanoke if not,
perhaps, to the hard work of keeping up a little homestead
with a small, rolling pasture, freshly turned soil for a garden
in the flat area near the house and a chicken coop beyond. He
couldn't see the goats, but he heard them well enough.

And then there was the dog.

Dave Hunter spent his days tracking down children, facing
predatory human monsters and occasionally lending a hand
in his family's privately funded security business. He'd seen
the darkest alleys, the filthiest warehouses, the slimiest side

of human nature. He'd built a reputation for success, for his commitment to finding children and for his unyielding values.

But he didn't like dogs.

This was a mutt, a big one. He stood between Dave and the house, head lowered slightly, tail tight and high. He had a long white-and-reddish coat and a broad, handsome head with alert ears, and he looked very much in command. Dave stood beside the car and eyed the wraparound porch with some longing.

As if you're going to give up after coming all this way to talk to this woman.

Dave looked back at the dog. "That's enough now. Go away." In spite of the cool day—a perfect day, actually, with a bright sky and the sun just warm enough to offset the mild breeze—he felt sweat prickle between his shoulder blades.

The dog didn't appear to be sweating. The dog appeared to know just exactly who was in control. He growled softly.

Maybe she's not home.

And maybe Dave didn't have all the time in the world. Maybe a little boy's life hung in the balance.

Looking the dog directly in the eye, Dave took a step forward.

The creature dove for his ankle, gave his pants leg a good yank and backed off again before Dave could even react. Dave froze, heart pounding loud and fast. The damned dog probably knew it, too.

"Standing still is the first smart thing you've done."

The voice was quiet, a smooth whiskey alto. Dave moved only his eyes to find her—there she was, leaning against the porch post with her arms crossed and no apparent sympathy for his predicament. He looked back at the dog. She made a tsking noise and said, "Stop meeting his eyes. You're challenging him."

He looked away, reluctantly so. The growling quieted. Off balance and not used to it, he should have known to keep his mouth shut. "Will he really bite?"

"What do you think?" Amusement colored that voice. He didn't remember it being so low, so completely self-assured. In fact, he remembered a woman who often hesitated before speaking.

"C'mon," he said, and his desperation leaked through. "Cut me a break." And then at her silence, he jerked his gaze over to her and said, "You don't remember me, do you?"

"Remind me," she said.

He fought to regain some composure. A little dignity, perhaps. "Dammit, call him off."

She might have smiled. Hard to tell from here. Without moving, she said, "Dewey," and the dog trotted back toward the porch. But he sat in front of the house, with his uncompromising gaze on Dave.

With effort, Dave looked away. *Don't challenge him.*

He looked at Ellen Sommers instead—and abruptly blinked, confused by the sudden impression that this wasn't Ellen at all. Except…she had Ellen's face, a lean face with a wide, expressive mouth. She had Ellen's hair falling below her shoulders, the same deep brown with honey highlights. And she had Ellen's dark, expressive brows—not plucked thin to be fashionable. But in the few conversations he'd had with Ellen Sommers, she'd kept her face smooth of expression. Now she looked at him with one eyebrow quirked in question.

No. In demand.

Well, country living certainly seemed to suit her, top to bottom. Before, she'd seemed thin. Now her jeans hugged an athletically lean figure, and under a sloppy hooded sweatshirt her baby-doll T-shirt showed a strip of toned belly without quite showing her belly button.

He wondered if she was an innie or an outie.

He closed his eyes, and breathed out slowly. "Dave Hunter," he said. "I spoke to you about fourteen months ago."

"Did you?" She said it negligently, as if it wouldn't have mattered one way or the other. Okay, now *that* stung. If she didn't remember him specifically, surely she'd remember why they'd spoken.

"About the missing boy? Terry Williams? It was right before you moved." Not that he'd had any trouble tracking her down. It was what he did, after all.

She hesitated. He took the opportunity to ease a few steps closer. Not so close as to set the dog off again, but close enough to see she did indeed have Ellen's eyes, a piercing gray-blue. Those distinctive brows drew together, leaving her with a disturbed expression. Finally she said, "Shortly after I moved here, I was in a car accident. I'm afraid there are some things from that period that I just can't remember. You seem to be one of them." At his surprise, she added a sardonic, "Don't take it personally. It was a pretty bad accident."

Held at bay by a mutt, lost for words before he even started...and a faint hope fast turning into a fading hope. If she didn't remember...

But he had to try, or it'd be Terry Williams all over again, lost and never found. "I do consultation work with various legal authorities—FBI, most often. Missing persons cases. Kidnapped children."

The eyebrow went up. "Not kidnapped adults?"

"These days," Dave said, somewhat reassured to hear the

familiar dry tone in his own voice, "kids can use all the help they can get."

Her eyes widened but went so quickly back to normal that he almost missed it. Her assertive stance softened slightly, and he didn't miss that, either. "I see. And you were asking me about—?"

Finally. "Terry Williams—an eight-year-old who disappeared in Melton Run Park. You were there, not far away. We discussed who you'd seen there, and you looked at some mug shots for me."

She nodded vaguely; he wasn't sure if that meant she remembered or simply that she understood. When she looked at him again, it was with such an intense expression that it took him unaware. "Did you find him? The boy?"

Ah. She really didn't remember. Regret tightened his chest. "No."

"I'm sorry," she said, and this time she wasn't sardonic or assertive or distant. Her honest response created a sudden connection between them, one strong enough to make Dave blink. And then it was gone, and she added, "But I don't know why you're here now. I do know you've interrupted my work and upset my dog, and that you'll gain nothing from it."

Upset her dog. Right. Even now the damn dog eyed Dave, looking for an excuse to start it up all over again.

But at last, they'd come to the point. "I'm here because I still think you might have seen something in the park that day. You might not even know it was of importance—"

"What does it matter now, if he's dead?"

"Because now seven-year-old Rashawn Little is missing. I think the same man has him, and I need your help to find him."

* * *

"You must be desperate." That's what Karin had said to Dave Hunter, but she might as well have said it to herself. Why else would she have let him on the porch, suggesting he have a seat on the picnic-table bench while she fixed some sun tea?

Yeah, she was desperate, all right. Desperate to pull off her Ellen role in front of someone who'd known Ellen. Not someone who'd known her long or well, but a trained investigator. A man who drank in details—and remembered them.

She'd seen his hesitation. He'd known she wasn't the same woman. She'd managed to overcome the doubt with pure brazen bluffing, but deep down he still knew. He'd figure it out if she let him stick around, and then he'd figure out there was a California warrant out for her arrest.

Problem was, she knew too well what it was like to be a child in trouble with no one to turn to.

Problem was…she couldn't afford to draw attention. To give Rumsey any excuse to contact her again—or to realize that Karin lived, in spite of the information the police had given him when he'd called after the accident.

A year ago, maintaining Ellen's identity wouldn't have been so much of a problem. Ellen hadn't known anyone here long enough to have close friends—and Karin had been careful to emulate every subtle thing Ellen had been. Finally she'd let the Karin side of her nature blend in. And she'd never intended to connect with anyone from Ellen's city life, people with whom Ellen had cut ties so sufficiently that no one even called her in the hospital.

You might have warned me, she told her sister. *All that time in the car, and you couldn't come up with one little word about something like this? About* someone *like this?* She

dropped a few ice cubes into a tall plastic cup—very classy—
and closed her eyes. Broad shoulders meant to carry a suit,
elegantly lean build, gold-glinting blond hair just long enough
to get mussed, expression all business…

At least, until he'd seen Dewey. She smiled, dropped ice
into a cup for herself and smiled again. He'd tried so hard to
look casual, standing there doing all the wrong things.

But her smile was gone by the time she returned to the
porch. She pulled Ellen's sweatshirt closer and leaned against
the house beside the bench on which Hunter sat. The bright
March sun wasn't enough to touch the chill of warning along
her spine. She couldn't afford the interest an investigation like
Hunter's could stir up. But she couldn't send him away with a
simple refusal; it would be like throwing away a boomerang.

If he wasn't the persistent type, he'd have gotten right back
into that car when Dewey Lake showed those capable teeth.

"Look," she said, finding just the right note of reluctance,
"I'd like to help you—"

"But you won't," he finished for her.

"I don't think you were listening." She kept her voice quiet.
She couldn't backstep all the way to Ellen-ness, not after the
greeting he'd gotten, but she could lean that way. "What
makes you think I can remember anything about that day?"

"I don't know," he said, and he sounded so reasonable,
sitting there on the hard picnic-table bench in his suit, that she
became immediately wary. "You could look at some pictures.
You could talk about it. Maybe you don't remember because
you haven't tried."

Karin's natural reaction was to snort. *Wouldn't it be nice
if the world worked that way. If only you try hard enough—*
She covered it by quietly clearing her throat. "I've never been

able to recall any of the things I forgot. And you might well imagine I've tried—there are things I *still* haven't been able to find since the move."

"Well," he said, and smiled in a most charming way, "that happens to all of us."

Karin didn't roll her eyes. Instead she let Ellen smile back, and decided that she'd just keep saying no. No, no, no…for as long as it took. Besides, that smile of his didn't charm her one bit. She knew when she was being played. She ought to. "It's been over a year," she said, and took a sip of tea. "What's gone is really gone. Even if I did remember a moment or two, I'd hardly be your best witness."

She hadn't realized his eyes were such a piercing ice blue, not until he turned them on her so directly. "I don't need a *witness*," he said, and he held everything in that gaze—the conviction, the determination…the commitment. "I need to find that little boy. I need your help to do it. *He* needs your help."

Holy crap. She'd been a kid in need, once. What if a man like this had been looking out for her then? Maybe Ellen would have stayed…maybe Karin would have made something of herself. Something more than living her sister's life. *If only for now.*

Dangerous thoughts. Regret only got in the way of survival choices.

And besides, they were only eyes. No matter the emotion behind them or how that emotion touched her…they were only eyes. And the eyes of a stranger at that.

Eyes that still watched her, waiting for reaction. For decision. *The decision was made long before you got here, Dave Hunter.*

That she didn't kick him right off the porch was Ellen's

doing. She restricted herself to the slightest shake of her head. In return she saw only a flicker of disappointment, followed close on by determination.

"Look," he said. "Let's give the subject a break. I've got to eat—why don't you come into town with me, have a late lunch?"

She took a deep breath. And she was about to shake her head, more emphatically this time, when an unfamiliar car came around the curve just beyond her house, moving slowly. "Cree-ap," she muttered. She took three long strides and tucked herself in behind the nearest porch post. It meant standing straight and tall—and it meant that Dave Hunter would give her away if he so much as asked her what the hell she was doing.

He didn't ask. He took a gulp of tea and rested his elbows on his somewhat spraddled knees, looking out over the little farm. Only when the car had moved out of sight did he say, "That was interesting."

"They don't belong here." As though that were explanation enough, she clicked her tongue at Dewey. It was enough to call the dog from his snooze, and she opened the screen door for him.

"Probably not." He'd straightened from his relaxed posture, setting the drink aside on the bench. "No dust on the car, that's for sure. Should I be grateful you didn't hide from—"

By then she'd followed Dewey inside the house, hesitating in the mudroom to slant the blinds. The first car, not a big deal, especially not when she'd scoped Dave out from the dormer before greeting him. But two strange cars on this road in the same day? This wasn't a main road; it wasn't even a shortcut between here and there. It was the kind of road on which Karin could recognize every car she saw.

She shouldn't have hesitated. By the time she turned away from the window, Dave Hunter had invited himself inside after her. There wasn't enough space for him to keep his distance; he was right up close when he trained those sharp eyes on her. "Ellen. What's going on?"

Some of the Karin in her sparked out. "You tell me," she snapped, and gave him a little push back, remembering only at the last moment to moderate the force of it. Ellen might well push, but she wouldn't shove.

But he didn't step back. He moved up on her, so quickly she didn't realize she'd given ground until she was already backed up against the washing machine. He didn't cage her in his arms, but she found herself just as trapped. Just as startled, looking up into his face with her mouth open in surprise.

In that instant, everything changed. She saw it hit him— saw his eyes widen slightly, his jaw hardening and his shoulders going tense beneath the perfectly tailored suit. The air between them solidified into something alive; it tingled off her skin. Her chest ached and—*breathe, Karin, breathe.*

He shook his head as though waking from a daze and shifted back slightly, a scant inch of relief.

Because a normal tone of voice felt oddly as if it would come out as a shout, Karin whispered again, "You tell *me*. How often do you think two strange cars travel this road?"

He didn't whisper, but his voice stayed low. "So you hid. Sure. Doesn't everyone?"

She shrugged. It was much more casual than she felt. The sweatshirt slid off her shoulder. "I like my privacy."

He gently tugged the sweatshirt back into place.

She closed her eyes and pretended not to notice. "They're looking for you, aren't they?"

He responded evenly. "It's just a car, Ellen."

Right, and this is just a conversation. Just any old conversation between two people who've just met and God, I can't believe how much I want to—

She overrode all those impulses to say, "I'm right, and you know it. You just won't admit it, in case you lose one last chance at my cooperation. Well, there *isn't* a one last chance."

"I can't accept that." But he turned away, leaving a tangible absence.

Dewey took this first opportunity to get between them. Karin put her hand on his head. "Did you see that slow crawl? They're looking for someone. They saw you on my porch, and they'll be back for you." *Or for me.*

He shook his head with finality. "I'm not exactly hard to find. There's no reason for anyone to come *here* looking for me. But…" He looked out the door, and his unfinished acknowledgment was clear enough.

So was the sound of a slowly approaching car. An instant later, Dewey growled. Dave Hunter muttered softly, "Son of a bitch."

Karin pushed past him to confirm she'd heard someone making the turn into the driveway. "Son of a bitch," she repeated, in a voice much sharper. "Dewey, let's go—basement."

"Basement?" Hunter asked.

"Damn straight, basement. I'm going to deal with these guys on my own terms." That meant scoping them out before they saw her. Not dealing with them at all wasn't much of an option, not with Dave's car in the driveway. She led Dewey through the kitchen, toward the little shelf-lined reading den in the front corner of the house. "You're welcome to come, if you don't mind getting that suit messed up."

"Your dog has already seen to the suit."

She gave a little laugh. "He told you not to come any closer." She pulled open the den's closet door even as she glanced out the window. The car had stopped behind Hunter's, and the occupants seemed engaged in conversation, but the driver already had his door open.

"Charming," Hunter said from behind as she reached down to the small rectangular rug on the floor of the closet, pushing aside winter clothing. "Your stairs are in your closet?"

"It's an old house." Karin teased a tab out from beneath the edge of the rug and when she pulled it, up came a big square of the floor. "It didn't come together all at once. And I'm not sure I'd call these *stairs*." More like a ladder. She'd had it put in shortly after she'd taken Ellen's name—and her house, and her dog, and all the rest of the things that came with her life. She might have picked up where Ellen had left off, but Karin never forgot she was a woman in hiding—a woman who might one day have to go on the run.

Having a rug-covered floor hatch suited her dry sense of humor. She told Hunter, "I'd rather you came down than stay out where you'll give them more to think about, but it's up to you."

Again, she'd surprised him. The car accident had changed her, all right...and it suited her.

Or maybe it just suited him.

He met her gaze, saw the impatience there. Reasonable impatience, given that they had only moments to get out of view. "You just want to keep an eye on me."

"You could say that." She crouched, knees open, and held her arms out. Damned if the big mutt didn't walk right up and put his front legs on her shoulders. She wrapped her arms around him and stood, staggering slightly under the weight. Undismayed, the dog wagged his tail.

And here Dave stood, looking at the dog. "Do you want me to—?"

She laughed, a short sound but with true amusement. "Do you really want to?"

Hmm. Maybe not.

But she didn't wait for a response backing down the ladder. For a moment, Dave hesitated—he had no reason to duck these men, and plenty of reasons to ask blunt questions of them. But as the crown of her sun-streaked hair disappeared into the dim hole, he found himself compelled to follow. He pulled the rug-topped door closed as he descended, and by the time he hit the uneven dirt floor, she'd put the dog down and left him to scent the air at the front of the basement.

Dave took in the lay of the basement—ceiling low enough so he had to duck the joists, a hodgepodge of pier supports, steel shelving and a big workbench along the back. Some of the walls were dirt; some were concrete block. The furnace and water heater sat up against a surprising stone interior wall, one that closed off a small room. Hand-set stone. Older than old.

But most importantly, there were two doors. One at the back corner, and another on the front.

Dave fought the sudden impulse to climb right back out and approach the men head-on. So far he'd kept a low profile as a special consultant in the FBI's investigation—in truth, the feebs were putting up with him. Don't make waves, he'd been told. And he needed to know more before he could define just what might make waves.

Ellen went to the front of the basement, where a dirt wall

ran next to the porch itself, offering a small crawl space. She looked back and gestured to him—*come on over*—and he did, just as the men mounted the steps to the porch. It was eavesdropping of a most creative sort.

Dave leaned close to Ellen. "You're sure a simple conversation wouldn't do the trick?"

One man went to the front door, and another to the mudroom; both knocked. She said, "Aren't you the trusting one?"

He muffled his short laugh. "Far from it. But I think you've got me beat. You're sure nothing's happened to you besides that car accident?"

She closed her eyes, took a sudden sharp breath…let it out slowly. "The accident was enough."

A second thought sobered him. "Your former boyfriend hasn't made any threats, has he?"

That drew her gaze, hard and sharp, the blue-gray a haunting shade in this dim light. He could have sworn she was going to say, "My former *what?*" But then she gave a short shake of her head. "Not that I know of."

"You didn't—" He stopped, cocked his head slightly. "Or maybe you did. Watch me when I first got here."

"Upstairs window." And then she held up her hand. *Listen.*

"I'm not sure this is the place," one of the men said, a gravel-toned voice full of doubt. "He said she was the mousy sort. This place…someone's *working* it."

"So maybe she hires out."

"He said she had a little money. What woman would live like this if she could afford a decent lifestyle?"

Dave didn't even have to be touching Ellen to feel her irritation. He had the uneasy feeling she'd turn out to be right after all—this visit had everything to do with his own arrival.

The second man immediately confirmed his guess. "Who cares why she's here? We're supposed to find her, and we have. Too bad we didn't beat Hunter to town, but we shouldn't have any trouble."

Ellen stiffened. She turned to Dave with a glare that should have cut him in half; it struck unexpectedly deep. He shook his head slightly, just enough to tell her he had no idea who they were.

Though he was getting one.

The first man gave a little snort. "No, she shouldn't be any trouble. That was the whole point of dating her, he said."

Ellen looked up at the porch with brows drawn, that wide mouth set in a hint of scowl. Dave leaned down, just enough to reach her ear, just enough to brush her hair. She'd been working that morning, all right; the salty scent of her skin tickled his nose just as her hair tickled his face. He murmured, "Do you know him?"

She drew back from him, gave him a look he couldn't decipher and finally shook her head. "Can't remember," she said, barely voicing the words at all. Just a hint of whiskey alto on the air.

The men argued for a few moments. Ellen abruptly pushed away from the wall, moving silently through the basement. "What're you—"

"I've heard enough." She picked a few gardening hand tools off the workbench—gloves, a trowel and a clawlike cultivator. "They'll be back if they don't talk to me now. At least this way I get to choose the moment."

"And you want me to just—"

"Watch my back." She raised an eyebrow. Expressive. "You can handle that, right?"

"Yeah, and I can also go out there and *ask*—"

She gave a sharp shake of her head. "I want answers, not confrontation."

He thought of how badly he needed his own answers. "I can—"

Apparently she wasn't in the habit of letting people finish what she thought would be stupid sentences. "Look, this isn't your choice. You may have brought these two down on me, but I'll decide how I deal with it."

Dave closed his eyes. He'd been in dim basements—some of them ominous, some of them stinking of the very person he'd hoped to find alive. And he'd dealt with irate witnesses. But not once had he envisioned himself lurking in a basement while the irate witness went out to play some sort of game with the questionable gentlemen who'd come to find her.

But she was right. It was her home...her choice. And maybe, just maybe, she'd get answers that they wouldn't give him. *Watch it, Hunter. Don't put her at risk for those answers.* That wasn't how he worked. He opened his eyes to find her impatient and somehow even less like the Ellen he remembered.

"I'll let you know if I want a hand," she told him. Still softly, as had been all their conversation. Still very aware of the men on the porch—who now banged on the mudroom door hard enough to make their true intentions clear. Ellen told the dog to wait and then told Dave, "Just be ready."

And with that she marched to the nearest door, leaving him with a plethora of unanswered questions, a definite sense of skewed reality, his hands wishing for the weight of the Ruger he'd left in the car. *Ready for what?*

To judge by the purpose in her stride, he was about to find out.

Chapter 3

Karin paused at the basement's side door, hefting the hand cultivator. She stuffed the worn leather gloves in her front jeans pocket and the trowel into her back pocket, and she glanced back at Dave Hunter. Assessing him.

She needed him to wait, but she also wanted the backup if things went badly. She wasn't sure if he'd do either.

He stood in the filtered light, the posture of a man who was fit, who knew himself and knew what he could do. But she didn't need him barging into the discussion, not when she still might chase these fellows off without too much fuss.

Not a very big chance. But still a chance.

He shifted his weight back. He'd wait, then. And in the end, he'd do what everyone did—serve their own best interests. She turned away, hesitating just long enough to swipe her fingers along the dirty windowsill and smear the dirt across her cheek, tugging a few strands of hair loose from her low ponytail.

When she walked out the door, she put on an air of distraction. A woman at work, thinking about frost dates and soil preparation and just how many zucchini would that one plant produce, anyway? She walked uphill toward the porch steps, for the moment still hidden from the men—but only for a moment. They moved heavily down those concrete porch steps; they had none of Dave Hunter's lightness of foot.

Too much bulky muscle.

She took a deep breath. God, they were big. And though she knew how to take care of herself, she was no wonder woman. She talked and flirted her way out of trouble. And even if she'd done fine when she'd had to get physical, she'd always known Rumsey was there.

If nothing else, Rumsey had known how to protect an investment.

And there. Now they'd spotted her. They stopped at the bottom of the steps and she slipped into her role. She started, raising a hand to the base of her throat as Ellen had often done when confounded. "I didn't know—" She pressed her lips together as Ellen might have done, too. "Can I help you?"

The two exchanged glances. At eye level, they turned out to be a Frick and Frack pairing—one swarthy, wavy black hair slicked back in…jeez, was that some updated version of a mullet? The gangster mullet. Great. The other fellow had the look of an ex-boxer, nose and ears damaged, his hair in a dull brown crew cut. It made his head look like a pasty football.

Do not underestimate the pasty football.

They made their tacit decision—yes, she was the right one— and the mullet-haired one said, "Barret wants to talk to you."

"I'm sorry…I don't think I know—"

The ex-boxer snorted. "He said you wouldn't want to come."

"Look," she said carefully. "I was in an accident. There's a lot I don't remember. I don't know who Barret is." And dammit, she didn't.

Although whoever Barret was, Ellen had come to his attention because of Dave Hunter.

"Doesn't matter," said the ex-boxer, both to his partner and to Karin. "Barret wants to talk to you. So let's go. He said you could pack a bag." He looked her up and down, gaze hesitating at her artful smudge of dirt and then again where the breeze caressed her exposed stomach, and his lip lifted slightly.

She couldn't even begin to pretend that the rising goose bumps were a byproduct of that breeze. These men weren't here to talk. They were here to fetch her to Barret, and they were already bored. Still, she got the distinct impression that they'd been given a hands-off directive. The ex-boxer had sneered at her appearance…but not leered.

"I can't go," she said, hunting for strategy, finding nothing. Damn, these guys looked bigger every moment. And Barret, whoever he was, sounded like a man used to getting what he wanted.

"I can't go," she repeated, a little louder. Just to make sure Dave Hunter knew exactly what was going on here. *Just be ready,* she'd told him. If Ellen's memories really mattered to him, he'd try to protect them—and, by default, her. She gestured with the cultivator. "I can't miss the planting season." She cocked her head, pretending she didn't see the impending escalation of the situation. *Saint Arthelais, this potential kidnap victim could use a little help here.* Thanks to Rumsey's habit of creating absurd saints for his own purposes, she'd made a study of the real ones. She knew just who to invoke, if perhaps not as reverently as she might. "Can't he just call me?"

The ex-boxer rolled his eyes. "Not gonna happen."

Oh, Ellen, why didn't you warn me?

As if she'd had the time.

Karin struggled to contain her resentment, channeling it into Ellen's wary fear. "I'm sorry," she said, lifting her chin slightly, a gesture opposite to her own habit of looking up from beneath her brow. "I don't know you and I don't know your boss and I want you to leave now." If Dave Hunter didn't take *this* hint, he was deaf and dumb—most particularly, dumb.

"Let's go," the ex-boxer said, but he spoke to his companion, jerking his head toward their car. "We're wasting time. She can pick up some things when she gets there."

Run, Karin, run. Surely they wouldn't have her stamina. And they'd never find her once she hit the woods—

Karin blinked down at her biceps, suddenly engulfed in the ex-boxer's grip. Not so slow after all. And it *hurt,* dammit.

Karin snarled—her own voice, her own words. "I said *no!*" She tightened her fingers around the cultivator as she jerked against his grip, feinting toward the obvious target with her knee. He looked smug as he straightened his arm, pushing her out of reach and leaning forward a little to do it.

Not so smug as she whipped the cultivator up and buried it into the side of his face. *Oh God.* Blood spurted from somewhere near his eye. As he screamed, high and thin and disbelieving, he wheeled away from her and jerked the cultivator out of her hand.

In his eye. Into his cheek, into the side of his nose—

Oh God.

His buddy leaped to reclaim her, his fist raised for a blow—

and then hesitated. Karin had only an instant to register the blur of white and red fur before Ellen's dog—*her* dog now— launched himself at the man's forearm.

Not a trained attack dog, no. But a dog who knew how to do battle, who regularly brought her groundhog and possum, undeterred by his own battle scars. The man scrabbled away as the ex-boxer hit his knees, his hands over his face to pluck at the cultivator with horror, still screaming. *"My eye! My fucking eye!"*

Somewhere inside her own horror, Karin realized the second man was hunting for a gun, hampered by the twist of his ugly sport coat as Dewey hung from his arm. She snatched the trowel from her back pocket and threw herself at him, slamming the dull blade viciously into his arm. It bounced right off the rock-hard muscle, but it must have hurt wickedly all the same because he roared and shook them both off. He took assessment of his partner and of Dewey crouched ready to spring again, his lips pulled back in a horrible snarl—and he pinned Karin with a furious gaze. Then he dragged his partner to his feet.

The ease with which he did it sent fear spearing through Karin's chest. He could have smashed her down and carried her one-handed to the car...and she'd *gone* for him. *Oh God.*

He hauled the ex-boxer back to the car, shoved him into the passenger seat and threw himself behind the wheel, backing up with such angry haste that the wheels spit gravel the whole way.

They'd be back. She might not know who Barret was or why the hell Ellen had been acquainted with him; she might not know any of the things Dave Hunter wished she did...but she knew these men would be back.

Well. At least one of them would be back. The other…

Karin looked down at her hands, found blood. And down at the cultivator, lying where the ex-boxer had dropped it…more blood. Back at her hands, to discover them shaking. *Of course they're shaking.* She'd never attacked anyone before. A slap, a shove, some bluster to establish she wasn't to be trifled with. Rumsey had wanted people's money? Fine. She'd done what she had to, what she'd *thought* she had to. She'd even learned to enjoy being good at it, and to ride the jazz of a good scam coming together. She sure hadn't hesitated to steal from Rumsey, to take her sister's name, to lie her way through life while she decided *what next*.

But she'd never hurt anyone before. Not truly. Not violently, with spattered blood and screams.

She had to get her rifle and get it loaded. She had to double-check her escape stash in the trunk, make sure that she could run at any moment if she had to, even if she didn't plan on it. This was her home, now—a life Ellen had given her, and which Karin didn't intend to waste. Still, she'd be ready.

But first she had to get this damned blood off her hands.

She crouched on jellied knees, wiping her hands on the lawn. Scrubbing them. Dewey came to her, uncertain; he ducked his nose under her forearm and flipped up, his not-so-subtle request for reassurance. Blood smeared his muzzle.

Crap.

When Karin stood, her knees steadier but a cold sick spot at her stomach and her thoughts still tumbling around from one extreme to another, she finally spotted Dave Hunter.

Over by his car.

Well, crap. She'd thought better of him than that.

He turned away from the road, heading for her with long strides—any faster and he'd have broken into a jog. "Gone for now," he said. "I thought for a moment there he was going to come back and ram my car, but…hey, are you okay?"

She didn't have any warning. It just happened. As soon as he pulled up in front of her, her bloodstained, grass stained, dirt stained hand whipped out and slapped him. Hard.

Unlike her actions of a moment earlier, it felt right.

He stared at her, stunned. Hurt, even, in those ice blue eyes. "What the hell—?"

"What part of 'just be ready' didn't you understand? What part of 'just be ready' sounded like 'run away'?"

"Hey," he said, and the hurt had sparked to anger, "if you'd let me in on your plans before you went charging out, I would have told you my gun was in the car."

"And there's a handy two-by-four next to the basement door, so don't aim those baby blues at me. You didn't have to leave me hanging, especially since you brought them to this party." Okay, maybe she wasn't being quite fair. She was the one who'd come outside alone, preferring to handle things her way. But the feel of the cultivator sinking into flesh made her scrub that hand against her jeans again, and he *had* brought them here.

Even if you could never really call those eyes "baby" anything.

He looked at her, his face going still as he processed the moment—her anger, and the turmoil beneath. His shoulders relaxed slightly. "I saw the size of those guys. I think the two-by-four would have lost. Besides, I wanted to get between them and their car in case they dragged you off." He tipped his head, not so much in inquiry as in observation. Maybe even dry humor. "You took care of them well enough."

She hadn't *wanted* to take care of them at all. Not like that.

"Dewey took care of them," she said shortly, bending to give the dog another tight hug. His tail thumped. "And they'll be back. So if you'll excuse me, I need to go think about that."

"You're kidding," he said, blunt in his surprise. "You can't stay here and *wait* for them."

But she had nowhere else to go, not unless she abandoned what Ellen had died to give her. Rumsey would still have all his feelers out for her, for *years* he'd have his feelers out for her. Let him figure out that she lived, and he'd rat her out in an instant.

And that meant she couldn't simply leave. In fact, she couldn't do anything out of the ordinary for Ellen.

Dave shifted his weight, hip-shot and out of place on her lawn. He looked like a model who'd been torn from a catalog, not someone who should be in her life. Not before her escape from Rumsey, not after. "Look," he said. "You're right. I brought them. I'm here to save a child, and I'll never be sorry for that. But I'm sorry they followed. I can find you a safe house until this is over."

She'd *had* a safe house until he'd gotten here. "You don't get it," she told him, only then realizing that she'd totally lost her Ellen-ness. Too late to go back now; maybe he'd rightly chalk the change up to the shock of it all. But it rattled her; she couldn't remember losing character before. "This *is* over. I can't help you. I don't have the memories you need." Literally.

"You haven't even tried."

She stood, letting her hand trail off the dog's ear. She couldn't help but sound tired. It was a chance to ease back into character. "It's been a year. What I've lost…I've lost."

Too true. Just not in the way he thought.

In fact, his expression glinted with stubborn refusal to believe her. She forestalled the impending argument. "Who is this guy, anyway? Barret? What's he got to do with me?" And then as something changed in his face, she added, "Or maybe I don't want to know."

But she did.

His face still stung from her slap. He relaxed only with effort, with his body still pounding at him to finish a fight he'd never really started. She was right enough; he'd left her to it. Not by design, but it hardly mattered. The most he'd done was release the dog. Also not really by design; he'd been headed for his car. So she'd been left alone, and first she'd softened into the woman he'd met a year before, and then she'd—

Wow. Boy, had she.

Ellen Sommers. Who'd have thought it?

They said sometimes head injuries caused a change in personality.

She dropped her chin, looking at him from beneath those expressive brows in a way that deepened the gray of her eyes. He recognized an ultimatum when he saw it. "Barret Longsford," he said, "is the son of a senior senator, being groomed to take his mother's place. He's also a player. He likes money, he likes power...he likes to get his own way."

"And he likes little boys? I dated a man who likes little boys?"

"Likes them and hates them," Dave said, unable to help a flinch—there, at the corner of his eye where it always seemed to come out—at the thought of Terry Williams. He did his damnedest to make sure his cases didn't end like that. "The FBI profiler thinks the perp is killing himself."

She looked a little baffled, and the ultimatum turned to a

faint knitting between her brows. "That just doesn't seem—
I mean, I just can't imagine myself dating a man like that."

Dave shook his head. "He's fooling a lot of people, and he's
doing it every day."

"And you're sure I—?"

"I'm sorry. Yes."

"Doesn't sound like my type," she muttered, and gave him
a deliberate glance. An up-and-down glance.

Good God. The hair on the back of his neck stood up.

It came only as a second thought that she'd done it on
purpose. Manipulating him.

Oh, yeah, Ellen Sommers had changed all right.

She moved on before he could call her on it. "I still don't
remember any of it. And why haven't the Feds grabbed him?"

He grimaced, a fleeting expression. "You think it's easy to
close in on someone with his influence?"

The dog decided Dave wasn't part of the problem and
ambled over to the shade cast by the porch, flopping down to
maintain his alert watch from there. Ellen let him go; her
narrowed gaze stayed pinned to Dave—and then she lifted her
head with dawning understanding. "No one else believes you."

He did little to hide his annoyance, both because she was
right, and because she'd figured it out at all. "They can't
afford to believe me. Not with the little evidence we've got."

"But you know better," she said flatly.

He did. He was the only one who'd received a phone call
from Barret Longsford, a condolence call for Dave's failure
to find Terry Williams in time. On the surface, a perfectly
normal call, made by a man with political aspirations who'd
been questioned simply because, like Ellen, he'd been in the
park the day Terry disappeared. But his voice…

Something in his voice had chilled Dave on the spot. He'd made the required polite small talk, all the while his mind racing, trying to make connections…

He couldn't. Not then, not now. Not the solid connections necessary to push an investigation, not when the feebs had already been warned to tread lightly—and when they were just putting up with him after his failure.

Good health insurance, good retirement benefits, a chance to keep jobs about which they were otherwise passionate…Dave didn't blame them for their caution.

But Dave paid for his own bennies. He had nothing to lose. *Nothing but an already damaged reputation.*

Ellen waited, more patiently than before, and he nodded. "I know better. And you're my chance to prove it. You were with Barret the day Terry was taken from Melton Run Park. You know his habits, his emotional buttons, his private hangouts. You might well not remember, but somewhere in your head are all the details I need. Because Barret Longsford has Rashawn Little."

Ellen stirred uneasily—and then she winced, looking down at her bruised arm in surprise. The man who'd grabbed her hadn't been gentle. When she looked at Dave again, she left her eyes in shadow. But her voice was resolute. "Then you'd better get back to the city and find him," she said. "Because I can't do anything to help you."

Chapter 4

I remember my funeral. Closed casket, of course.

It should have been about you, Ellen. Your name being spoken, your life honored. Instead it was all about me. The platitudes, the niceties…the tears. And a few people who couldn't see past the bruises the accident left on me to notice it wasn't you at all. Of course, I told them I'd broken facial bones. No point in taking chances.

The cop was about me, too.

I was so caught up in it all. Losing you *hurt*. More than grief…guilt and an unbearable sense of *wrongness*. It was wrong that you died, helping me run from Rumsey. It was wrong that you didn't even have your own funeral, your own headstone. God, yes, it hurt. The cop noticed, though I didn't see him until he stepped up and took my elbow. I suppose he thought I was going to faint. Maybe I was.

He was nice enough. He asked me about the accident. He asked if I'd known you were wanted.

(That would be me, again. The wanted one.)

I couldn't believe it. Since when? Rumsey knows how to cover his tracks. I mean, sure, the locals knew we were active, just not *how* active. But he knew how to play them, tossing just enough dirt their way to keep himself useful and harmless.

But it looks like he wasn't careful enough. Maybe my escape rattled him. But somewhere along the line, the cops must have gotten close—and he pointed the finger at me.

That bastard.

I don't even know what I've done. The cop wasn't talking. So I guess it was bad enough. You know, I had planned to be me again. I planned to give you back what's yours. Your name. Your own headstone, for God's sake. But now it's just about staying out of Rumsey's way until he doesn't care anymore. Now I'm Ellen...at least long enough to find out what I've "done." And to hope the statute of limitations is...*limited*.

Crap.

Well, you'll have your headstone one day. I've already made arrangements. When I'm beside you, they'll swap the headstones. Then things will finally be right again.

But until then, I'm you. Even if poor Dave Hunter can't understand why Ellen Sommers isn't even willing to try.

* * *

Karin closed the journal, her hand lingering over the sturdy leather binding.

No cheapo little diary for her letters to Ellen, oh no. Deep burgundy leather over thick, sensual pages, a blank book already half filled with her impossibly tiny, impossibly tidy handwriting. A book she shouldn't even be keeping, given the risks of it…but a book she couldn't stop herself from writing if she'd tried. Her final connection to Ellen.

She shouldn't have taken the time today. She had decisions to make and livestock to feed. But the book had drawn her— the day's events gave her reason to think of Ellen. Of the funeral. Of her new life here, now threatened.

Anyway, the rifle was up here. So were the cartridges. And from here Karin could look out over the driveway, watching Dave Hunter refuse to leave while she went about her business. Which—aside from sending a quick "just in case" e-mail to Amy Lynn, the neighbor who swapped chores with her—meant double-checking her retreat options and varied stash of IDs.

Pack a suitcase, Dave Hunter had said. If only he knew. She was packed and ready to go, but not with him. If she could help with this investigation, she would…and she half wished she could. But putting herself into the middle of it when she had nothing to offer…nope, not in the plan.

Karin slipped the journal into her big leather courier bag, next to the lining pocket she'd created for her IDs. She slung the strap over her shoulder and picked up the .22 rifle, heading down to the main floor to deposit her things by the door.

At the rumble of a male voice, she discovered Dave Hunter on the porch bench, yellow pad of spiky-scribbled notes balanced on his knee as he spoke into the phone. Tea sat on the bench beside him, condensation trickling down the glass and a blue steel and black composite semiautomatic pistol looking incongruous beside it. *Ruger.* The porch wind chime stirred only enough for a trill of notes, then silenced again.

He didn't notice her. Because surely if he had, he'd have lowered his voice. His peeved, impatient voice. "I don't know how long, Owen," he said, rubbing the back of his neck with his hand. "Does it matter? After that business in Pittsburgh and Kimmer Reed, I think I've earned enough family player points to get myself a safe house for as long as I need it."

Owen, whoever he was, must have said something conciliatory. Dave sighed. "Ribs are ribs…they take a while to heal. Collarbone's taking a while. Wouldn't set properly…I don't know. No—no, I—"

Interesting. Family player points. And someone who not only interrupted this strong, straightforward man, but who got away with it. *Older brother.*

"Okay, I hear you. It's not gonna happen, but I hear you. Now—that safe house?" He straightened on the bench, closing his eyes with evident relief at the response even as he winced, rotating his shoulder without lifting his arm. "Good. Great. Thanks. I'll let you know more when I have it." He closed his phone and tipped his head back against the siding. She watched him, resting her eyes on his profile—a nose for which the word *aquiline* had been invented, and a jaw angled sharply from ear to chin. Misleadingly, really, given the width of it. Maybe that was why he had those little parentheses of dimples that lay quiescent in repose.

They'd be there all the time when he got a little older, she

decided. It would be a nice look. Mature without being weath-
ered. One of her favorites.

For what it was worth.

Rumsey supplied her with the answer to that. *Absolutely
nothing*. Wasn't cash, wouldn't save her hide, wouldn't catch
her an advantage. If anything, the opposite. It'd be too easy to
go *mmm, nice* and lose track of her priorities, especially the one
that said the sooner she separated from this man, the better.

Karin nudged the door with her foot, opening it farther. She
knew it would squeak; she counted on him to notice, whatever
deep thoughts ran behind those closed eyes.

Squeak.

His eyes flashed open, eerily, icily blue in the afternoon
light. His gaze landed unerringly on hers. She kept her voice
soft, but the words had no give to them. "Making plans?"

"Trying to." He placed the iced tea on the porch floor, tucked
the Ruger into his coat pocket. "Come out and talk to me?"

She came out, but she didn't sit down in the spot he'd made
for her. "Come out and be talked into something, you mean."

He didn't bother to deny it, though it did give him an instant's hesitation, a double take. Recognizing something other
than Ellen, not knowing what to do with it. "It doesn't really
matter what you remember. Longsford isn't going to let things
rest once they've gone this far."

She couldn't argue with that. "His errand boys sure didn't
seem to be empowered to consider it."

"And that means you must know something that can
damage him—something that can help me."

She dropped her head to look up at him. "Or it means he
thinks I know something. Or maybe he just doesn't want me
spilling the beans on his other endeavors. What did you call

him? A player? Likes his money, likes his power? He's probably got plenty of things he doesn't want me to talk about."

"It doesn't matter what he's protecting. We've got to get you somewhere safe until I work this thing through."

"We're agreed on that," she muttered, knowing full well that his concept of *safe* had nothing to do with hers.

He looked up at her, hope showing in his eyes. "Then you'll come with me now. I've got a place just outside Alexandria—"

"*Now?* You think I can just walk away from all this?" She gestured around the yard, realizing it would mean nothing to him. The animals and the garden were half hidden beyond the trees and the hill behind the house.

He didn't back down. In fact, he stood up, moving in on her until she retreated to the screen. Not intimidating…just *close.* Close enough to take in all the personal things. The scents, the small white scar in his brow nearly hidden in the blond hair, the faint gust of breath on her lashes. She should have been annoyed or offended or concerned. She wasn't. Instead, a smile lurked at the corner of her mouth.

"We think he keeps them alive for a while. Long enough to manipulate and control. And that means I've still got a chance to find Rashawn—but I can't risk scaring Longsford into moving too soon. And you're—" He blinked. "You're *smiling.*"

Karin glanced down, as if she could see her own mouth. "And you…you're *close.*"

It startled him. He looked at her, he looked at himself. Then he said, "Huh." As in, *look at that.*

She didn't ask him to move. He didn't. He lowered his voice and he said, "I need you. I need your help."

She pitched her own voice to match, meeting his gaze with

a boldness she was quite certain Ellen had never shown. "And what if I don't remember anything? Ever?"

"Then you'll have tried. *We'll* have tried."

She didn't immediately respond. For the second time in a very short day they stood within inches of each other, fully engaged in their silence. That connection zinged to life again; Karin felt her smile fade.

Flirting was one thing. Appreciating…even flinging. She was no stranger to the semicasual fling, though she'd avoided the totally random fling and the formal fling. Semicasual suited her. Suited her life.

But her life had changed. And there was nothing casual about this moment.

She slid aside, leaving him in communion with the screen door. "Even if I leave, I can't just walk away. I've got to make arrangements."

He backed up until his calves bumped the porch seat, putting distance between them and rubbing one eyebrow as though he weren't quite sure what had just happened between them. "Then you'll come to the safe house? Revisit Melton Run Park?"

She gave him a shrug that looked like assent…and was anything but.

Like most marks, he saw what he wanted to see.

He tagged along on her chores. She set him to pumping water from the old-fashioned hand pump by the goat shed and left him to ration out alfalfa pellets for the two nanny goats, one of whom had a young kid at her side.

"You should wait—" he started, stopping only when she cocked her head at him, raising an eyebrow in clear *excuse me?* fashion. "I'd prefer to keep you in sight."

She snorted. Not at all genteel. "You think Dewey is going to sit quietly while anyone unfriendly approaches?" At his name, the dog waved his plume of a tail, on his way to the crest of the hill that overlooked the property.

He grunted, still pumping. "Not likely."

She unabashedly watched the play of muscle beneath his rolled up shirtsleeves. His jacket lay on the fence in a spot that no man familiar with goats would have risked, and the Ruger now sat in a belt holster. "If you think these guys are that much of a threat, then why aren't you calling your feeb friends?"

That got a wince. "I'm not high on their list right now." Still pumping, still looking good. "They'd send someone out, and then they'd shut me down."

"Wow." She kept her voice light. "You do lay all your cards on the table, don't you?"

He stopped pumping, straightened. "As opposed to re-assuring you that everything's under control, blah blah blah? That's just what I don't want to do. I want you to leave with me as soon as possible, not dawdle here over a billy goat."

"They're girls," Karin informed him primly. "And be nice to them—you'll be drinking Agatha's milk tonight at dinner."

He didn't seem to have a response for that. Just as well. She ducked into the shed, where she clattered around measuring pellets, tossing hay out the back for the beef cow and the sheep and nabbing a stool and then a milk pail. She tossed pellets into the ground feeder for Edith, and Agatha jumped to the raised milking stanchion in anticipation of her own meal and milking. Dave watched with a distracted fascination.

Off on the ridge, Dewey got to his feet, glanced back at Karin with another acknowledging wave of his tail, and trotted down toward the end of the wooded hill. "He's okay," Karin said, before Dave could ask. "Just a squirrel or maybe a snake."

"A snake," Dave said, quite abruptly checking the ground at his feet. "You're not just saying that to—"

"Copperheads," Karin said cheerfully. "Rattlers. We got 'em. And who is this Owen guy, anyway? Your brother?"

He lifted his head to stare at her. "How did you—"

"Because you talked to him like a brother," she told him briskly, pulling the pail out from under Agatha so the goat could finish eating in peace. The kid eased warily around her legs; Karin dipped a finger in the milk and gave it to him. "Like a big brother, actually. A big brother who can supply a safe house. Now there's something you don't find every day."

"No." Dave's features closed down. *No trespassing.*

Except she'd never been one to heed the signs. *Stay off the grass, no trespassing, members only*…those were for people who didn't bother to get around them. Karin did what she needed to accomplish her goals, signs or no signs. "What's that about?" she asked. "You two don't get along?"

He shook his head, short and sharp. "It's irrelevant."

"Oh-ho," she said, scratching the kid behind the ears and heading for the gate, a solid wood slat gate that stood up under any goat onslaught. "You think you can break into my life, bring along some goons, push me about lost memories I have no desire to regain, and then draw the line at answering a question or two? I don't think so." She felt not a moment's guilt that they weren't her memories. It was her life now, and that was enough. "Fair's fair, Mr. Hunter."

His impatience turned to outright annoyance. "That's the way it is. I'm the investigator, you're the witness. One of us asks questions, and the other answers."

She gave him one of Ellen's shrugs just to keep him off balance; made her voice into Ellen's softer tones. "Except you're not in the best position to make the rules, are you? You can't even go to the FBI—not until you have the proof you need. So really, whether I feel like helping depends on you."

Dave jerked his gaze to hers, eyes deep with disbelief. "A little boy's life—!"

"Exactly," she said. He stared; she added another shrug.

He shook his head. "You're not like you were," he said, out loud for the first time, though Karin knew he'd been thinking it. Just as well. Face the issue head-on.

"Yeah," she told him. "You might say it was a life-changing accident."

True enough.

He narrowed his eyes. "If you really don't want to cooperate, I can just walk away. Leave you here. Of course, I don't think you'd be alone for long."

Karin couldn't help it—she burst into laughter. *Not this man.* She knew that much already. "But you wouldn't."

He stared at her a moment longer and then broke away, muttering a series of indecipherable words under his breath. French words. Huh. He looked as if he wanted something to hit, but even in the height of the moment obviously realized he'd only break his hand on the stout post beside which he stood. He repeated the curse and turned back to her—hands on his hips, and completed the Ralph Lauren Polo model image with the simmering anger behind his glare. "Owen and I 'get along' just fine. I was supposed to go into the family business. I didn't. He hasn't given up."

And what, exactly, was the family business?

But she'd pushed enough for now. She didn't want him on

edge. She wanted him confident and comfortable with her.
She wanted him off guard and trusting...and she wanted that
space so he wouldn't see it coming when she walked away.

Chapter 5

Dave looked as though he didn't quite believe she'd let the conversation drop. He didn't move as she headed toward the house. She had to reach Amy Lynn and leave credit with her at the farm store…and she'd call the farm store and let them know this particular part-timer wouldn't be in to work this week.

For starters.

Myriad things ran across Karin's mind as she opened the gate, slipped through and latched it again. Which way to run. When to do it. She glanced at his pistol and considered the impulse to acquire it before she left.

He'd been watching her with silent and somewhat wary attention, but now his head snapped around, responsive to Dewey's angry bark.

Karin said, "It doesn't have to mean anything. We get kids cutting through now and then. They tease him sometimes."

Dave did a double take of horror. "They *tease* him?"

She knew it wasn't for Dewey's sake; he just figured the kids must be insane. "Shh," she said out loud. "I'm listening." Trying to gauge…yes. Dewey was heading for the house. "Probably not kids," she said out loud, and then did a quick count on her fingers. "If that guy dropped his pal off at the county hospital and came right back…"

"Timing's right?"

She nodded, met his gaze. "Especially if he opened the car door, shoved his friend out and turned around." She scowled in the direction of the house, a view obscured by winter trees. "He must think I'm an idiot, if he supposes I'm still there."

Dave cleared his throat. "You *are* still here."

She waved him off. "I'm *here*. That's different. Besides, even if I was there, I'd be *ready*." She spoke more glibly than she felt; the barking clearly came from the yard, and she could only hope Dewey's dislike of guns would keep him safe.

She suddenly realized that Dave had unsnapped his holster, already turning toward the house. "Hey," she said. "No!"

"You want to wait for him to find us?"

"I think I can keep that from happening." She took his hand, leading him on the narrow path between the barn and the currently unoccupied pigsty. He didn't resist, his fingers firm on hers; when they parted, she'd smell of gun oil.

When they emerged from between the two outbuildings, she gestured at the small, crooked building at the end of the path. The grass and weeds grew more heavily here, and the woods had crept up to enfold the building. At one corner, a stunted-looking tree embraced the narrow wood slats, drooping over the door. "There's the spot," she told him. She tucked the half-full milk pail behind the goat shed, behind the rain barrel there.

"Come on. Even if he comes looking, he'll never find us here."
Not to mention the way he'd pay for his snooping.

"He won't find us, because…there's an interdimensional
transport inside that building? It's damned sure not big enough
for hiding."

"Have faith," she said, and tugged his hand. He pulled free
to head for the shed door, one hand already reaching to brush
away the leaves.

"No!" she said sharply, relaxing somewhat as he heeded
her tone and stopped short. "Definitely a city boy."

"Mostly," he agreed, glancing behind them as the barking
grew louder. Closer. "Not always, but…it's been a while."

A year ago, Karin had been the city girl. Immersion learning—and one bad rash—had taught her this particular trick
of nature. "It's poison ivy. That door doesn't open anyway—
that's the beauty of it. Come on around back." She caught his
hand again and tugged.

This time he came less readily, still staring at the drooping
leaves. "That's a *tree*," he said, disbelief coloring his tone.

"It's a big happy bush," Karin told him, and tugged harder.
"I leave it alone and it leaves me alone. Come *on*—if that
guy's serious, he's going to find his way here fast enough."

He followed, if not happily. "I can handle him."

"Oh, be smart. Why bother?" She led him to the shadowed
back side of the building, barely accessible within a thatch of
staghorn sumac. A small door in the far corner had been
meant for chickens. "See? There's our way in."

"You're kidding." His voice held utter disbelief. "It's a pet
door. Do I look pet door–size to you?"

She gave him a deliberate, critical squint. It would be tight,
all right. Whipcord lean wouldn't do him much good when it

came to those shoulders. Still, there was a bright side. "You look…flexible."

"I—" He stopped, apparently truly without words, and said, "You go. Get out of sight." He looked over his shoulder, as if he expected their visitor to make an appearance at any moment. "I'll take care of—"

She gave his hand a yank to cut him off. "Really? Are you going to shoot him? That'd be nice and inconspicuous."

Noisy, that's what it would be. Noisy in an official way, a law-enforcement-looking-closely-at-Karin-being-Ellen way, when Karin-being-Karin had a California felony warrant hanging over her head.

"He's going to come back if he doesn't find us, too."

"Right. And then we'll be *gone*. So give me your jacket and pull off that holster and take your damn car keys out of your pocket if that's what it takes, but get in there!"

Definitely closer, that barking. Definitely heading this way.

Dave closed his eyes, said his bad word under his breath and shoved his jacket at her. She thought he'd lose a little skin. Definitely put a tear in that sleek shirt. "Let me go first—I can help."

"Fine," he grunted, unclipping his holster and moving faster as Dewey's furious barking marked their visitor's progress. "If I can't make it, you'll already be in."

"You'll make it," she promised him. And they might even both fit inside, hidden among the junk and old feed sacks barely visible through a proverbial knothole. She'd meant to get that door unjammed and get this place cleaned out, but now…

Just as well she hadn't.

She shoved the little door open with a terrific squeak of hinge. A glance behind showed Dave drawing himself up with tension, the holster in one hand, the Ruger in the other.

Yeah. Getting closer. Bless that dog, anyway—smart enough to keep from getting hurt, persistent enough to let them know just where the interloper was.

Even so, she jammed a stick through the door first and listened for the sound of movement. She had no wish to come face-to-face with some rodent, but even more she didn't want to come fang-to-fang with a copperhead. Then as she pulled herself into the small available space—a dim enclosure turned into a visual zigzag of tools and old shovel handles and buckets and straps and items that defied identity at a glance—she felt a firm hand on her posterior.

A shove, if it had to be said. He planted his palm solidly on her ass and pushed.

Karin sputtered dirt and cobwebs and pulled herself along, tossing the jacket to the side so she could bring her feet through and angle herself out of the way, quickly arranging the shed contents—the pails, the musty burlap feed bags, old chicken wire—between the front door's knothole and their small retreat.

Dave didn't hesitate; he stuck his hand through, gun and all. Karin neatly relieved him of it and tugged. For Dewey was at the goat shed and still barking, and Dave, angling his shoulders through the door, had taken on a sudden look of desperation. Karin turned to face him, braced her legs against the sturdiest parts of the old foundation footers, and grabbed his arm for one swift, powerful yank.

Dave made a soft, pained grunt of protest, something ripped…and he popped through. His legs followed quickly enough. They took opposite corners along the back wall, scrunching down low, legs stretched out calf to thigh and cramped at that. Karin padded her back with the until-now very nice suit jacket, and pulled the Ruger out to rest on her stomach.

Dave gestured for it; she ignored him. She squinted at the engraved model number on the slide. P95DAO. Double action only semiautomatic, a 9-round clip, no external safety. That meant a long, hard trigger pull and release, but she could do that. As long as there was a bullet in the chamber, she could fire this gun any time she wanted—with haste or deliberation.

Dewey had moved into the old pigsty, still barking. Not a frantic bark, but an angry one. Karin exchanged a long glance with Dave, sinking even farther into her corner. He held out his hand, twisting sideways to stay low and behind the screen of junk she'd created; this time she handed over the gun. His fingers curled around the grip with easy familiarity, his trigger finger resting over the guard.

He didn't like hiding this way. That was plain enough. He wanted to go out there, confront the man and get this over with. As relaxed as the hand around the Ruger might be, the rest of him fairly trembled with tension—a condition that Karin knew very much for certain, given the juxtaposition of their legs.

The building gave a sudden little shudder. Karin jumped, unprepared for the intruder to be *here*. She shrank inside her skin, trying to grow small, except her heart had suddenly grown bigger, pounding so hard there couldn't possibly be room for it. *Be small. Be very small.*

Dave lifted his chin, just enough to catch her attention. Just enough so he could nod at her, a bare fraction of reassurance that somehow made a difference.

The old henhouse gave another shudder. The brute, trying to yank the door open. No way. It would take a shovel and crowbar to clear that thing. But she could easily picture the man—one hand yanking at the door, one hand braced against the door frame. Braced against the huge old poison ivy bush, grown to treelike proportions. She smiled.

Dave must have thought she was losing it. He put a hand on her lower leg, gave it a reassuring squeeze. Even with the building shifting around them and dirt raining from disturbed cracks between slats, she still smiled.

Another thirty-six hours and this man's hands would be swollen with a weeping rash. If Barret Longsford wanted men hunting Ellen Sommers, he'd have to send out a new crew.

Didn't mean he wouldn't.

That thought took the smile off her face, all right. She was going to have to hide out for weeks, maybe even months. She'd lose her planting season, and she might have to give away the livestock. The thought made her downright grim.

Dave's hand squeezed her leg again, and she scowled at him. *I'm not frightened, you overprotective caveman—I'm mad.* As mad at Dave Hunter as anyone. Mad at Ellen, too, for not warning her about this boyfriend.

Not that she'd had a lot of time to talk.

Another jerk on the door, this one in frustration. And then, unexpectedly, something slammed up against the wall beside Karin's head. She jumped, nearly levitating, and only barely avoided a startled squeak. Had he simply been frustrated? Or maybe even trying to flush them out. Maybe they'd left too many clues. Even a city boy could read crushed grass.

An equally startling voice bellowed, "Damn dog, shut up!"

Shortly thereafter, Dewey did. *God, please let him be all right.* Please let that mean the intruder was moving away. She started to sit up and Dave squeezed her leg again, kept his hand tight until she looked his way and he could shake his head. She responded in kind, a denial, and he leaned forward enough so she could hear his barely vocalized words. "We'll be sitting ducks when we leave this place. We have to know he's gone."

Okay. Score one for him. Karin settled back against the slats and observed that he'd acquired an artistic slash of dirt across one cheek, but the cobweb in his hair just looked yucky.

And then the sheep darted across their paddock, the soft tickety sound of their cloven hooves catching Karin's ear; the cow, too, trotted heavily away. *The goats.* Edith's bell rang wildly, her startled bleat cutting through the air.

This time Karin did sit up, straight up. "Son of a bitch!" she whispered. "He's not messing with my goats!"

He sat up to grab her arms, neatly trapping her. "No," he said. *"We can't leave now."*

"We damn well can!" So what if hiding had been her idea in the first place. She wasn't about to sit back and listen to the man mess with her livestock. She jerked against Dave's grip, accomplishing nothing, and subsided to a glare. Just for the moment, but it was long enough for him to lean close.

"Listen," he said, his voice low.

"Listen, nothing. Hiding only works as long as he's not taking it out on—"

"No, I mean...*listen.*" He cocked his head.

Karin swallowed a protest and closed her eyes, shutting out the visual distraction.

Silence.

"He's not hanging around," Dave murmured.

She opened her eyes again, drawn smack into his gaze. Even in this dim light, his eyes seemed bright. "Dammit," she whispered. "I should have known better."

And she should have. She was raised to know better—she

was raised to play the games herself. She took a deep breath; his hands on her arms relaxed. "Ow," she said, feeling it then. "That big carnival geek already left his mark on that arm."

"Sorry." He looked abashed and gently rubbed the arm in question. "Carnival geek?"

"Yeah, one of those guys who bites the heads off live chickens." She scowled. "He'd better not—"

He grinned, ducked his head. The cobweb looked back at her, tangled in hair cut just a little too long to be conservative, just a little too scruffed. "I'm sure your chickens are safe."

"Easy for you to say." The scowl deepened. "And don't think I've forgotten why all this is happening. You got ol' Barret worried—you made him come looking. He's been out of my life since before the accident, and now he's back and not in a good way. And *then*—" she narrowed her eyes even more "—you put your *hand* on my *ass* and you *pushed*."

He took said hand off her arm and regarded it in a bemused way. Then he looked up at her, no visible regret. "Yeah," he said. "I did."

When had they gotten this close?

The moment he got here.

"You like this with all your witnesses?" she asked him, not pretending it didn't hover there between them, contact about to happen. Or that she didn't want it or that she *hadn't* wanted it since he'd braced her in her laundry room. Had nothing to do with why he was there, only with the energy that tightened between them at every inopportune and inappropriate moment.

She liked it. It made something inside her hum. A hum in need of use.

He considered the question, giving it a respectful amount of thought. He gave a definitive shake of his head. "No," he said. "I'm like this with…" Another moment for thought there, and then he turned those blue eyes on her full bore and said, *"You."*

It was a simultaneous thing—the leaning forward, the head-tipping, the perfect mesh of skin and lips, fingers in each other's hair, breathless gasps at just the right time to say *more of that please right now.* Cramped together in a filthy old henhouse, surrounded by junk, the carnival geek lurking…

It was perfect.

Totally perfect.

Totally mind-blowing, lips-blowing, body-tingling—

His hands left her hair and slid down her sides, up and under her shirt, up her back to span the width of her shoulder blades, tugging her closer. Hands that saw enough work to be callused, not so much they were sandpaper rough. *Perfect.*

Karin made a wordless noise of demand and hitched closer to him, dropping one hand to the inside of his thigh. He groaned something…it took her a moment to realize it was a noise of heroic determination, and by then her fingers had crept upward. On a quest, those fingers. He jumped, pulled his hand out from beneath her shirt and clamped it onto her wrist. "Now!" he managed to say, just barely, before dipping back into the kiss.

Now was perfect, too. Right now. *This* now.

Except what he'd said, she realized, hampered by her lips as he'd been, was actually *not now.*

And then she was thinking again, pulled back to stare at him from only inches away, her pulse pounding in all the right places. Places that wanted attention. Immediately. But she was thinking again and she knew he was right. Not with their unwanted visitor still lurking, their retreat not yet arranged. She had to call Amy Lynn. She had to…she had to…

She had brains somewhere. She'd find them before they reached the house. Somehow. For now she looked at his mouth with complete regret, raising a thumb to caress the damp corner. He closed his eyes and his nostrils flared and she had the feeling that thumb came *this close* to being nibbled.

"Ew!" she said, startling both of them. His eyes flew open; he looked almost relieved, if offended. Karin flapped her fingers, trying to get the stringy cobweb off her hand. Eventually she gave up and scrubbed her hand along her thigh— *her* thigh, because she had just enough mercy to spare him that, given the distinct remains of his erection.

When she looked at him again, he repeated with no little regret, "Not now." He looked very much as if he was trying to convince himself…and was failing.

"Right," she said flatly, and saw his head lift slightly with wariness. She leaned forward and added in tones of pompous import, "This must never happen again."

He stayed wary, that shadow of hurt in his eyes, a crinkle of uncertainty in his brow.

This one would be so easy to play. But…she didn't want to. "Do I *look* serious?"

"You look…" He paused. *"Flexible."*

"Ohh," she said, a purr of a word, "I *am.*"

Dewey, his timing impeccable, stuck his head through the hinged chicken door. Foamy white liquid lined his lips. "Oh my God," Karin said, all one word, "You *didn't*. You're not coming into the house for a week, Dewey Lake!" A great big glut of goat's milk and adult dog digestion. She'd need a gas mask.

But that's right. It didn't matter. She wasn't going to be here. It didn't matter that she intended to back this man into a tight corner at the first opportunity, the first moment they were safe enough so she could lose herself in what waited between them. Because at the first opportunity, she also intended to be out of here. Gone. Running. Being someone else for a while. Not likely ever to see Dave Hunter again.

And wasn't *that* just perfect.

Chapter 6

Dave's feet encroached upon the end of the twin bed, a constant reminder of his unfamiliar surroundings. His mind raced toward morning, eager to get Ellen to the safe house. She'd made all the arrangements; she'd seemed resigned as she set her suitcase at the back door, but thoroughly convinced.

For Barret's errand geek would be back. Whether Ellen recovered her memories or not, for now she needed to hide. He didn't blame her for her anger. She was losing a year's worth of crops, and losing her tidy little life as well.

Even if she no longer struck him as someone who was well-suited to a tidy little life.

He tried to imagine the Ellen he knew kissing him as she'd done him today—holding nothing back, not embarrassed or ashamed or reluctant—and couldn't. Of course, thinking about the kiss at all was a big mistake. A huge mistake.

Growing bigger by the moment. And the way she'd looked at him as they'd parted ways for the evening—no, don't think about that, either. Not how she'd dropped her head and watched him with those smoky blue-gray eyes under those strong and expressive brows, licking the taste of their whiskey nightcap from the corner of her mouth.

I am an idiot.

Too true.

Think of the whiskey. It still warmed his throat, an intense, peaty twelve-year-old single malt. He hadn't expected that of her, either—that they could small-talk the evening away with whiskey-tasting memories, or that they'd both been to that unexpected little shop in northern California, walking away with single malts neither could afford. Her voice matched the whiskey, he'd realized. It had that same slow burn.

She'd never inspired those thoughts before.

Of course, the last time he'd talked to Ellen Sommers, she'd been dating Barret Longsford. He just didn't remember thinking he wished it were otherwise.

Okay, so thinking about the whiskey didn't do any good. Thinking about the close calls they'd had today didn't do him any good, either. His mind's eye had a perfect view of Ellen facing those two men, no hint of her concern in her voice and then no hesitation when push literally came to shove.

He supposed he should be lucky she'd kissed him instead of wielding some other gardening implement at his head. Because she was right. He *had* brought this on her.

Then he'd just have to fix it. And while he was at it, they'd find Rashawn Little and put good old Barret Longsford behind bars. Perhaps he'd work on world peace next.

A pipe dinged somewhere below. She'd warned him that

the house would settle, creaking and banging and knocking in its own little musical composition. "Don't pay any attention unless you hear Dewey bark," she told him, lingering at the bottom of the stairs, whiskey glasses in hand and her hair still damp from her shower. The regret in her eyes as they separated had been palpable.

Certainly it had become instantly palpable to Dave, who retreated up a few steps. "Be ready," he'd told her, already turning away. "We'll get an early start."

"Oh, I'm ready." She'd said it in that low voice she sometimes used, the one he hadn't heard over a year earlier. She'd said it in a way that made her double meaning clear. And then she'd walked away, glasses clinking in her fingers.

I am an idiot.

But sleep was coming anyway. And even though he wanted to linger a bit on his plans for the morning, sleep claimed him, two modest fingers of whiskey hitting home at the end of a long day.

Hitting home...too hard...

Baseball bat. Check. *Forged ID.* Check. *Clothes to match.* Check. *Amy Lynn, ready to feed tomorrow and for as many tomorrows as it would take, well compensated.* Check. And there went a chunk of her hard-earned savings, too.

Karin leaned her forehead against the steering wheel of the truck, careful not to bump the horn. The darkness of the old cinder-block garage—set at the end of the driveway a hundred yards from the house—enfolded her. Made her doubt her decision.

She'd chosen this midsize cab-and-a-half Dakota to replace Ellen's car—one of the few things that were now hers, and not Ellen's. Most of her belongings had been ruined in the crash. Her new identity had come at a high price.

And that was what leaving was all about, wasn't it? Protecting what Ellen had given her. It wasn't as if she could help Dave's quest in any event. She'd been through Ellen's things when she first arrived, and hadn't seen a thing about Barret Longsford.

She ignored the whispered mental suggestion that she might have missed something in her hurry to assimilate Ellen's life. Or that with new context, she might see the importance of notes or photos or bills that had once been meaningless. It wasn't a convenient suggestion. Not at all.

Get an early start, Dave had said, but the poor man had had no idea. She'd gone to her bedroom to wait for him to fall asleep upstairs. Between the whiskey and the drugs she'd added, he hadn't stood a chance. Within the hour, she'd crept through the dark house, grabbing her things by the door. She'd had some things waiting in the garage—always waiting, her Just In Case kits—and though the truck was full of junk, she wouldn't take the time to dump it. Rusty leg-hold trap, an old mattock, a roll of electric fence wire…no big deal.

At the garage, she pressed her lips together on another wave of regret. *Sorry, Dave.* What stood between them was potent…but it was all about possibilities. Karin knew to take the sure thing. And there was nothing she could do for the missing boy but offer rusty prayers. Saint Arthelais, indeed. If ever there was a kidnap victim in need…

She started the engine and hit the automatic door opener. But she didn't turn on the headlights when she backed out onto the road. She put the truck into Drive and hesitated just long enough to give the house one last look. *I can't help you, Dave Hunter.*

And then she drove away.

Karin headed west, through Jefferson National Forest and toward Bluefield, West Virginia. She'd been to Pipestem State Park a couple of times…she thought she could find some work around there. Not enough to live on, but better than just spending down what she had with her.

The terrain gradually changed around her, starting as long, folded ridges of earth with plenty of valley—graceful formations, in harmony with each other. But slowly the mountains took on a different flavor—craggy, the formations harsher and struggling for apparent dominance, one over the other. The valleys started to narrow into hollows, and humans took themselves to live upon the sides and tops of the ridges instead of down in the bottom. And every now and then…the roadside view turned spectacular, offering long, uninterrupted vistas of the mountains fighting with one another to be king of the hill. Sometimes there was even enough shoulder available to form an official scenic viewpoint.

Karin drove for three hours, crossed I-77 on Route 61, and found herself one of those spots. She'd made some distance. Unless Dave—or the persistent geek—had tied themselves to her bumper, they weren't going to find her. By the time she settled in somewhere with her hair dyed, her eyebrows plucked into bare existence, and a horrible home perm…

"The sacrifices we make," she grumbled, cutting the engine after her bumper tapped the guardrail.

Come daylight, she'd want to get moving again. But finding

a place to settle wouldn't happen in the wee hours of the morning, and she needed sleep as much as the next refugee.

Temporary refugee.

Out of habit, she reached for her courier bag, pulling out the journal. Until now the leather-bound book had had an easy existence, sitting in one spot on the same desk in the same room. Now it was about to take some dings. "You'll have character," she told it, rummaging for the pen.

Dear Ellen,

Boy, has your life gotten adventurous in the last twenty-four hours. How could you have failed to mention Dave Hunter? I can understand why you might have left Barret out of the picture. But Dave...okay, I would have talked about him if I were you. I wish you were here so we could talk about him now.

Too bad I can't give him what he needs, and there's no way I'm staying in a safe house with him. He's no dummy. He's an *investigator,* and he's already noticed I'm not quite you. Put us in the same house for more than a few days and he's going to start investigating who I am—and he'll figure it out, too. I have the feeling he's damned good. And then he's going to put my name in the system just to see what it spits out, and why I'm pretending to be you.

On the other hand...it might be nice to know what my lovely little warrant is for. Here I am on the run, and I don't even know why.

Well, except that here in your life—the one that's gotten adventurous—there's a very big man who's looking for me. And Dave is going to look, too—and even if his reasons are totally admirable and all that stuff, I don't need the attention.

So I'll make sure neither of them finds me. But stayed tuned. The next couple of days aren't going to be about chores.

Karin rolled the truck window down a crack for the fresh air, but only a crack. She'd driven up to a higher elevation, where the nights still regularly nudged freezing. She pulled on a thick knit cap, wrapped a scarf round her neck and pulled an old wool army blanket over her legs. Oversize mittens on top of her insulated work gloves, a good wiggle to scratch her back against the truck seat, and she was ready for napping.

But oh. She added that one final touch—she reached for the rifle. If anyone came tapping around her windows, they'd be in for a surprise.

She warmed herself with decadent thoughts about that moment in the henhouse with Dave, and fell asleep.

Something shattered, raining shards down upon her. Karin barely had her eyes open when the truck door pulled out away from her, and fingers clamped down on her arm through her old army surplus coat. She was yanked up and out; something in her hand tangled with the steering wheel. Only after it was torn from her grip did she realize she'd lost the rife; only then did she remember why she'd been sleeping in the car at all. Sleeping deeply, after a long, hard day and gone straight through to the wee hours of the morning.

How—?

How didn't matter, not when she was flying through the air to land on the hard grit of the one-vehicle parking area. Another car jammed in beside her truck, engine still running, lights still on. Karin threw her hand up against the light, blinded, but it wasn't a good move—it only gave her still-unseen assailant a convenient handle. He snatched her up and gave her a little shake. "You're a real pain in the ass," he growled.

Errand goon with gangster mullet. Oh crap.

"If Barret told you I'd be easy, that was his mistake," she gasped, her feet barely touching the ground. She'd lost her oversize mittens and her scarf skewed to cover one eye; her world whipped back and forth as he shook her. She had to get to the truck, to the rifle or the baseball bat or even her keys....

"You're done running now," he said.

She squirmed, still breathless. "Tell him you couldn't find me. I can make it worth your—"

He shook her again. Hard. "I'm not being paid enough to listen to you."

"Ohhh," she groaned. "I'm going to..." And she gave a convincing heave. He thrust her away, slamming her against the side of the truck. She floundered, reaching into the bed of the truck, hand groping for...for *anything,* any tool small or large, any hard object....

She came up with a handful of hay detritus—dusty, prickly little bits of dried grass stems. *What the hell. What you've got, you use.* She flung the dust into his eyes and dove for the open truck door.

He snarled—the real thing, a nasty, animalistic sound—and blindly scooped her up on the run, a hand clutching the material between her shoulder blades and another hand grabbing her jeans at the hip and he *flung* her—

Right over the guardrail.

Right over the effing guardrail....

Flashes of the night Ellen died hit Karin head-on, tangling with reality as she bashed into a small outcrop, *smashed up against the windshield,* scraped against a verticle of dirt and vine and stone, *tumbled in the rolling car,* cold air on her face, *cold rain on her face—*

Impact.

At first she couldn't breathe. Diaphragm frozen, lungs empty of air and burning, straining—*I'll never breathe again and I'll die right here and now*—and then the air rushed back into her lungs with a great whoop. The outrage began to sink in. How the hell had he found her? How fair was *this,* to find herself thrown over another embankment?

From above—far above—came a nasty string of words.

"How do you think *I* feel?" she muttered. But she got the idea. He hadn't meant to throw her over the edge of anything. He probably still needed to return her to Barret. *"Cree-ap."*

A moment of silence passed, during which the errand geek was presumably contemplating his options. Karin took the moment to assess her situation, carefully not moving, not until she had a feel for the width of this uneven little outcrop. She stared up into the night sky, glad enough to see the waning moon. Slowly, she picked out vague details of her surroundings, allowing her peripheral vision—the best night vision— to feed her the details. The stunted rhododendron above her, the thick fall of foliage beside it that could only be invasive kudzu, the occasional glimpse of treetop in the otherwise open space to her left.

But mostly, just that open space.

Using only her fingers, she felt out toward the left and found gritty, sloping rock. She allowed her hand to creep over, and then her whole lower arm. She had about a foot before the ground rounded off and fell away.

A pure luxury of space. Ha.

Still, she thought she'd just stay as she was for a moment longer. A moment to get her breath and to listen in on the man who'd put her here.

"Mr. Longsford—"

The man's voice rang out clearly, all deference and apology. Karin could picture him on his cell phone, leaning over the guardrail. There came a few ingratiating phrases of apology, and then he spelled out the situation.

Actually, he fibbed. "She ran right at the guard rail," he said. "She musta lost her bearings."

Well, she couldn't blame him at that. Why take the heat? Parts of her, formerly numb from shock, started to hurt. All of her, actually, except the middle of her back, which just itched. She did a quiet inventory of fingers and toes, only then considering the ramifications of serious injury.

Everything wiggled. She sighed with relief and found a few new aches in her ribs. Cold from the ground seeped through her jeans.

"I can't see where she is. But it's pretty steep." A pause, and then his voice grew louder. "Hey! Can you hear me?"

She shouted some anatomically improbable suggestions.

"Yeah, she's down there." His voice faded slightly as he stepped away from the guardrail. "She's pretty far down. Nah, there's no other traffic—hasn't been anyone by since I got here. No problem, it's a pull-off…people park here all the time." As if he knew. The creep. Just trying to cover his own ass, now. "She might last a day, I guess. It's awfully cold here."

You can say that again. Karin eased her knees up and left her feet flat on the rock, getting her legs off the cold ground.

The man's next few comments were just a murmur, and then he stuck his head back over the guardrail to say clearly, "You should have just come with us in the first place, you stupid bitch. Maybe in a day or two they'll find your body."

"You're leaving me here?" she said, more startled than she expected. She sat up, one hand gripping the roots closest to her—and in the process discovered shooting pains in her wrist. She vaguely remembered landing on the heel of that hand sometime during her fall.

"Like I said, you should have come with us in the first place." He didn't sound the least bit sorry. Great. He'd not only thrown her down a gorge, he was being mean about it.

Left on the ledge? Alone? With no one the wiser? Karin shuddered. Time to get to work. "Don't go!" she said, and fought back on edge of panic. "You need me."

He snorted.

"You think I'm kidding? You've been exposed to a deadly disease." Her mind slid right into scam mode, forgetting for the moment her precarious physical situation.

"I don't think so." But he was a little closer now; she'd hooked him.

Karin smiled into the darkness. "It's new. The CDC has been keeping a lid on it. Mad Sheep disease. Why do you think my one goat has a bell collar on? She's over it, but she's still contagious—that part of the property is in quarantine. I've been vaccinated, of course."

"I'm leaving." The disinterest in his voice wasn't feigned. She was losing him.

"What about the rash?" she said, talking fast and trying not to sound desperate. "It's a little early for it to be a true rash, but I bet it itches." Maybe not. He'd have to be terribly sensitive to the poison ivy oils to show symptoms this soon. *Be sensitive,* she thought at him. *Be really, really sensitive.*

And after a pause, he said, "Keep talking."

"It's only going to get worse. And it spreads along the nerve pathways—it can reach your brain in a matter of days." Okay, so that was conflating shingles and poison ivy...but it sounded good. "Very few doctors know anything about it. I can tell you where to go for treatment." She hardened her voice. "Of course, you'll have to haul me out of here first."

And then what? He wasn't likely to simply let her go.

It doesn't matter. It would be better than clinging to the side of a gorge cliff in the middle of nowhere, with no one the wiser and no one looking for her. She'd handle the *and then what* when she got there.

Except he gave a snort of a laugh. "It's not much of a rash," he said. "I'll go get myself some magic ointment at the drugstore. Meanwhile, you have a nice life. Or should I say, have a nice death."

"Bastard," she muttered, but not so he could hear it. Not now. Now that he'd decided to leave her here, there were plenty of ways he could make this situation worse. She wanted none of it.

And he wasn't bluffing. His car engine started...and the vehicle drove away.

Karin took a deep breath, ignoring the twinges in her ribs. "Cree-ap!" she bellowed into the open darkness.

"Ap-ap-ap," the darkness echoed back.

All right. Think. So far, she was for the most part whole, especially considering how many things could have broken on the way down here. Her wrist would be a problem, but it wasn't a jagged-bone kind of problem.

Maybe things weren't as bad as they seemed. Maybe she was already nearly at the bottom of this particular gorge. If she could slide her way to the bottom come daylight…

Or maybe in daylight, she'd find a way to climb out, bum wrist and all.

One thing she couldn't afford to do was wait. Sure, people were going to notice her car, but this wasn't a back-and-forth kind of road. This was an out-of-the-way, going-from-here-to-there road, the kind of road no one traveled twice in the same day or two. And she bet it would take a couple times of spotting her car before something bothered to think something wasn't quite right.

So…maybe things weren't as bad as they seemed. Karin scrabbled around for a decent rock, something she could toss without effort but still big enough to hear on the way down. "Have a short journey," she told it, and kissed it for luck. Then she tossed it out over the edge of her little cranny and listened to it bounce and hop.

And listened.

And listened.

And slumped back against the cliff, not bothering to listen for the end of it. Softly, she said, "Oh, crap."

Chapter 7

He wasn't certain what woke him, not until the dog barked again. Even then, he almost let himself drift back into sleep. But the dog barked again, and Dave pried his eyes open.

That he had to work so hard to manage it was enough to get him sitting up. The way he staggered when he got up…that triggered all his warning systems.

What the hell had she put in his whiskey?

And *why?*

Dave acted without thinking, stumbling down the stairs in his boxers to check Ellen's empty bedroom, and then straight to the bathroom where he cranked the shower on full and cold.

The icy blast hit him hard; he managed to stay beneath it but only by snarling his best string of curses. Once he'd been through the litany twice, he figured enough was enough, and stepped out sputtering, reaching blindly for the nearest towel.

It smelled of shampoo and of Ellen.

Okay, *that* woke him up.

Peeling off the wet boxers was no fun at all.

From there he ran up the stairs—ran, because whatever she'd given him still hung in his system and he couldn't afford to slow down—and pulled on clean underwear and a pair of jeans and an old Rochester Red Wings sweatshirt. He gulped down two of the caffeine pills he kept with his razor and ran back down the stairs and around to the back door, checking his watch on the way. *Hours. He'd been asleep for hours.*

He didn't have to know what she'd given him, or why. He only knew he had to find her. She was more than his best hope to help Rashawn. Now she was in trouble, and it was his fault.

He shoved his way out into the cold night and discovered that leaving his coat in the car hadn't been his best idea ever. The cold hit his wet hair and damp skin hard enough so his goose bumps might never fade. He fumbled for the car keys in the side pocket of the overnighter, hit the unlock key, and was never so grateful for the automatic interior lights. First things first: he threw his bag into the passenger seat and pulled on his dark Gore-Tex parka, listening to his teeth chatter.

The next step was pretty clear, too. He slid in behind the wheel, firing the engine up—but he didn't crank the heat up. It wouldn't do to get too comfortable. Not until whatever Ellen had slipped into his whiskey was totally out of his system, and the caffeine had kicked in. But he was a man with a mission nonetheless; he reached into the passenger seat and pulled out his laptop, putting it aside to boot up while he grabbed his USB receiver. Then he found his glasses, knowing better than to try to work without them when he could barely focus in the first place.

Oh, yeah, he'd felt guilty enough about that bug, even if at the time he was bugging her for her own protection and didn't tell her only so she wouldn't worry. As if she were still the old Ellen. Now his guilt dissipated somewhat, especially when the results of his two receivers—the GPS and the short-range RF—told her she was nowhere in the area. He took a closer look at the GPS map on his screen.

What the hell was she doing at the border of West Virginia? She didn't know anyone there…had no ties to the area.

Running. Running like a rabbit.

No, he told himself quite suddenly, listening to the gut instinct that had been poking at him since his arrival. Not like a rabbit, not anymore. *Like a fox.*

But a fox who didn't know she'd been tagged.

The receiver beeped; he almost dismissed it in his attention to the laptop. But the beep meant the automatic scanning receiver had found success, and that made no sense. There was no way its range extended over a hundred miles. Dave alt-tabbed his way to the open receiver window and stared at it.

Oh, shit.

It was him. This car. Somewhere in the back half of it, probably under the wheel well.

Barret's man hadn't given up at all. He'd just come back to bug Dave's car, hang back and wait.

Dave pushed the laptop aside and slid out of the car, running cold fingers along the inner wheel well, the bumpers, the second wheel well…and there it was. He pried the thing free and took it back to the car, flicking on the overhead light to get a better view of his prize.

It was an impressive little device. Not as tiny as the beyond cutting-edge tech he'd planted on Ellen, but if the receiver was anywhere near this quality…

Then Longsford's man would have picked up the motion-activated bug on Ellen. If he was alert, if he was in the car…he could easily have followed her, staying in range. And that meant Dave somehow had to reach her before it was too late.

God. I'm gonna need more coffee.

"Dear Ellen," Karin said out loud, speaking into the darkness. The moon had set; dawn couldn't be far away. "Your sister is in a mess."

For one thing, she'd lost her hat, and then she'd lost most of her body heat through her uncovered head. She'd lost part of her scarf, too, but only because she'd used it to strap up her wrist. And then she'd ended up on a west-facing slope. This spot wouldn't see warm sunlight until the day was half over.

It wasn't as if she could keep moving to generate body heat.

The errand geek was right. She might last a day. If she was lucky.

Daylight. She just needed to stay functional until daylight, until she could truly assess her situation.

Helpless. Plain and simple helpless.

When was the last time that had happened?

Never, she told herself…but even to her mind's inner ear, the protest came too strongly.

"It wouldn't feel familiar if it was a first," she said out loud, just in case it would make herself listen more carefully.

But it did feel familiar. In a sly way, a trickle of feeling that was oh-so-hard to identify. A feeling she wanted to ignore. Under other circumstances she would have sprung to her feet and found some busywork, if only pacing. *Now...really not a good time to take up pacing.*

So she kept her feet still, and she sat with her back against the earth and her face buried in her arms as she hugged her knees, trying to keep warm. Familiarity didn't make sense. She'd never been helpless. She was the one who took to Rumsey's games, at least until she realized the consequences of the games, from the charity scams to the good old ketch-up-squirt scams. She'd been good at playing backup for Rumsey.

At first, just by being there. Just being a little girl, engaging their interest for the investment scams or charity scams—the long view, when Rumsey needed a whole cast of characters. As she got older she'd carried his messages, muling not drugs or money but information. She interacted with the marks themselves, filling in while Rumsey was busy with some other scheme. And she'd even handled fenced goods and bartered information with their more felonious acquaintances.

If Karin needed something, she got it. If she was in trouble, she got out of it.

Until today, anyway.

Now she had a wrist that was badly sprained if not broken, and she clung to the side of a mountain in the dark. And it felt...

Familiar.

And because she wasn't afraid of anything, not even some damned elusive feeling, Karin shut her eyes and followed it. She let it well up inside her.

Until suddenly she was eight years old, waiting for Rumsey to fetch her, because he was preparing to make one of his special visits. And she didn't want to go. *She didn't want to go.* How she wished her mother were still there! And she almost turned to Ellen to cry about it, but she already knew that Ellen wasn't strong enough for Rumsey's games, and if Karin didn't go along then Ellen would have to do it.

Didn't anyone know? Couldn't any adults see what was going on, the lies he made her tell? The fake smiles he made her smile, pinching the back of her neck when it looked like he was putting a proud hand on her shoulder?

But no one had ever seen through the lies Rumsey told about her, about Ellen. No one had ever seen she wasn't a perfectly happy, normal little girl with her perfectly normal family.

Helpless.

It didn't take long to figure out that the best strategy for surviving—for thriving—was to put aside her reluctance. To become so good at scamming that Rumsey counted on her…that he did decently by her and Ellen in other ways. Food in the fridge, money for clothes…except later, when she really got good. She and Ellen had stolen their first bras together.

Karin shivered, wrapping her arms more tightly around her knees. An emotional as well as a physical huddle, with helplessness smothering her in a wave of unwelcome feeling. "Okay, it happened," she muttered, ready to be through with it even if it wasn't through with her. "I made choices. I got past it. I'm not eight any longer."

No, she was twenty-six and she was stuck on a cliff.

I wonder if Rashawn feels this way. Helpless.

The thought came out of nowhere; it made her suck in her breath and then forget to breathe out again. No child should feel like this. It wasn't something she could understand as an eight-year-old, but as a fully grown woman she understood plenty. None of that should have happened. Not to her; not to Rashawn.

But I'm not Ellen. There's nothing I can do to help.

There's nothing.

Dave bought coffee at every opportunity, filling his thermos. He therefore also stopped to get rid of coffee at every opportunity, grateful that the amazing scarcity of gas stations was offset by cover at the side of the road. It was harder finding enough shoulder in which to pull over…these two-lane roads ran narrow, ofttimes barely notched into the side of a ridge. The mountain rose on one side, dropped away on the other.

But Karin hadn't moved, and he steadily gained on her, though he didn't quite understand it. Unless Barret's man had inexplicably lost her, he'd practically been on top of her all this time. But if he'd made a move, Karin's tracking device would have reflected it.

Unless Dave was too late, and Barret had instructed his walking wall of muscle to get rid of her.

Dave hated being too late.

Too many late-night drives hadn't ended well. They now vied for his thoughts, from that very first dead boy—the one who'd set him on his life's path—to last year's young victim. Plenty of successes in between, but those weren't what ever came to him in the darkness. They weren't what came to him now as he raced not only to save another child, but to save his witness.

To save the woman who'd kissed him senseless in the crude confines of an old henhouse.

Dave's leg gave a sudden cramp; he discovered his fingers

crimping on the steering wheel. Too much caffeine, too much tension. Whatever Karin had used to dose him was wearing off. He'd probably be lucky if he wasn't up for three days in the wake of all that coffee.

Then again, if he didn't get to Karin in time, he'd be just as glad to avoid the nightmares.

Dave shook his hands out, and drove on toward dawn.

The first hints of light came as a surprise; one moment Karin stared out into darkness and the next she could see the jumble of hills across the gorge. She worked on deep-breathing exercises, those she'd taught herself in the early days. She rarely needed them anymore; she could just drop right into whatever persona the moment demanded, playing her mark with experience. Playing *anyone,* if it suited her. If it got her what she wanted. Needed.

Except…

It had been over a year. A year of sinking into the most convincing role she'd ever needed. Deep immersion…but only a single role. And that left her out of practice, even when it came to fooling herself. In this case, fooling herself that she wasn't, in fact, terrified.

"I am a mountain goat," told herself, staring out at the slowly brightening land. "Breathe deep. *Ommm.* Be the goat." Not quite right, that last. She summoned up an imitation of her youngest goat. The easiest. "Beh-eh-eh," she said into the mountain air. Yeah, that was so much better.

But she couldn't distract herself from her situation. Straight down, just as far as she would have expected from the endless fall of her tossed stone during the night. Karin's mouth went dry at the thought of the pure dumb luck that had landed her on this small outcrop; she had to lean her head back and swallow hard a couple of times.

All her survival skills were urban-based. Just because she'd lived on a tiny working farm for the past year didn't mean she was ready to free-climb this cliff.

Or you could just sit here and wait to freeze to death. Or fall asleep and roll off. Or dehydrate and faint and roll off....

Didn't seem like much of an option. She dug her fingers uselessly into the outcrop in a search for security as she slowly tipped her head back to see what lay above her.

Not quite as bad as she was expecting. More of an angle to the ground, more vegetation handholds. Of course most of it was rhododendron with shallow rhododendron roots....

Ugh. She didn't want her life to depend on them.

Then you'll just have to be careful.

But first things first. She wasn't climbing this cliff with a full bladder. At least she was too frightened to feel the humiliation of peeing right out there on the exposed outcrop. But she was shivering before she got her jeans refastened—face it, she had been shivering for a long time now. It didn't add to the security of the situation any.

Finally she stood, turning to face the cliff in tiny little steps, never taking even an inch of ground for granted. She contemplated her best path...up to the rhododendron, over to the kudzu, try to avoid the greenbrier, and then there was another, smaller ledge where she could dig her toes in and re-evaluate the situation. She squinted up at the rhododendron, working up nerve. Her wrist throbbed fiercely and she'd be lucky to use it. She sure couldn't count on it in a pinch.

Deep breath. Reach up to the stunted bush, tug and test. Breathe. Now or never....

The rhododendron held.

She made it to the kudzu.

The kudzu not only held, it offered her regular root knots. The narrow waterfall of vines—not quite suited to this elevation or it would have been a full-size blanket of growth across the hillside—had deep and sturdy roots, and the root knots sat above ground, spewing vines everywhere and most importantly giving Karin something to grab. One step at a time, always testing, her injured wrist held closely to her chest where she could feel her heart pounding even through the insulated canvas of the old army jacket. She kept her eyes on her goal, kept focused on the feel of the ground beneath tangled vines as it came through her cheap sneakers. The vines grabbed at the fingers of her work glove, and she disentangled her hand with care, pressing herself against the woody growth like a lover and taking hold with her teeth when she had to.

It can't be this easy.

Not that it was easy in the least. Not with knowing how far and long she'd fall if she lost her grip, or the way the treetops had looked as they swooped away beneath her former perch. *Idiot. Don't think of—*

Her foot slipped. She cried out, snatching at the vines with her injured arm and then crying out again when she made contact. Her foot scrabbled, got purchase, lost it again. Her world narrowed to a bright point of pain at her wrist, the emptiness beneath her searching feet, the burn of stressed muscle in her arms, the sound of her own harsh, irregular breathing....

There. There, she'd found purchase. She leaned against the vines and rock, panting, suddenly not cold at all.

Just a little farther.

Karin sighed deeply. Her face itched and she rubbed it

against the vines, surprised to realize she'd scraped away a tear. She was not prone to crying.

So one whole tear slipped out. Boo-hoo. She still needed to reach that ledge. Her next step was to move sideways, abandoning the kudzu altogether and making her way over a patch of greenbrier. Great. Nature's version of barbed wire.

On the other hand, it wasn't likely to break on her.

Her wrist was already screaming but the choice had become a no-brainer—use it, or risk a fatal slip. She needed all the security she could get. Good thing the greenbrier thorns were so big they dug right into her gloves. Ha. Karin ground her teeth together and snarled at the thorns, gaining mere inches of ground at a time. "I laugh at your puny thorns," she told the vines. "I sneer at—*ow, crap*—them. You need thorn Viagra, all of—*dammit*—you!"

There, finally—the next ledge was only a step away. So much smaller than her original perch, but so much closer to the top. She made herself slow down, taking the time to wait out the edge of panic that made her movements jerky and uncertain. She had to wait out a bout of the shakes—her muscles tired and flooded with fear and lactic acid both, already getting cold again. But that last step was a doozy. No way to get there without releasing both handholds to reach for the rock across from her.

So Karin breathed deeply, and she did visualizations, watching her good hand hit home in that safety over and over. Feeling the smoothness of the movement, the security of the ledge beneath her feet.

And then she simply…

Did it.

Once there she had to tip her forehead against the rock and

breathe "OhGod ohGod ohGod" a few times. Too bad she hadn't been a better little Catholic girl. She'd given up on church when she realized she could scam a priest as easily as anyone else. It was best if she just dealt directly with God since He was the only one she *couldn't* fool. But at this moment…she'd have been happy enough for saintly intervention. The patron saint of hanging off the side of a hill by your fingernails. That's the one she needed. Saint Bernard would do it.

But when she opened her eyes, she discovered she needed more than that.

She hadn't let herself even consider what would happen once she reached this spot.

She hadn't thought there'd be nowhere to go.

Almost there. Jittery with caffeine and hours of worry, but finally closing in on the beckoning map. The sun had risen, flashing low into Dave's rearview mirror, there and gone again as he navigated the twisting roads.

He'd closed the laptop to conserve battery power, checking the tracker in intervals. The stability of the signal gave as much cause for worry as for relief—what if she'd found and ditched the transmitter over one of these mountains? Owen would kill him, for one thing. Theoretically he was field-testing Hunter Agency equipment, but it was truly more of a lure. Owen never gave up.

And if she'd ditched the transmitter…he'd never find her. Or more precisely, he couldn't afford the time to find her. He'd have to return to Alexandria, scrape up new leads….

He didn't think Barret Longsford's latest victim had that much time.

Or what if Barret's man had caught up with her as Dave

had fully expected him to do by now? Caught up with and disposed of her. Another midnight chase to failure. The ultimately wrenching failure, the one that made him feel like a kid again—and a kid definitely wishing he hadn't smuggled himself into his father's car to see what excitement the late-night call held. Except Ellen Sommers made him feel like anything but a boy. Ellen Sommers already meant more to him than any witness should. It was crazy and stupid and undeniable. And stupid. He tapped his thumb against the steering wheel in a restless rhythm. Yeah, definitely stupid.

The computer beeped at him, a warning that he was getting close. He slowed, took the next hairpin curve and then dipped down an unexpected incline.

If he hadn't been watching for her, he would have missed it. But there it was…her graphite-colored truck with the black trim. He hit the brakes and skewed into the tiny slice of a parking spot, leaving the corner of his rear bumper exposed to traffic but parking there anyway.

His stomach got hard and cold and sick in a way that had nothing to do with the sloshing of coffee…he tossed his glasses onto the dash and jumped out of the sedan even though he'd already seen what he had to. She wasn't in the truck. She wasn't in the truck, yet the transmitter was here somewhere.

Barret's man had her.

And Dave had no way to find her.

Chapter 8

When the car pulled up, Karin almost didn't notice. Her teeth were chattering loudly enough to obscure all but the most obvious sound—and by the time she got them clenched long enough to listen, there was only silence from above. *Great. A chance to call for help and I missed it.* She would have banged her head against the rock, but she was so stiff and cold she was afraid even that would throw her off balance.

Coincidence was her only chance now. Someone stopping to answer the call of nature—inspired by view or bladder, she didn't care What she might have attempted in good condition, she now couldn't even consider. Here she'd be on this ledge, pressed up against cold rock, until she could get someone's attention or until she quite simply toppled off. The turkey vultures flocked to the strong thermals in these hills…maybe they'd get someone's attention when they started circling her.

Gloom and doom.

From above—not so very far at that, just no way to get there from here—she heard the slam of a vehicle door. She started, lost a moment of attention as her foot slipped, and pulled herself together just in time to hear a uniquely familiar string of French words, a phrase that had not so long ago amused her and now sent an invigorating spark of hope through her cold body. Except—first Barret's man and then Dave?

"Hey!" she shouted up, her voice full of suspicion. "How the *hell* did you find me?"

His reply came instantly. "Ellen? Where—" And then she knew he knew, for his voice grew louder, loud enough so he had to be at the guardrail and looking down. No suspicion there, just pure, joyful relief. "Are you—"

"Yes," she said, droll for his benefit. "I'm down here."

"How—" he started, and in her mind's eye she could all but see him shake his head as he cut himself off.

"Can we just say the mean man threw me over by mistake and then left, and get to the details later?" She waited a moment, then added, "I made it back up this far, but…I'm stuck."

"I'm calling 911," he said, no doubt dialing as he spoke.

How long would they take? Could she even hold on?

And if she did…there were sure to be cops.

"Dave," she said, and had no trouble getting her voice on the edge of tears, no trouble at all, "I'm cold, my lips are chapped to hell, I'm stiff, I think parts of me are broken, and I'm standing on a tiny little ledge. How long—"

He cut her off. "Okay." A silent moment, and then, "I don't have any rope."

Jumper cables. She had jumper cables tucked behind the half seat of the truck. Or… "Check in the truck bed," she told him, thanking her own laziness. "My tire chains—"

"Gotcha."

She heard the bumping around, the chains dragging over the side of the truck. "Got 'em!" And then silence, which she didn't mind because it meant he was linking the chains together. In the end Karin would have a nice narrow ladder made of chains, perhaps not so different than climbing kudzu. "Hold on!" he called down, as if she might just spontaneously let go. After a pause he added, "Sorry. That was dumb."

Or not so dumb. Her fingers were numb, her feet cramping, and her legs stiffened into clumsy, uncoordinated appendages. She felt more like a patchwork of cold, dead sausage than a functioning human. "Dave?"

He must have heard the uncertain note in her voice. When he asked, "What?" he was as close as he'd ever been, literally leaning out over the guardrail. Had to be.

"I don't think…"

"How broken?" he asked, understanding before she even got there.

"My wrist. Or arm. I'm not sure which. But that's not— that is, I'm just so cold—"

"Okay," he said. "We'll deal with it."

"We'll deal with it," she repeated to herself, curling her fingers hard against the rock to steady an unexpected sway, all the more frightening because she hadn't seen it coming.

And her thoughts stuttered to a halt, because the end of the chain came slithering down to head level and if only she had two good hands, two *warm* hands, she could reach out and snag it, and if only her arms weren't already trembling with fatigue, she could actually *climb* it—damned if safety wasn't that close, and yet still out of reach.

A rustling came from above; dirt and pebbles rained down on her head. By the time she realized what he had in mind, Dave was already there. He hesitated just above her, and then lowered himself down alongside her; by the time she'd gathered the words to ask, his intention was obvious. He moved in behind her, one arm strong on the chains, his feet braced on her little ledge, and the other arm gathering her up.

His coat was open.

His chest against her back was *warm*.

Karin groaned in the luxury of it, tugging the edges of the coat around herself, greedy for the warmth and the human touch. He dropped his head so it rested against hers, and that, too, offered warmth. Karin soaked it in, sandwiched between Dave and the cliff. For the first time since her rude early-morning awakening, she knew that for this moment, at least, she wasn't going to fall. For this moment, she was safe. Protected.

Safe enough, in fact, to inch herself around to face him and thread her arms around him beneath the coat, reassured by the steady strength in his chest and arms, and by his breathing. He pulled her in and let it be, so steady she'd never have guessed he was in any way vulnerable, braced against the cliff that had tried to spit her off all night.

And a different kind of warmth stole through her from the inside out. *No longer alone.* More than that. He'd come from safety to hazard, and now he hung here as if nothing were amiss, offering her support and comfort, his free arm holding her close.

No longer alone. Could she even remember that feeling? As if for the moment, nothing else mattered. Just her arms around him, feeling the unexpected strength in his frame and knowing it was there for her. That *he* was there for her.

"God," she muttered into his chest. "This is such a mess."

He laughed, so low she wouldn't have known it had she not had her face on that chest. "Warm yet?"

"I'll never be warm again." But she took a deep breath, pulling back enough so she could see his face, instantly missing their connection. The concern she saw—and the confidence—seemed a fair trade-off. "Warm enough. Wait a mo." For now that she'd gotten circulation back, her back itched abominably. She found a little knob of rock at her back and wiggled slightly against it, perforce wiggling against him so she thought when his eyes widened slightly she'd inadvertently—

But no. "Wait!" he said, just as she heard the tiniest little crunching sound and froze. Dave sighed, the most quiet of sounds. Then, ignoring her surprise, he snaked his hand up the back of her jacket to the spot that had plagued her all night. Right between her shoulder blades, just above her bra strap. When he withdrew his hand he held it up in the scant space between them. Not quite close enough to make her go cross-eyed looking at the little flat, round object.

"What—" she started, stopped by her own incredulity as she realized what she was looking at. A bug. Electronic surveillance. "That's a—you—*you*—"

"Yeah. And it's how our mean friend found you," he said. "On the bright side, it's how I found you, too."

"You—" It was hard to be mad when she was still greedy for his warmth, his touch and the security of his body blocking out her view of the sky. Hard, but not impossible. *"You—"*

He shrugged and tossed the bug over his shoulder. "It's dead, now."

"You...*litterbug!*" She scowled fiercely at him, but as her own words sank home she couldn't keep it up and the corner of her mouth twitched even as he let out a mild guffaw.

"Yeah," he said. "And we'll talk about that later. Now how about we get you out of here? I'll give you a boost. Once you get started, it's an easy climb."

"And why do I have the feeling this *boost* business will involve more of you putting your *hands* on my *ass?*"

"Waste no opportunity," he said, straight-faced. "You ready?"

More than. She turned around in still-careful increments, reaching to get a good grip on the tire chain, one-handed or not. He crouched, wrapping his free arm around her hips; Karin gave a little bounce and jumped even as he pulled her up. They worked in tacit accord to repeat the procedure, silent except for their panting and Karin's gasp as she hit her wrist and Dave's grunt of effort as he finally did get his hand on her bottom to *push*—

And then she was over the little jut of rock and damned if the guardrail wasn't practically within reach. She scrambled up, gaining enough momentum to lurch right along on all threes, and then crawled under the guardrail, rolling over to stare up at the bright blue sky and the vultures circling overhead.

If only she was in the sun, she'd never move again.

"Okay?" Dave called up to her.

Oops. Yeah, she probably should have let him know. "Okay!" she shouted back, still not moving.

Someone snorted, followed by a clanking at the guardrail, a grunt of victory and the rattle of tire chains coming up. She sat straight up, wrist cradled to her chest.

Barret's errand geek.

Oh my God. He was back, his car jammed in against her

truck; he must have arrived while she was busy grunting and breathing and climbing the cliff. He was back and he'd pulled the tire chains up from Dave, who even now called to her. Karin could only stare. "Oh, no-o," she said to the gangster mullet. "You had your chance. You *left*. It's not your turn anymore."

But when he turned to face her, she knew just why he'd come. She'd played him with that Mad Sheep story and in the end she'd gotten to him. Or rather, the poison ivy had gotten to him, blooming profoundly along the side of his face and over his hands.

"Ellen!"

"Company!" she warbled back down at him, a false June Cleaver note that ought to let him know in one word or less that she'd run into trouble.

Trouble with looming intent. "You said you could help me."

"Sure." She scooted backward a bit to lean against the side of the truck, trying to visualize how'd she'd left things inside. She frowned at the jumbled memory of the night before, of the rifle caught in the steering wheel. No easy access there.

But behind her, in the half cab…

The man loomed over her now. God, he looked terrible. The side of his face was bright red and weeping less than twenty-four hours after he'd gotten into the poison ivy, when most people were just realizing they had a problem.

She didn't feel the least bit sorry for him. "It's too late."

Always best to play someone based on the truth. And truth it was; he'd have had to wash that oil off within twenty minutes of exposure to stop the course of the poison ivy rash.

"No," he said, and his fear came out in anger. "It's only been a few hours. It *can't* be too late."

"A few *hours?*" She snorted expressively. "Trust me, I was out on that cliff for more than a *few hours.* More like a lifetime. For you, too, it seems." She pulled herself up the side of the truck, startled by just how quivery her legs had turned. *Don't show it.* With as much nonchalance as she could muster, she reached for the door handle. Maybe Dave had freed the rifle…maybe she'd find something else of use.

"Don't turn away from me," he snarled, yanking her away from the truck. She'd had her fingers under the handle, and the door opened behind her as he flung her back toward the guardrail. "You want to go over again? See if you can get lucky twice?"

Hell, no. This time when she went down, she stayed low. If he wanted to toss her over the edge, he was going to have to start from scratch. "Mad Sheep disease," she said sagely, and her heart beat such a race of fear she wondered just how long it could hold out. "See? Feel feverish, don't you?" Her fingers scrabbled against the hard ground, hunting purchase; instead they landed on knobby chains. Now *there* was luck. She shoved at them as though still finding her way. Shoved *hard.*

They slipped over the crest of the slope, slithering away…still anchored here at the base of the guardrail. *Hurry!* she thought at him, and then shrieked as the man bent over her and snatched her right off the ground. Her thoughts skittered in terror, certain he'd throw her over the edge again…certain she'd die this time.

But he slammed her up against the truck instead, eliciting protest from every bruised rib in her body. "This is me in a *good* mood," he said, sticking his heavy features far too up close and personal. But he'd put her where she could reach inside the truck. Her bad wrist, yes. But she did it, even as she kicked him away. Not a nice swift martial-arts kick, but the kick of a woman with no strength left and no particular training to start with. Just good heavy farmwork and a fierce desire to survive.

Actually, more like a woman frantically flailing her sneakers in the direction of someone's groin, shrieking all the while. Then her hands closed on the old leg-hold trap from the truck and she scrambled away, around the tailgate and then around the end of his own car, crouching there to step the trap open.

"You're wasting time," he said, sounding really annoyed this time. "You can take me to your doctor and live, or I can beat his name out of you and leave you here to die—again."

"Someone will see you," she said, breathless. He just laughed. She didn't blame him. No one had yet driven by. She hunkered down behind the back fender of his car, the trap in hand—in both hands, actually, no matter how it hurt. Now for the bait. "Dave has a phone, you know. We're not going to be alone for long."

"Long enough," he said, striding around the end of the car, reaching down for her—

She leaped up to meet him, thrusting the trap out before her. His hand skidded off the trip plate and the trap slammed closed around his arm and this time *he* was the one who shrieked. *He* was the one to lose his balance, stumbling backward to tip over the guardrail at a gentler part of the outcrop. His cry stopped short as he crashed through the branches and finally hit something strong enough to hold him.

Karin dismissed him, at least long enough to hop around holding her wrist and crying, "Ow, ow, ow, ow, *dammit, ow!*"

"Ellen!"

And here came Dave, roaring around the end of the car, his

face flushed and his hair totally ruffled, his coat still flapping open to reveal a sweatshirt with the absurd logo of a red bird flexing impossible muscles. He stopped short, just as she halted her little pain dance. He said, "Where—"

Karin gave a haughty little nod at the guardrail. "Turnabout is fair play."

In some disbelief, he leaned over the guardrail. When he straightened, he was shaking his head. "He'll need help getting out of *that.*"

"Call for it," she said. "But I'm not waiting. I'm all bent up and I'm *still* cold and I'm starving. I'm driving on to Bluefield." She headed for her truck.

"You're—oh, *no.* Not alone, you're not."

"Then follow me. You've probably got a sneaky way to do that, right? Some other little tracker thing?"

At first abashed, his expression hardened. "Hey, you want to talk sneaky—what the hell did you put in my drink?"

Improbably, she felt her cheeks pinking up. Ellen's Xanax, that's what. "Didn't hurt you," she muttered, mustering exhausted dignity to pull at the tire chains.

He grabbed them away from her in one big mass and dumped them into her truck bed. "I'm not kidding. You're not going anywhere alone. I'll follow you to a safe place to leave that thing and then I'll take you to the Bluefield hospital."

"I'm not waiting," she told him, opening the truck door to fumble around for her keys. She could drive one-handed if she had to, even on these curves. For a while, at least. And somewhere in here she had Goldfish crackers.

He stood frozen a moment, then gave a bemused shake of his head. "Hey," he said. "About that cliff thing. You're welcome."

"Yeah," she said, climbing in behind the wheel. "About

getting those tire chains back down to you while Mr. Mad Sheep Man was tossing me around…you're welcome."

He shook his head again. This time it looked like a more subtle version of throwing his hands up. "I'll catch up with the local LEOs later."

She couldn't help a smirk. "Let him explain about the leg-hold trap on his arm…yeah. And oh—tell them he doesn't *really* have Mad Sheep disease, whatever he says."

That stopped him short. He held her gaze a long moment. "Okay," he said. "I'll tell them. But boy, do we have to talk."

"Yeah," she told him. "That goes both ways. And I want food *before* we go to the hospital. No way I'm going to wait on an empty stomach. And no way I'm eating hospital crap."

This time he held up his hands for real, total capitulation. "You win."

She gave him a victory smile. But as she shut the door and started the truck, she looked at what her life had become and she suddenly wasn't so sure.

Dave took Ellen to a truck stop just outside of Bluefield. She ordered a huge breakfast and savored each bite. For a while he just watched her. The way she ate, the way she interacted with those near her, the way her gaze flicked around to keep tabs on those around her. If he hadn't known she'd spent the night out on a cliff face… Oh, her appearance was ragged enough—scuffed, torn and dirty clothing, her cheek scraped, her left arm tucked protectively into her lap. Her eyes gave away the most—no longer piercing, but rimmed with exhaustion. Not quite the same face as the one he'd once interviewed…but she'd mentioned that the accident had broken some facial bones. Not the same demeanor, either.

In fact, she was someone a little bit different with everyone to whom she spoke. To the older man who'd seated them, she'd been a daughter figure. To the waitress, a sister. To the trucker who'd hesitated long enough to give her a questioning once-over, dismissive enough so the man had turned away, not so blatant that he'd taken offense.

So there was plenty to look at. Plenty to ponder. And Ellen, even stiff and battered and grimy and exhausted, was still striking enough to catch Dave's eye by surprise time after time. More vibrant than she'd been before. It made him wonder if she'd been abused by Longsford...if now he saw what she would have been like without the man's influence. Or if—

"The accident really changed you," he said, though he hadn't meant to speak out loud at all.

She looked at him with one of those dry expressions, the eyebrow raised, her wide mouth quirked up at one corner in a way that emphasized the unusually straight line where her lips met. "You're just now figuring it out?"

"I'm sorry about the tracker," he said, and took a sip of his coffee. Unleaded, because he didn't need any more caffeine for a week. Maybe two. "It was insurance against Longsford's men. I didn't mention it because...frankly, I didn't want you to think I was concerned about keeping you safe."

"I'm sorry, too," she said crisply, taking a slug of milk. White foam traced the left half of her upper lip. "There's only one moment you could have planted that thing, and I'm *really* sorry that you even thought of it. I know I was thinking about other things."

He winced at her words. "Trust me, it wasn't—" And then he fell silent, caught in her gaze as she looked up at him, her expression making it perfectly clear what she had been thinking about. He stuttered to a stop there, and then finally took a deep breath into aching lungs. Slowly, he sat back in his chair, still holding her gaze. He thought about the conflict of interest and he thought about professionalism and he gave an abrupt shake of his head, freeing himself from the moment.

The scary thing was, he wasn't convinced. Not where it counted. Witness or not, he *wanted*—

"You've got a milk mustache," he told her.

Calmly, she licked her lip clean and went back to her pancakes.

It wasn't until later that he realized they'd never talked about why she'd run.

At the hospital emergency department, Karin fell asleep with her head on Dave's leg, curled up on the padded bench seat while she waited for her turn. She woke to the sound of Ellen's name to discover his hand resting on her hip, his head tipped back while he snored gently. He still wore that silly sweatshirt and his jeans were as ragged as hers, but...he somehow still looked as if he'd walked out of the pages of a catalog.

She slid out from beneath his hand and he didn't wake. No little wonder, after the crash course of drugs his system had gotten. Might as well let him sleep on. He'd taken it pretty hard that she'd gone over the cliff as a result of his tracking bug. She guessed that his out-to-save-the-world directive didn't leave much room for nearly getting someone killed.

She followed the nurse in Igor mode, stiff and pained in every muscle she had. An interminable length of time later, she came back out, somewhat less stumbly and somewhat more floaty. Painkillers were a wonderful thing. Dave waited for her, bleary-eyed and rubbing his neck; she guessed that he'd only just woken up.

"Sleep well?" she asked him, and couldn't help but grin.

"Ha," he said, and rubbed his neck again. Served him right. He nodded at her wrist, where a short arm cast enclosed her arm from elbow to halfway up her hand. "Broken?"

"You must be an investigator of some sort." But she relented and gave a short nod. "It's not bad. One of those little wrist bones. Or two. They gave me pain meds and told me to see my family doctor when I get home."

"About that—"

She gave a sharp shake of her head. "I don't want to talk about it right now. I want to find a hotel—you'll have to drive, by the way—and I want to sleep until I wake up. Then I want decadent room service and an old black-and-white movie. And then I'm going to sleep again—until sometime tomorrow, at which point we can pick up my truck here, and I'll drive myself home."

He stood up; he was closer than she'd meant them to be. "There's more than that," he said gently. "There are things we're not done with."

She'd figured. But pretending otherwise…it had been worth a try.

And then she thought of that moment on the cliff, when he'd come to help her. When he'd closed his strength and warmth around her and she'd had that flood of relief and she'd thought *this is what it's like*. To be frightened and to know you're trapped in your desperate situation…and to have someone come along and make a difference.

And to know there was still a little boy out there, and his only chance was if someone did the same for him.

Dave knew it, too. She had the feeling Dave never let himself forget it.

So she sighed and she rubbed a finger over her brow and she looked back at him with the slightest of nods. "Okay," she said. "But not now."

"Okay," he said back. "Let's find a hotel. One with really heavy curtains and good soundproofing."

Damned if he wasn't doing it again.

Making a difference.

Chapter 9

Karin woke to a muttering television and the tickety-tacking of a keyboard. She followed the low light in the room to find Dave in the corner, ensconced with his laptop and that yellow pad of paper. He slouched in a chair by the room's little round table, his feet propped on the double bed Karin hadn't fallen into upon arrival and a pair of wire-rimmed glasses settled firmly on his nose. His eyes looked slightly larger than normal through the lenses...huh. Farsighted, was he?

"Hey," she said, and it sounded like a frog being stepped on. She sat up in the bed—carefully—and reawakened every single bruise anyway. "So were you wearing contacts before, or do you do the vanity thing and leave the glasses off?"

He finished a few more keystrokes and looked up at her. "More like I break them on a regular basis if I leave them on.

Never could adjust to contacts. Doesn't matter…unless I'm using this thing or tired, I'm just fine."

"Working late," she observed, discovering the clock on the bedside table between them. Just after midnight. No wonder her mouth tasted so vile. And ugh…that smell…was that *her?*

"I caught up with my sleep a little earlier," he said drily. "It seemed wise to get in a report to the local LEOs as soon as possible." He nodded at the foot of his bed. "There's a sub in there for you. Didn't know what you'd like, so I went for blah."

Surprised gratitude twinged through her. "Thanks. Blah is fine. *Anything* is fine. I think…I'm going to take a shower first." Yeah. That smell was definitely her very own.

"I talked housekeeping out of a garbage bag and some rubber bands." He looked back at his computer, typed a few words. "For your cast."

"Jeez, who are you? An ex–Boy Scout?" She hadn't meant for her words to come out so sharply.

He looked up again, catching her gaze for a long moment. But when he looked back at his work, he said simply, "There's a sweatshirt in there, too. It's all I had…it'll be too big, but it's clean."

She plucked ruefully at her own long-sleeved waffle-weave shirt. "I can't believe we didn't bring my bag."

"Other things on our minds." It was a noncommittal reply, and she knew she'd hurt him with her sharp words after all. No big surprise that someone who was so fixated on helping children would have a heart big enough to be a target.

Well, so be it. She wouldn't be in this mess if it weren't for him.

And he's only trying to help a little boy.

With much care, she left the bed and went into the

bathroom, leaving the sound of his swift keystrokes behind. Her inner wince of contrition followed her right on in.

Under any other circumstances, it would have been a luxurious shower—hard spray, hot water, lots of lather. But tonight, it was merely a challenge to avoid the bruises and abrasions. She washed out her jeans and underwear and then hung them with the stern admonishment to dry overnight. The small fine-toothed comb he'd left would do nothing but foul up her hair, so she left it to dry uncombed, knowing she'd pay for it later. And though his sweatshirt hung down below her hips, she wrapped a towel around herself anyway. She surveyed herself in the mirror—tangled hair down around her shoulders, gray eyes wary and pained, abrasions artfully scattered around her face. The sweatshirt had another Red Wings logo on it—a ball with wings—which at least stiffened the cloth and obscured her breasts.

Sort of.

Turned out she wasn't that brave after all, and she kept one hand at the twist of the towel as she left the steamy bathroom. Just in case. She rummaged in the open television cabinet, coming up with the hotel stationery and a pen, snagging the food on the way back.

"There's a soda on ice," he said, not looking up. Or rather, desperately not looking up. She caught his eyes following her, heard the slight strain in his voice.

She was about to say, *you do think of everything,* but stopped herself. "Thanks," she said. And when she put it all down on the bed and sat, safely tucking the covers around her, she popped the top of the soda, fiddled with the tab a moment and said, "Thanks for getting me off that cliff, too."

This time he looked up. And again, he didn't answer right

away. Then he nodded, and said, "You're welcome. And you're right. It was my fault."

Startled, she nearly spilled the soda she'd just put her lips. "I didn't say—"

"But you've thought it. More than once." He shrugged. "It doesn't take a mind reader. I'd think the same, if I were in your place. But…I thought we were on the same page. About the safe house. I didn't think you'd—"

"Drug you." She said it without remorse. "The safe house probably seems like a great idea to you. But it wasn't *my* idea, was it? I can take care of myself."

"So I saw." He shook his head, but he smiled a little as he did it. "You certainly do rise to the occasion."

"I could say the same of you." It was an attempt to divert him, but it was lame and she knew it had failed when he just looked at her. Then faint amusement crossed his features and he said, "So. Mad Sheep disease?"

She couldn't help it; she snorted, raising a hand to keep the current swallow of soda in her mouth where it belonged. "Hey, he'd just tossed me over the cliff. He didn't mean to, but he was getting ready to walk away—with Longsford's blessing. I figured he'd have a little rash starting from the poison ivy, an itch or two. So I told him he'd been exposed by my sheep."

He thought about that a moment, then shook his head…but it was a gesture of amused admiration. "Good try."

She shrugged, tearing off a corner of the sub. Hardly stale at that. "Didn't work. Made a mess, in fact…I had no idea he'd be so sensitive to poison ivy. It came on strong enough to make him believe me after all."

Dave tapped a few more words into the laptop. "Means he's in custody, though." He got serious with his typing for a moment, and Karin ate her sub in silence. It didn't take long before she pulled the pad of paper to prop on her knees.

Karin Sommers's Substitute Journal, March Something

> Next installment in our exciting story. I'm here in a hotel room with a hunky guy in glasses that make him look even *more* sexy—if it can be believed—and I'm not even wearing underwear. Gosh, what do you think will happen next?
>
> Nothing, that's what. Because I hurt too damn bad. I'm in trouble, Ellen. Real trouble. I can't help that boy as you could have, because we neglected to do one of those memory transference things as you died. I might be able to do something as me—Rumsey's lessons come in handy now and then—but I can't be me without throwing away the new life you died to give me.
>
> And considering that warrant, without throwing away what's left of the old…

And didn't that just sum it all up.

Karin ate another bite of sandwich, savoring it. When she looked up she found Dave watching, his laptop closed, report submitted. "What did you tell them?"

He assumed a straight man's face. "That he didn't have Mad Sheep disease, no matter what he said." He watched as she tucked another morsel of food into her mouth, then gave himself a slight shake. "Actually, I didn't. I figure if he's babbling about Mad Sheep disease, they're not likely to give whatever else he says much credence. I just told them we'd found him when we stopped to stretch our legs, but that my companion had hurt herself while trying to help. Once we realized we couldn't, we called 911 and went to get you medical attention. And that I would be happily cooperative about answering any questions."

She narrowed her eyes at him.

He shrugged. "I don't think we'll have to. The man tripped and fell over the side in the dark, that's all. He's not the first they've rescued from that little patch of ground and he won't be the last. And whatever he says, you can bet he's not going to admit that Barret Longsford sent him to kidnap you, or that he threw you over the side of that mountain and then came back for you. Unless he's got a warrant lurking, he'll be headed back to Barret soon."

Karin stopped chewing at *warrant lurking* but immediately forced herself to continue, even if the food had gone tasteless. Swallowing, she took a sip of soda lest the bread get stuck in her throat, but after that she had her game face back. Even if she did push the sandwich aside.

If he noticed, he misinterpreted. "Don't worry," he said. "If something comes up, I'll handle it. Working with the local LEOs is something I do all the time—you think I had a contact in Bluefield out of coincidence?"

She'd wondered, actually. "So the errand geek is still on the loose," she said, drawing her knees up to grow pensive.

"Sidelined for a while, I should think," Dave said. "That rash…it's going to take him out of work for a while."

Karin pictured the man, allowing herself a small, tight smile. "All over his hands," she said. "Ol' Barret's gonna have to send someone down to get him."

Dave looked at her another long moment, rubbing a finger just below his lower lip in a thoughtful gesture. "Seriously," he said, "we could have pressed charges. But I don't think you could have stayed low-profile, and I'd rather have Barret wondering just where you are. I've gotten the impression you feel the same."

She took a sharp breath at the thought of being discovered. Longsford would *know* Karin wasn't the woman he'd dated. Fooling Ellen's casual acquaintances while leaning on the changes wrought by the accident was one thing…fooling someone who had been intimate with her was something else again.

"Hey," Dave said. She looked at him, for the moment only blinking. Here she was with the man who'd inadvertently turned her life upside down, the night after her life had *literally* gone topsy-turvy over the side of a mountain. She'd survived that…she'd survive this. She'd survive being unable to help Rashawn Little—and she'd survive being wanted by Longsford as Ellen and in California as Karin. She'd survive, because it was what she did. But right now…

Right now it all piled up around her in an implacably suffocating way.

Dave made getting-up noises, and rummaged in the overnight bag he'd dropped to the floor on the other side of his bed. "Hey," he said again, standing there looking as rumpled as she felt, damned adorably rumpled. And in his hand…a flask.

"Ooh," she said. It was an expensive flask, leather covered. It promised…

Single malt.

"Just a taste," he said. "It's cask strength, and you've got pain drugs in your system."

"They've worn off. Trust me on that." She watched—more listened—as he retrieved two hotel glasses, rinsed them and reemerged still shaking them free of excess water; he put them on the little round table. Then he rummaged in the room's minibar and brought out a bottle of purified drinking water.

"Ooh," she said again. "We're going to do this right."

"Damned straight we're doing this right. This is a twenty-six-year-old Cardhu. Distilled in '76, bottled in 2000."

She dropped her knees back into a cross-legged position, leaning forward a little. "If I didn't hurt so much, I'd bounce. Twenty-six-year-old Cardhu? Let's get married."

He grinned. "Ah," he said. "A true believer. I'm surprised this didn't come out when we spoke last year."

"We weren't talking about pleasant things," she pointed out, ignoring her little frill of alarm. This detail wouldn't be the one to out her. "*This* is a pleasant thing. A *sublime* thing."

He tipped his head in acknowledgment, trickled a finger of scotch into each glass, and handed her one, sitting on the edge of his bed. Not so far away, as they each swirled the amber liquid, taking in the smoky scent of a cask-strength malt. Karin sighed with appreciation, then took the smallest sip, holding it on her tongue as it warmed. Woody and citrusy and just a hint of smoky aftertaste when she swallowed.

She stole a glance at Dave, found his eyes closed and his nostrils slightly flared and suddenly fell just a little bit in love with a man who could savor such simple pleasures.

If scotch at nearly two hundred dollars a bottle could be called *simple.*

When he opened his eyes, he smiled, a self-aware sort of smile. "It's better shared, I always thought." He uncapped the bottled water and tipped it at her, and Karin held out her glass, wincing a little at what the movement did to her muscles.

"Never mind," she said, as he eyed her with concern. "This

will help." She waited for him to pour a splash of water, swirled and took in the aroma all over again. The taste turned smoother, sweet honey on her tongue with a side of citrus and a peaty, smoky aftertaste. "Oh yeah."

He grinned suddenly, still taking in the expanded aroma from his own glass. "I had a feeling it wouldn't be wasted."

"Oh?" She let the glass warm between her hands as he warmed a mouthful of the drink. "How did you come by that?"

He nodded at her sandwich. "The way you eat," he said. "You enjoy it. You take your time. You…it's…" He cleared his throat. "It caught my attention."

Karin let another sip of whiskey sit on her tongue, regarding him from beneath lowered brow. Too observant, this one.

Too engaging.

Too tempting.

And if she was going to hold herself together, to protect her new life…just plain too dangerous.

In the morning, Karin donned her dry underwear and her not-so-dry jeans and held back conversation in favor of ordering room-service breakfast. She had him worried, she knew; now he knew better than to take her for granted. And she caught him watching as she lingered over her spicy sausage and couldn't believe herself when she flushed. *Get a life, Sommers.*

Of course, that was the whole point.

She knew he'd insist on escorting her back home, and he did, following her truck with the casual skill of a pro. She knew he'd insist on coming inside, and he did. She knew they'd have another conversation about the safe house and her memories and the boy…and she knew he was running out of time. One way or the other, he'd be headed back to Alexandria soon.

She hadn't known he'd left his boxers on the floor of her bathroom. She tossed them at him and he caught them without comment, stuffing them into his overnight bag. Didn't even blush, darn it. She picked up a crumpled towel— more evidence of his attempts to shake off the drug she'd given him.

She could also take it as evidence of his frantic reaction to her disappearance. Probably somewhat like Rumsey's reaction…only she found she didn't mind. Not this time.

She let Amy Lynn know she was home but that she wasn't likely to stay, and she pointed Dave at the living room where he could make his phone calls. Then she went into her bedroom to peel off his sweatshirt—how could it still smell enticingly like him when it had clearly been freshly laundered?—and do what she'd been studiously not thinking about since her interminable night on the cliff.

She went up to the dormer.

To the storage off the dormer, where she'd carefully packed away Ellen's most personal things.

Not before she'd had a good look at them, of course—the amnesia defense could only take her so far. The official stuff— bank information, old taxes, insurance papers…she'd kept those out in the file cabinet just as though they were hers. By default they *were;* she paid the bills and made decisions and signed Ellen's carefully forged signature. But in storage… notes, old letters, photographs…

She'd taken a couple of ibuprofen, made herself a stiff cup of coffee, and disappeared upstairs.

"We have to talk—" Dave had said to her on the way by; she'd merely lifted a hand in acknowledgment. She'd told him she wanted to check her things, to try to jog her memory.

Close enough to the truth. She figured she had until dinner to sort out what came next.

Dewey had followed her up the stairs; now he curled up beside her as she sat cross-legged beside the half-height door to the eaves storage. Ellen's old letters had told her next to nothing; she wasn't a woman who'd made close friendships and as Karin looked at the stack—a few holiday cards kept through the years, one wistful note from a former coworker and several of Karin's quick missives from the years before e-mail and library Internet access—Karin suddenly felt awash in the sadness of such a solitary life.

And then she realized she had even less to show for herself, closed her eyes long enough for tears to form but not long enough for them to fall and set the letters aside. She flipped through Ellen's photo album—scenic shots from a handful of vacations, several parties from work… And here were several captioned photos clipped from the society page, with Ellen on the arm of Barret Longsford. She was dressed more expensively than Karin ever would have guessed. *Longsford must have provided those glittering gowns, that cocktail dress….*

Karin ran her finger over a picture that showed Ellen in detail. Her makeup, flawless…the dress, formfitting. Like Karin, Ellen had a lean figure…lean unto boyish, Karin had always thought, but there was nothing boyish about Ellen in this dress. "Wow," Karin whispered at her sister. "You look amazing." *And I never knew….*

Beside her, Longsford had a publicity smile pasted on his face, his hand at Ellen's elbow and the other hand giving a princely wave to the media. He wore a tux for this particular benefit event, his hair—blond or light brown, it was hard to tell in the black-and-white photo—conservatively styled, his teeth straight and white, and just enough smile lines at the corners of his eyes to look both dignified and a little dashing. She tapped the picture, tapped his face. "And do you really steal away little boys, Mr. Longsford? Do you kill them?"

And if he did…would Dave be able to prove it?

Stashed with the society clippings in the back of the album, loose photos sat unorganized and unsecured. More from the Longsford days. Exclusive resorts, a cruise ship, several outings that appeared to be more mundane trips to local parks.

A careful study of those photos revealed nothing of significance. Ellen and Longsford, his arm over her shoulder, a fountain behind them. Or a bandstand with band, or a sculpture…Karin would have guessed them to be events of political significance except for their dress…always casual, jeans and a polo shirt for Longsford, light sweaters and pretty shirts over slacks and jeans for Ellen. Longsford always had dark glasses on, always a cap of some sort.

But hey. Even an aspiring politician, son of a U.S. senator, and social gadfly needed some time to himself. Maybe that's why Ellen had taken these pictures…reminders of her private time with a public man.

Still. They did nothing to prove Longsford was a monster. They did nothing to pinpoint where a small boy might be stashed.

"Crap," Karin said into the quiet room. Dewey's tail thumped twice on the carpet in response. "Crap," she repeated, just so he'd do it again. Then she kissed him on the head and piled the albums, letters and loose photos away in their box, and pulled out the next one.

The old date book. Hmm, this could be promising. It had been on Ellen's desk when Karin arrived to this unfamiliar house that was suddenly her home. At first she thumbed randomly through it. Plenty of days with Longsford's name on them. Karin settled in to turn the pages, swiftly but in order. A doctor appointment, an office event…blah, blah, blah…and then a series of Realtor connections. The bank. The moving date. Long before then, Longsford's name ceased to show up. Karin wasn't sure if it reflected the assimilation of the man into Ellen's life, or the breakup. If she'd spent enough time with him so she no longer noted it on the calendar, then there was no telling when they actually broke up.

Maybe it had been when she first talked to Dave Hunter. She had it in the book, right before the evidence of her intent to move.

And again, the day before she had left to meet Karin in California. *Call Dave Hunter.*

But she hadn't. Karin had called *her* late the night before, asking for help.

So what had triggered her intent to contact Dave?

"I'm not meant for this," she told Dewey, who of course thumped his tail at every word. "I'm meant for creating situations, not untangling them. What a good boy." And he understood those last words as she'd meant him to, and offered up a flurry of wild thumps. Therapy dog.

Karin flipped through the remaining blank pages in frustration. Bad enough she'd had to look through all these things—to immerse herself, once more, in the loss she'd barely accepted.

A photo fluttered out.

"Hmm," she muttered, reaching for it. "And why aren't you with your little photo friends?"

The date on the back stamped it as being from one of the last batches, one of the park photos. And when Karin turned it over, she saw exactly why it had been pulled aside.

There was Longsford, leaning over to talk to a small boy. Karin turned the pages of the date book, tearing paper in her haste. There. The discussion with Dave Hunter...dated only a week before these photos were developed. Too bad the picture itself didn't bear a digital time stamp; there was no telling the exact date of the event.

But what if that little boy was Terry Williams?

Dave would know.

No. She couldn't show it to Dave. Not just yet. He'd have questions she couldn't answer...and it wouldn't bring him any closer to finding Rashawn Little.

The photo trembled in her hand. God, she didn't need to show it to Dave. She *knew.* Why else would Ellen have pulled this photo? Why else would she have planned to call Dave? Karin didn't know if Ellen had realized the photo's exact significance, but she'd clearly put two and two together.

Dave was right. Longsford was his man. And while Longsford's willingness to let his errand boys push her around—and then leave her on a cliff to die—had been pretty damning, they spoke only of the man's ruthlessness. Not of his guilt in the kidnapping and murder of little boys. This photo...

This photo drove it home.

Longsford was a predator.

Ellen would have been able to help nail the bastard.

But Karin...all Karin could do was hand over this photo and shrug. Somewhere out there Rashawn Little was sitting on a figurative cliff, helpless. Waiting for someone to drop him some tire chains. To give him that wondrous feeling Dave had given Karin...that for one moment, she wasn't alone in the world.

As Ellen, she couldn't help at all.

But Karin had resources Ellen had never even imagined.

Chapter 10

Dewey warned Karin out of her deep contemplation by lifting his head from his paws and then stalking out. By the time Dave got there, she was waiting for him—still sitting cross-legged, still holding the clues Ellen had left. Things that had meant nothing to her when she'd packed them up but now suddenly meant everything.

Dave waited in the doorway, as if sensing this was her most private space. More private, even, than the bedroom.

Not that she'd had visitors to either.

"Hey," he said, leaning against the door frame, a casual posture for someone who couldn't possibly feel casual inside. "I'm sorry to interrupt, but...we need to talk."

"Hey," she said. Odd to see him there, draped in the doorway with all his innate grace and still wearing his sweat-shirt as though it were designer goods. She could feel his presence from here…a baffling awareness. What was she supposed to do with that?

Enjoy it.

She blinked at the unexpected little voice in her head.

Huh.

He rubbed that spot below his lip, just above the cleft in his chin. Not a Kirk Douglas dimple, a more subtle thing at the bottom of an angled jaw. It balanced his nose—a strong nose, at that—and somehow always drew her eyes to his mouth.

At least it did when he hadn't already caught her gaze, holding it in silence as he so often did. Like now. Then that mouth went wryly crooked. "I know you've been through a lot, Ellen, but…I'm running out of time. Rashawn is running out of time. I've got to go back…and I want you to come."

She gave her next line on cue…the line that would make sense if she was who she'd told him she was. "You still think I'll remember something?"

Dave gave a one-shouldered shrug. "I don't know. But it's not safe for you to stay here by yourself. Not now. And that's my fault."

"Yes," she murmured. "We've established that." Not that he had any true idea of the potential ramifications. Of course, he was so damned honest that if he had even an inkling of her warrant, he'd probably put her on a plane to California himself.

That's not fair, said her pesky little voice. *He might believe you didn't do whatever Rumsey claims you did. He might even help you.*

As if she could take the chance.

She was hardly the innocent. She might not have done what the warrant claimed, but she'd done plenty. The long-term scams were her specialty, but she'd pulled plenty of high-pressure investment scams. She'd muled for Rumsey, she'd picked pockets when she was younger…she'd done plenty. She'd done it to survive and she felt no particular guilt even though she'd been ready to leave it behind.

That, she suspected, would bother Dave most of all.

She savored the physical tension between them. If he wasn't leaving until tomorrow, then there was the rest of the afternoon…the evening…

Take what you can get.

It had always been a motto of sorts.

Her glance fell upon the items in her hand. She looked over at him, gestured with them.

He took the invitation, coming in to kneel beside her when he saw the nature of what she had, exhaling with the surprise of it. She offered the photo; he took it, holding it out at a distance.

"Need those glasses?" she asked.

He shook his head, his mouth gone tight. "Do you know who this is?"

"Longsford," she said, her inflection saying *isn't it obvious?* even if her words didn't.

His finger—abraded and bruised from the cliffhanger antics—stabbed at the picture. "No. The boy. Terry Williams."

Karin looked away. "Crap." And then, still looking away, said, "Check the date book."

He did. Something like wonder came into his voice. "You were going to call me." It changed to demand. "Why the hell didn't you?"

Karin pointed at the next day. "There," she said. "My sister reached me. She…was in trouble. She lived with my stepfather. But my stepfather isn't a nice man, and she finally needed a way out. I left that day to get her." So odd to talk about herself in that way…but somehow also a relief. She could tell him of herself without truly revealing anything at all. Her finger then traveled across the page, stopping at the day Ellen had died. "Here. The accident. By the time I got back home, that note meant nothing to me. 'Hi, is this Dave Hunter? Who are you, and do you know why I was going to call you?'"

Dave ran his finger over the photograph. "Damn," he said softly.

"Isn't that photo enough? Won't it help?"

He stilled, thinking about it, and then shifted beside her, settling into a cross-legged position like her own. He didn't need to shake his head for Karin to know the answer. "Someone else, we might pull in for questioning with evidence like this. Longsford is too highly connected. When we go for him, we've got to have the case already made. But this is one more piece." He flipped the photo over, checking for notes, and then gestured with it. "Can I take it?"

"It's all yours."

He nodded his thanks. "If I'd had any doubts about him…"

That surprised her. "Did you?"

His smile was grim and weary. "No. But I'm the only one. There's a reason they didn't officially bring me in to consult."

She realized for the first time that he was doing this on his own time. Scraping around without Bureau resources, trying to find Rashawn before it was too late.

He looked over at her—caught her eye in that way he had. 'You'll come with me?"

She hesitated. She didn't need his help…she could easily wait until he left and then do what she'd planned in the first place, hide out as someone else until the threat was over.

But if Longsford wasn't caught, then the threat would

never end. Not now, once he'd decided she was a threat. Especially not if he wanted to continue his little hobby.

She was going to have to tell Dave. To offer him the help Ellen couldn't give him.

And when he learned who she really was, what she'd really done with her life, this man who now sat so comfortably beside her, who'd offered her his warmth and his kisses…then he'd look at her in an entirely different way.

Take what you can get.

Something must have shown on her face. The wistfulness…the *want*. And he had it, too. He said, "Hey." The same way he'd announced himself at her door, but somehow an entirely different word.

"Hey," she said softly. Had they moved closer together? Yeah. Definitely. With the *want* growing between them, reminiscent of their connection in the henhouse and quickly going beyond. She said what she'd said then, trusting him to catch it. "You like this with all your witnesses?"

Give the man credit, he didn't need a Clue Bat. "No," he said, meeting her gaze. "I'm like this with…*you.*"

They reached for each other at the same time, fingers tangling in hair, lips meeting with inexplicable familiarity. Her cast rested awkwardly against his neck, but when she ran her fingernails over the skin behind his ear he still froze for an instant. Then he nudged her backward, shoving the box out of the way. She went gladly and brought him with her, no hesitations…just *want*. She offered him full, hard kisses, half trapped under his body—and she suddenly felt bereft from the waist down. No warmth, no weight…no *heat*. Then his hand slid down her ribs—carefully, still somehow thinking of her battered state—and up her shirt and already she strained, lifting herself with the expectation until his hand cradled her breast. *Oh, yeah.* She dropped her head back, giving him free access to her throat.

Mistake. That Dave Hunter integrity was still at work, and she'd given him just enough space to think about it. "Ellen," he said, and the doubt came through clearly enough.

"Don't even think it!" she said fiercely. "I'm not even a witness anymore, not really. And you're *not getting away this time.*"

He laughed, propped on his elbow long enough to clear her face of the hair that had somehow become tangled between them; gently, he disengaged a strand. "Gee," he said, amused in his mild sarcasm. "If you're *sure*..."

She put his hand back on her breast—as close as she could get it, hindered by her cast—and pulled his head back down. Firmly. His lips barely touching hers, he murmured, "I guess you're sure."

In response, she levered herself up and rolled them both over. It was noisy and ungraceful and full of intent, and when she was done she straddled him.

Dave didn't appear to notice. Too busy helping her yank his sweatshirt over his head, and then too busy hissing through his teeth as she found the flat of his nipple and scratched it lightly; he thrust up against her to create instant lightning in all the places that were rapidly becoming the most important parts of her body. Except...

Too many clothes. She wiggled in a wordless demand and his hands clenched on her hips, his head tipping back and a delightful groan working its way through clenched teeth. A man who knew what he liked...who knew how to let go and enjoy it. But still too many clothes. "Off!" she demanded, reduced to one-word sentences. She unsnapped her jeans, fumbling to unbutton his until he took over. They separated long enough to shuck their jeans and then she was right back with him, sinking into the satisfaction of almost-contact, wrapping herself around the heat of his erection through his dark boxers. She moved against him, body thrumming, and gave no quarter as he reached for his jeans, his wallet—and then arched in helpless reaction as she reached behind herself to give him an intimate tickle.

So she did it again, and then leaned down to nibble the throat he'd just exposed.

"Lord!" he said. "You—"

She laughed into the curve where his neck met his shoulders, taking in the scent of him. But he hadn't lost himself entirely; he dropped his wallet to grab her hips and lift his own, angling them together so perfectly she cried out at the intensity of it. "Two can play that game," he told her.

She groped for that wallet. This was what she'd wanted, what her body had been reaching for, each and every time she'd felt the connection between them. Across the room, in a crowded henhouse, over pancakes at breakfast…this was the silent language they'd been speaking to each other. "Now," she told him. "Now, now, *now*."

Panting, his ice blue eyes alight with laughter and desire, he said again, "If you're *sure*—"

She knew the only answer to that. She ran her hand up the inside of his thigh, sneaking in under his boxers. He instantly snatched the wallet up, pulled out the condom lurking within and covered himself, not bothering to remove the boxers. Karin did her best to make it a challenge, scraping her nails lightly up his thigh, high enough to make him react and gasp and tighten—but he laughed, too, short and breathless, enjoying her.

And then he didn't bother with her underwear, which she wouldn't have predicted anyone could just yank aside like that but who *cared*, not when they finally came together. *Together.* They spent a few luxurious moments learning the feel of each other—hard and soft, getting acquainted—and started to move. Nothing slow about that, not with the two of them so explosive, so full of coiling energy. Karin arched into him, braced her hands on his thighs and threw her head back. They danced together, fast and hard and quickly building, until all her strength drained from her fingers and toes and spiraled inward and Dave's thighs tightened beneath her hands, raising them both.

It was impulse that made her clench her knees to his side, stopping them in mid-thrust. Impulse that made her close down around him so he gave a surprised little cry, neck straining, fingers reaching and needy and headed for the juncture of her thighs. She did it again and he froze, arching upward, trembling, still reaching for her, pulsing in response to her.

A long moment she held them that way, neither of them quite breathing, the intimacy of their connection almost unbearable, a pulsing focal point of—

"Now," she whispered, and moved. He gave a great cry, a strangled sound...a startled sound. And he finally reached her, a single touch, and she cried out with him.

He should have been spent after that...Karin was, as limp as a noodle and not sure whether to fall forward or simply to finish falling backward to lie like an acrobat atop his knees. He made the decision for her, pulling her forward to kiss her with a surprising intensity. She thought it might be a thank-you...she thought it might be his way of making certain he didn't take her lightly. Either was fine with her and she kissed him back until they had so little breath left there was no choice.

She lay across his chest, taking a brief moment to regret that she'd never gotten her shirt off, never felt his hands on her bare breasts. *Next time.*

Except there wasn't likely to be a next time. She was running out of time. She'd have to tell him who she really was…and the man who thought he'd made love to Ellen might well not want to make love to Karin. Karin who'd lied to him…deceived him…

For once, quite suddenly, she was grateful to Rumsey. He was the one who'd taught her to grab opportunities, to rely on her instinct…to avoid thinking things to death when the moment was right. And nothing…*nothing* could be more right than this. Whatever happened next. Nothing could take this moment away. She kissed his collarbone, drawing on enough energy to run her hand down the crisp of blond hair that covered his chest. "I changed my mind," she said, lazy and satisfied. "This wasn't a good idea at all."

He laughed, as much as he could with her weight on his chest and a slight tremble still reverberating through his body, and he kissed the top of her head. "You're right," he said, and his voice tickled her ear. "That didn't work out well in the least. We should never do it again."

"Ever," she said…and prepared to do it again.

Chapter 11

Karin managed evening chores with an old sock over her cast to keep it from picking up unsavory farm substances, and with Dave by her side. "Yes," she'd told him. "I'll come with you. But we have to talk." So they fed the goats, and she taught him how to milk Agatha, leaning over him to wrap one hand over his, initiating just the right rhythm in his fingers.

He gave her a sideways glance, one sparked with humor. "You're enjoying this."

"Hell, yes," she told him, and licked his neck.

He carried the milk pail as she fed the sheep, apologizing to them for the whole Mad Sheep disease ploy. The sheep did not appear to care, and as they ate, Dave took a rake to the worst spots of the pen. He and Karin cast simultaneous glances at the old henhouse and she waggled her eyebrows at him, eliciting a somewhat smug grin. She drank it in.

She figured it was one of the last she'd see. That connection between them, so warm and nearly palpable…she figured she wouldn't have it much longer. Maybe that was why she pinned him against the barn for one last, deep kiss before taking him by the hand and walking along the crest of the hill. When she sat, ignoring the dampness of the spring ground, he followed suit. But he'd picked up on her tension.

"You're not changing your mind," he said warily, more a prod than a question.

Karin drew her knees to her chest and pulled her hoodie sweatshirt out to envelop them. Total coincidence if it looked something like a fetal curl. "I'm not. But you might."

He thought on that a moment and shook his head. "Nope," he said. "Too cryptic. You'll have to give me more."

She thought wistfully about his flask, but knew he wasn't carrying it. A swallow of that Cardhu would have gone down well, cask bite and all. "This Owen of yours," she said. "The family business. Are you all rescuers?"

That surprised him. He withdrew, looking down the slope of the greening pasture. When he glanced at her, his eyes were back to cool ice. She told herself to get used to it. He said, "The safe house tipped you off, huh?"

"Well, *yeah*." That was the truth, but not all of it…and here, on this hill, Karin was offering the whole truth. She added, "Not just that. It's the way you are. A rescuer. I figure you either come from a family of them, or a family of the opposite. A kick-you-when-you're-down family."

Dave snorted. "No, not that." He turned his jacket collar up, though it wasn't nearly cold enough to inspire the need. "Rescuers. I never thought of it like that before, but…yeah."

"So what's Owen's beef with you? He's a rescuer…you're a rescuer. I thought you said you weren't in the family biz."

"This day isn't about me." He tried to put some finality into his words. He didn't have much success. Not after what had happened between them that afternoon.

She leaned into him, bumping his shoulder. Did it again, until he looked over at her. Not happily. She shrugged. "Maybe it wasn't when you got here. But now, kinda…yeah, it is." *And besides, I don't think there's any way we're going to have this little talk after I spill the beans on myself.*

He scruffed his hand through his hair. It looked like defeat to Karin. "When my parents started the agency, they kept it personal. Small cases, affecting individuals. But once Owen truly had control, things changed. He got a few big jobs…he headed upscale. Instead of dealing with individuals, the agency manages big-picture ops. Saving the world, instead of just your neighbor." He shrugged. "It's a good agency. It's a *superb* agency. Their operatives are the best. But…they're *operatives*. I'm not."

She thought about that a moment. A long moment. Then she asked, "Why?"

He made a gesture of impatience. "Ellen, is this—"

"Yes," she interrupted, unrepentant. "If I leave with you, then yes. I want to know more about who I'm going with."

"You knew enough to…"

This time, her smile—a little wry, but undeterred—was enough to cut him short. She said, "Yes, I did. That was my *now*. This is about my future."

Dave did the hair-scruffing thing again. When he spoke, it was grudging. "Okay. Yeah. Look…there's nothing wrong with Owen's way. It's just not for me."

"But you don't mind drawing on the resources of the family agency."

He stiffened slightly. "No," he said. "I don't. What I'm doing is just as important. If my parents were still alive, they would have the same priorities. Owen might not appreciate the path that I've taken, but he understands that. It doesn't happen all that damn often, but if I need resources, I ask for them."

"And you help them, too." She filled in that blank; he gave her a disgruntled and impatient look. "You said something about Pittsburgh. Ribs...collarbone. I've got good reason to know how long ribs can stay sore."

His eyes had narrowed. "You're full of surprises."

Oh, ha. You're about to find out how right you are.

But he conceded her point. "Yes. I help them out when they need me. Which is just often enough to remind me what Owen thinks I should be doing, but not so often that I tell him to take a flying leap. He's good like that. Knows just where the line is."

"Where?" she asked softly, knowing he would be appalled that she seldom bothered to draw lines at all. Morally acceptable to unacceptable...she'd lived her life moving freely on either side of that line. "Or should I ask, why? What made you different? What made your work more important than what your family expected of you?"

Because this was one of those families. A family with obligations and expectations. Rather like Rumsey, only with an entirely different focus.

She thought he might object again. She said, "I've got the persistence to hang off the side of a cliff all night. What makes you think I'm going to give up on this?"

He said his bad words again. The whole string, under his

breath, not even looking at her. *Nom de Dieu de bordel de merde*. Then he said, "It was just one of those things. Everyone's got one or two of them." He glanced at her as though guessing what hers might be but she didn't flinch; he'd know soon enough. "I was nine. I took ride-alongs with my dad all the time—not the crucial stuff, nothing inappropriate. Meeting people he worked with, handling legwork. But I got greedy, and I wanted in on some of the exciting stuff. When you're nine, you can't even imagine…"

Well, yes. She could. Rumsey had hauled her everywhere, introducing her to the life. But she nodded anyway. "So you… what? Invited yourself along?"

He hadn't expected her to guess it so closely, but he got past his surprise to say, "Just that. Hid in the backseat of my dad's sedan one night. Turned out he was on his way to a body recovery." He looked at her without turning his head, just a flash of those bright eyes. "Little boy about my age, the son of a French diplomat who was touring our wine county. He'd been kidnapped and dumped. It was an ugly scene."

"I'm sorry," she said. "It must have been a shock."

"That's one way to put it." He shifted to look her straight on, obviously struggling to move past the memory. "Don't bother with psychobabble, by the way."

"Me?" She hadn't intended it. In truth, she was too lost in her own thoughts, in what came next.

"You. Anyone. I've heard enough of it—how it's too late to save that kid, and if I spend my life trying I'll just waste my time. The way I see it, I was pretty much headed for this business. I might as well choose how I go about it."

"I get that. I got funneled into the family business, too."

He frowned, golden eyebrows pulled together. Thick eyebrows, thick enough to avoid that pale-haired, eyebrow-free appearance. "You were a legal secretary."

"Okay," she told him. Now or never. "It's my turn to talk. And you just listen. Though you're not going to like it." She sat silent for a moment, thinking of his hands on her body, savoring that memory. Then thinking of his honesty in love-making. He didn't hide how she'd affected him, didn't play stoic…he'd laughed and cried out and shared himself with her.

He wasn't likely to hide how he felt about her words, either.

He didn't help, not when he reached out to tuck her cast-covering sock back into place where it had slipped toward her thumb. She'd miss that thoughtfulness. She'd only had it a short while, but she'd drunk it up and found herself thirstier than expected. Still thirsty. *Always thirsty, at this rate.*

Didn't matter; it was what she was used to. She knew how to live that way, and this was something she had to do. No longer even a choice, somehow. She'd help this boy as best she could. She had her own demons to drive her.

She lifted her head to look him in the eye as she spoke. She'd see it that way, the exact moment he realized the import of what she said. "A year ago my sister and I were in a car accident. No—" She shook her head sharply as his mouth opened, and made no attempt to retain any of Ellen's mannerisms. "No, you *think* you know this, but you don't. We were in that car accident, and my sister died."

"I do know—"

"My sister *Ellen.*"

Dave didn't hear her. Not really. He only stared, frowning. And she stared back, waiting. Impatient. Blue-gray eyes watching him from beneath her eyebrows.

And that was when it fell into place. So preposterous it had never even occurred to him, and yet it explained every lingering question he'd had since his arrival here. It explained how quiet Ellen had slammed a man with a hand cultivator; it explained how she'd had the grit to get through the night on the mountainside.

It explained why he'd reacted to her when Ellen had never inspired more than a professional glance.

"Karin," he said. It sounded like a question so he said it again, making it into a statement. "You're Karin."

She nodded, relieved and wary at the same time.

He managed another silent moment, before the questions and anger coalesced into the realization that this woman couldn't help him at all. Not only couldn't help him, had wasted precious days in which he might have been hunting Rashawn in other ways. Realization burst out, and it was loud. *"Why?"*

"Here's the way this goes," she said. "I'll explain, and then I'll help you. Or you can shout at me again and you can leave right now without me. Me, I'm leaving tonight regardless. The hounds you put on my heels are real enough."

"Just tell me why the *hell* you let me think—" He couldn't help it, couldn't keep the anger inside. Everything they'd been through…for nothing. Everything they'd done together… meaningless. And he was no closer to saving Rashawn than he'd ever been. Even the photo just told him what he'd already known.

Dark honey-brown hair spilled over her shoulder, trapped in the ponytail he'd helped her secure. He'd run his fingers through that hair…he'd loved it. But this new expression wasn't one he'd seen before. Harder. Perfectly resolute.

"That's two," she said. "You ready to listen yet, or should I go make my alternate arrangements?"

Dave put both hands over his face, ignoring the dirt from his recent farm chores. "I'm listening."

"Ellen is—was—my older sister. She moved away years ago, because she couldn't deal with the family business." Her voice was resolute. Implacable. And for all the emotion she kept out of it, the deeper husky notes of that voice throbbed with the price of this conversation. "Rumsey raised us to follow in his footsteps. I was eight when I took my first real part in a con game." She paused so he could take that in.

Took her part in a con game. Raised to be a scam artist. A thief. A player.

Thank God he had his hands over his face. No doubt she could still see his jaw clench.

"Ellen left as soon as she could. But by the time I was ready to go, I was in too deep. I had to run for it. Ellen intended to bring me back here so I could lay low and figure out how to move on. But when…" She faltered for the first time.

He dropped his hands, found her wiping some imaginary scuff off her jeans. She swallowed visibly, but then she was back. "After the crash, as she lay there dying, Ellen made me promise to take her name. I needed the time to sort my life out…it seemed like a good idea." She snorted, but the tears in her voice never made it anywhere near her face. Tough woman. "Hell, it *was* a good idea. It worked perfectly until you came along."

He shook his head and didn't even realize he was doing it until she gave him a sharp look. He said, "Why the hell didn't you just tell me I had the wrong woman?"

Her expression turned skeptical. "Did you listen to what I

just said? I'm *hiding,* that's why. And I dare you to count how many times I said I couldn't help you. I'd have booted you right off the place if Longsford's errand boys hadn't come in and complicated the hell out of things."

She brushed her knees off and stood. "As I recall, I even drugged you and ran off to keep myself safe, which is where I'd be right now if your sneaky bug hadn't been attached to my back. Safe. Keeping my little world together." She crossed her arms, awkward with the cast, and glared down at him. "Now my cover's heading for blown, Longsford is still after me and you're no better off than if you'd only *believed* me. Not to mention the whole thrown-over-the-cliff thing. That *really sucked.*"

Dave rested his forehead on the heels of both hands. The sense of betrayal went beyond reason, even when fair play reared its intrusive little head and reminded him that she was *right.* That everything she'd said was true. He'd intruded here; she'd told him she couldn't help. Repeatedly. With emphasis and conviction.

If only you'd told me the truth…

Then what? He'd already put her up against a wall. He'd already drawn Longsford's men her way, trapping her between running as Ellen or running as Karin.

And still…the lie twisted in his stomach. *And there's your conflict of interest.* Stupid, to end up in bed—or on the floor— with a woman connected to one of his investigations.

Yet in spite of the bitter twist, he couldn't quite regret it. He'd wanted her with a poignant strength that surprised him. Right from the moment he'd followed her inside the house, trapping her up against that washing machine so he could make his point. He should have known they weren't the same person, should have listened to himself, for the real Ellen Sommers had never interested him in the least. This woman, her sister…

She'd been more to him, more *alive* to him, from the moment he saw her. He lifted his head to see her standing there on the crest of the ridge. Unyieldingly straight back, chin raised as she looked out over the land, thick, straight hair escaping from the ponytail, long waist down to tight hips that held low-rise jeans, leaving a taut athletic curve of skin.

Yeah, he still wanted to pull her in close and kiss that belly, unsnap those jeans and tug away the practical underwear beneath. Some part of him definitely still wanted it, and wanted it *now*.

But those moments were past. Now he had to deal with where the situation had brought them. One man who was all about doing right by people, all about rescuing them…and one woman whose skill at deception still hadn't quite sunk in.

He should start with an apology. Whatever his intentions, he'd walked into the middle of a fugitive's cover situation and stomped it all to hell. But they already somehow seemed past that.

Or maybe just not ready to talk about it.

So when he finally cleared his throat and spoke, his rough-edged voice came out with, "How?"

She didn't turn around. "How, what?"

"You said you could help."

"That depends, really." Her voice might have been a little huskier than normal; hard to tell. She was no longer offering him any of those glimpses of the Ellen Sommers he'd known.

Dave pushed off to his feet, uncrossing his legs along the way. "Depends on…what? You have conditions?"

She glanced back at him. "No. This is something I want to do, for my own reasons."

"What, then?" An anxious twinge surprised him. Three days gone, and no closer to finding the boy he sought. Not even a clue. Being convinced Longsford was behind the kidnapping was one thing, and finding the boy was another.

She turned to face him then. "Whether I help depends on you. On if you can bring yourself to do things my way."

"I don't—"

"Look, the law's not getting anywhere. Your feebies aren't getting anywhere. You're all constrained by legal niceties. What you need is a way to slip up on Longsford from the other side."

"You?" His voice may have been skeptical, but something in him already believed.

She dropped her head ever so slightly. It emphasized the size of her eyes, the way she could use them to say whatever she wanted to say, entirely without words. *Yes. Of course me.* Out loud, she finally said, "If Longsford's as greedy as you painted him, I can rope him in with a layered long con. It'll get me close. Once I'm in…" She shrugged. "I know what to look for. I'll find Longsford's little hidey-hole."

"It takes a thief," Dave said flatly, unable to lighten his tone.

"No. It takes Longsford's greed and power thirst. Without that, I'd have nothing to exploit."

"You want to what—make him an offer an e-mail scammer couldn't refuse?" That was insulting, and he knew it.

She didn't pretend it wasn't. Her expression turned derisive—and then hard. "Whatever it takes," she said, and looked away, back out over the farm. "It seems Rumsey taught me well after all."

Chapter 12

Dave thought to say no, that much was obvious to Karin. He didn't want any part of her scheming.

She reminded him that he'd offered her the safe house. That she had to leave this little farm in any event. That he had time to think about it. If it occurred to him that he'd be making this decision while in the company of a woman who knew exactly how to get what she wanted, it didn't show.

And so they left the farm to Amy Lynn and Karin kissed Dewey goodbye and told him to watch the property, and they drove off toward Alexandria.

Karin Sommers's Journal on the Road, March 16

I'm getting used to the car. From the farm to the big city...lotta hours. And then there's Perfectly Gloomy

Gus, my travel companion. He thinks he's gonna dump me in his brother's safe house and rush on with his investigation. He thinks he's going to sift through the same old information and find a new trail somehow. Yeah, right.

He needs the angles I can work. And dammit, doesn't it seem only fair that Rumsey's teachings might actually do someone some *good?* Wouldn't he just be disgusted?

Perfectly Gloomy Gus has his knickers tied in a knot because of what happened between us. He forgets himself, responds to our *us-ness,* and then clams up tighter than a righteous virgin.

Poor guy. Mr. Straight-and-Narrow, stuck with Ms. Take-What-You-Can-Get, However-You-Can-Get-It.

It's not like I was born that way.

And it's not like I had any trouble leaving it behind. Some habits die hard, but jeez, Ellen, the most I've done since the accident is a little finders-keepers. And no, I'm not racked with guilt over what came before. We both took early beatings for ratting him out—such great imaginations we had, weren't we precious!—and I still have that scar on the back of my leg. So I didn't have a lot of choice. Not—and don't get all guilt-racked over this, but we both know it's the truth—not once you so dramatically opted out of the life. Me...I just opted out of high school early. Out of proms and slumber parties and sweet first dates...and a future.

Nothing comes sweet in Rumsey's world, not unless it's for Rumsey himself.

Dave doesn't get it. He doesn't get that I left that world behind. You know, I was thinking of getting my

GED. Of working in criminology, even. But things don't exactly bode well for that particular option anymore. Especially now that Mr. Straight-and-Narrow knows who I really am. He knows I want to keep your identity; he knows it's because of Rumsey. But the warrant—the one in my name, for who knows what except I damn well didn't do it—is the real problem.

Gotta wonder how long it'll take before Dave figures it out.

Karin fiddled with the radio stations, hunting for something between outright country and hard rock. Surely there'd be one little station with an independent bent, one that played music that crossed the lines...just like her.

Bored, bored, bored. She gave up and sat back in the car seat as Dave linked his laptop to his cell phone and checked out the Front Royal Yellow Pages. "There's a bed-and-breakfast that looks good," he said. He disconnected the laptop and dialed the cell phone as Karin contemplated the brick restroom building not far from them. "Going for a walk."

He hesitated, as though he might put the call through later and walk with her now. He might not like her scheming, but he fully intended to deliver her to that safe house.

What he didn't realize was that she no longer had a reason to run. She'd already lost what she'd been trying to protect. "Dude," she told him, "if I wanted to ditch you, I'd ditch you. And the whole escape at the bathroom thing has been done to death."

"Dude," he mused, one of those rare moments in this day when a genuine smile teased along his mouth. "Go, then. I'll see if we can get a suite at this place."

So she went, wrapped in her old army jacket and pretending she didn't know about the tears and scuffs the cliff had wrought. Her poor stiff body sure knew about it. Her wrist ached inside the cast, and every bruise and cramp protested her movement. She walked the perimeter of the area, stopping to watch as a boy played with the family dog. She realized, to her astonishment, that she missed Dewey. Ellen's dog had come into her life with no choice in the matter. Yeah, she missed him.

And the sheep. And even the demanding goats.

Great. She was homesick. *Farmsick.* And it wasn't even her farm to begin with. Then again, it wasn't even her life.

To shake herself free of the mood, she took another brisk tour around the perimeter. Hey, maybe her butt wouldn't be asleep forever at that. She put her mind to work on the scam she'd run if she had endless resources. All the extras she needed, all the finances, the best manager…she'd be the roper. She was always the roper. She'd weave her way into Longsford's trust, pulling him along by his greed.

Except in this case, the end goal wouldn't be the sting itself. It would be what she could learn along the way. It would be about saving one little boy.

Dave had parked at the end of the lot, and Karin broke into a jog, stretching her legs a little as she went back to join him. First things first…clothes. Surely Front Royal would have a store or two. Would there be anyone she could trust with her hair? With her eyes?

She arrived back at the car flushed with both the minor exertion and the major buzz of the con planning. She had to admit there was a real jazz to planning a long con, a pleasure in thinking through the details and putting the pieces in place.

A satisfaction when those pieces came together, especially if the grift was so seamless that the mark never truly realized he or she had been scammed.

There was, however, no sign of Dave at the Maxima. Not in it, not next to it…. *Okay, so…sometimes a guy's gotta go, too.* She waited, stretching with mini-calisthenics so as not to stiffen right up again.

No sign of him.

Huh.

She circled the car, looking for him behind the trucks, behind the buildings, along the tree line of the thick, early-spring woods.

Ah.

There he was, just inside the tree line, staring at the phone in his hand as if it could offer him much-needed wisdom. He rubbed the heel of one hand across his brow, never quite completing the gesture…just standing that way.

Huh. Again.

She walked across the spongy spring grass. He saw her and came to meet her, but there was no authority in his stride, no confidence. Karin slowed, wary even before they'd closed the distance between them, and then she got close enough to see that his troubled eyes were red rimmed, their expression…

Haunted.

By the time they stood face-to-face, he'd shuttered the depth of the emotion, but it was too late.

"Who was that?" she asked. "The FBI? You just got your walking papers?" But that didn't seem quite right, not quite in sync with the emotion he'd shown.

"Yeah," he said, and cleared his throat. "I did." He didn't meet her gaze, so unlike him.

Karin found she missed that blunt, quiet connection. "Doesn't mean anything. You can still—"

His look was sharp enough to cut her off. With rough, short movements, Dave stabbed his cell phone at an inside jacket pocket until he found the right opening, looking at her all the while. And although he hadn't moved back, he'd somehow put distance between them nonetheless.

It's me, she realized quite suddenly. He'd gotten news of her warrant, and there was no way he wouldn't take her in—

But he cut those thoughts off as easily as he'd cut off her words. "The search is over. They found him."

By then her thoughts were so tangled up that she could only stare at him, unable to take in the significance of his words. Her expression got stuck on full *duh.*

"Rashawn," Dave said bitterly. "Dumped."

From *duh* to disbelief. "But—you said you had time!"

He laughed, a harsh, short sound. "So I thought. Turns out my persistence got some attention…the Feds poked around in Longsford's life. That's what brought Longsford's men to your place." He shook his head, his eyes gone unfocused.

She had no trouble following his thoughts this time. She walked right through the barrier he'd erected since he'd learned her true identity, her hand landing on his elbow. "Hey," she said. "Not your fault. None of it."

He didn't even look at her. Didn't react to her touch. Lost somewhere.

"Call it *my* fault," she said. "If I hadn't asked Ellen for help, she'd have been in touch with you a year ago. When Rashawn went missing, you would have been ready. You wouldn't have wasted your time with me in Blue Ridge country."

He gave her a wry glance, then. "I only had to believe you

three days ago when you said you couldn't help. I could have been back in Alexandria before that day was over."

"Not once the geek boys showed up. You wouldn't have left me to face them alone, not after they focused on me. Well, focused on Ellen." She moved a step closer, bringing her hand up to brush at the dampness shining faintly on his cheek.

He closed his eyes at her touch, emotions flickering across his face. The reluctance to accept her touch…the inability to resist it. "I don't want this," he said, even as he put his hand over hers. "You know I don't want this. Can't trust you. Can't understand you. Can't even approve of you."

"Look on the bright side," Karin suggested. "Wouldn't it give Owen fits to think of us?"

That got a smile from him; he took her hand and kissed the palm, then enfolded it in both of his and put it to his chest, holding it there. "We aren't an us," he said, but the wry little smile had reached his voice.

"For right now we are, and you know it. Being angry at who I really am doesn't change that." She'd spent the car ride believing that part of him to be lost to her, but in the wake of his gentleness, she suddenly knew otherwise. She dropped her head to look up at him from beneath her brow, her voice deepening. "Sometimes it just *is*. For however long it lasts."

"Voice of experience?" He met the intensity in her own eyes and blinked.

"Voice of observation." She moved in closer, right up next to him. "You and I…we're still us, all right. The definition and duration of that us…it doesn't matter. Not right now." *Take what you can get. Enjoy it.* "What matters is *we're not stopping now.*"

He heard the change of tone in her voice, realized she

wasn't talking about them anymore. Not personally. "Ell—" He closed his eyes again, very briefly, this time to rein in his annoyance. "Karin. I'm off it. They've stirred up too much trouble with no results, the boy is dead…someone's got to lose their head. That, in case you hadn't noticed, would be me."

"I've seen you lose your head. I rather liked it, and I think we should do it again sometime." She leaned closer, close enough to kiss his jaw right where it met his neck and where his pulse pounded visibly. Then she stepped back. "But you're an investigator with or without them, right? You can get this guy—before he does this again. While he's still basking in the glow of thinking he's gotten away with it."

He shook his head; regret shone through in those piercing eyes. "It's not that simple—"

"In my world, it is. You do what you have to do. You take what you can get."

He stiffened; he understood her perfectly. An exchange of impeccable honor for the results he craved. Probably not something he'd ever even considered. He shook his head. Then he put a hand on either side of her neck and drew her in for what turned out to be a startlingly thorough kiss, one that baffled her, but which she didn't hesitate to allow to deepen. When he pulled away he still held her close, and after a moment gave her one last gentle kiss on the lips…and then he stood back. He shook his head again. "I can't do that."

"You wouldn't have to do all that much of it," she pointed out. "That's my gig."

"Thank you." He straightened his jacket, though it didn't need straightening. "For trying to help, I mean. But…no." He took her hand, starting them back toward the car.

She waited until they reached it and said, "You've got the

night to think about it. If we're going to do this, I need to start preparing before we reach the city."

He stopped her with that same grip on her hand, hanging back until she turned around to face him. "Just to be clear," he said. "By 'if we're going to do this,' you mean using one of your scams to get close to Longsford so I can find what I need to nail his ass to a cell wall."

"From what I understand, that particular activity will be someone else's pleasure," Karin said sweetly. "But yes. I mean scamming to get inside his world. That's what you haven't been able to do, isn't it? See his world from the inside out?"

Reluctantly, he nodded. "We're on the outside looking in. We can't even get disgruntled ex-employees to talk."

"Which should tell you something. Supposing you didn't already get the message with the Messieurs Ruthless at my place."

He let go of her fingers; he covered his face briefly and then let his hands fall away to expose the weariness, the awareness of the odds...the battle within. "I don't know," he said. "I really...I just don't—"

And that means you do know, and you don't want to face it yet. The best time to back off totally, to remove the pressure. "I'm hungry," she said. "I'm thinking lots of carbs. How about you?"

"I'm thinking of that Cardhu in the backseat of the car," Dave admitted. "But let's get some food on board first."

Karin nodded, getting back into the Maxima. Already playing the game, whether Dave knew it or not. The jazz of it returned in one big rush mixed with the way it would give her a chance—for the first time ever—to make a positive difference in someone's life. To give Rashawn justice and revenge.

But yeah. The jazz of it...

She took a deep breath, sinking deeply into the car seat as Dave backed out of the parking spot. *Oh yeah.*

She felt she could get used to it again, just that fast.

She wasn't sure she liked that.

In the past, she'd been able to blame Rumsey for how she lived her life. How she'd been brought up…what she'd turned into. But the truth was, once she'd stopped resisting Rumsey, she'd been too damn good at it. And now it looked like she just couldn't stay away from the life after all.

Chapter 13

Dear Ellen…it looks like I'm a little more hooked than I ever thought. But hey, maybe there's a twelve-step program. Maybe good old Saint Dismas, patron of reformed thieves that he is, will lend a hand.

Or maybe…it's just who I am.

Peripheral vision alerted Karin; she instantly recognized Dave's movement. Sure and masculine, but also with a strange sense of grace. By the time he sat down opposite her, she'd closed her journal and stuffed it back into her courier bag.

He noticed, of course. "It's never far away, is it?"

"What's that?" Useless misdirection and she knew it.

He nodded at her bag. "Your book. It's more than just a diary."

"Damn your investigative eyes," she said cheerfully, and then still didn't answer. The letters to Ellen were too private. Sharing the fact that she wrote them...too vulnerable. "Did you decide on your dinner?"

He looked at her long enough to let her know he wasn't stupid, but let it drop anyway. "The four-cheese burger," he said. "Lots of carbs. So what were you thinking?"

The menu suddenly seemed like too much trouble. Karin found herself tired, ready for an early bedtime or at least a hearty nap. "That burger sounds fine."

He smiled again, more briefly this time. "I meant, thinking about the situation. Your big plans." He reached for one of the miniature muffins that had appeared in a wicker basket while he was gone. Poppy seed, blueberry, carrot, zucchini...

Okay, yeah, she was still hungry. She went for blueberry as she pondered his question, slathering the muffin with butter. Reminded herself that he wasn't sold on the idea yet. Reminded herself that he was her partner, not her mark; she had no reason to withhold anything from him.

Except possibly the extent of her proficiency.

"Classic layered real-estate scam," she said. "I'll rope him in, but we'll need someone to play the inside man—phone ought to do it—and you'll need to fill in as an extra for a handful of minor roles. I assume he'll recognize you, but we can work around that."

He held the little muffin between thumb and finger and seemed to have forgotten it. "What makes you think he'll even go for it?"

Karin let his obvious skepticism sit unanswered a moment. "A couple of things," she finally told him, and then had to pause while he gave their orders to the waiter. Suited her fine. She drank down half a glass of ice water and licked the rim of it off her upper lip. As the waiter left, Dave raised an eyebrow. She shrugged. "You said it yourself...he's greedy. He likes to feel powerful. He's a player. Any scam depends on underlying greed. And to this one I'm going to add layers—the chance to do a big loud public good deed. The chance to make someone else look politically stupid for opposing that good deed."

That took him back. He thought about it a moment, until he remembered his little muffin, gave it a puzzled look and ultimately put it down on the bread plate. "That sounds almost too good to be true. What makes you think he'll buy it?"

She smiled. It wasn't her sweet smile, or her genuine smile, or to be mistaken for anything but the most predatory expression. "You're forgetting. We're not really doing this. He doesn't have to buy it, not in the end. He only needs to be interested." And there it came again, that little thrill. The anticipation of reeling in this mark, even if this time, it didn't actually include a payoff. "All I'm doing is buying *us* the opportunity to nose around his life from the inside out."

But Dave didn't respond to her certainty, to her enthusiasm. He sat over there with the muffin he'd somehow crumbled into tiny pieces along the way, and he didn't really respond at all.

"What is this?" she asked. "Is this you not trusting me, or not thinking I can pull it off?"

He shook his head, not taking his eyes off hers. "This is me thinking that you'll be in pretty deep when he realizes he's been had."

She took it as a personal affront. "Timing is everything in grifting. You think I don't know how to balance the pieces?"

He cast her an annoyed look, his ice blue eyes gone remarkably broody. "I *think*," he said distinctly, "that I don't want to take the chance. Not with you."

"You don't even know me." The words popped out of her mouth, and she instantly wished she could take them back. The best she could do was an angry twist of her perfectly innocent napkin as she admitted, "Okay, that was wrong. You do know parts of me. I just think there are other parts you might not care so much about. That you already don't care so much for."

His response was pure silent frustration, burning across the table at her.

Well, good. She had him off balance. She had him turned around so much he didn't know what he wanted or what he felt. And that was the moment of opportunity—the moment when she then got to make those decisions for him. She didn't do it blatantly; blatant was what got you caught. No, she just shrugged and said, "The truth is, I can do this with or without you. I can walk into that city and plug myself into the right circles and get the tools I need. And I'll have your information before I'm done."

Of course, if things went that way, Rumsey would find her all too quickly. And Rumsey would alert the cops, and that mystery warrant would come crashing down. And that was why she didn't really want to run this one on her own. That was why she backed off, eating the meal the waiter set before her, waiting for Dave to finish his own while deep in scowling thought, waiting for the complimentary sherbet dessert. Trying to make up her own mind about how badly she wanted to give Rashawn his justice…how much she really wanted to risk. Would she or wouldn't she?

And that was why she heaved a silent sigh of immense

relief when Dave finally scowled at her and said, "What do you need to get ready for this thing?"

And why she gave a casual, thoughtful lick of the sherbet on her spoon when she smiled at him, covering the relief fluttering through her chest, and said, "Plastic is a girl's best friend. Let's go play makeover."

Dave got them settled at the Woodward House, a bed-and-breakfast overlooking Front Royal. Then came the errands... sucking up beauty-parlor fumes at Eclips, not to mention the nail-polish lacquer. Dave sat in a comfortable spouse-oriented corner with his laptop, digging into news items on Rashawn. Doubting the path he'd chosen...doubting Karin. She offered him an opportunity he wasn't sure he could turn away.

He wasn't sure he could deal with it, either.

Lost in dark thought, he was taken unaware when Karin emerged and struck a pose for his benefit. He floundered in a double take, classic man-lost-for-words.

Her dark honey-and-chestnut hair had been cut and shaped into something shoulder-length and classy but with a definite kick. The darkest shade came from her former honey highlights; the rest of it was pure sunshine, and the carefully placed spike of bangs added an edge of punk. It was a style suited to the newly dark-eyed woman before him, with her bluntly manicured hands and waxed brows. Nothing here spoke of Karin; nothing spoke of Ellen. Even the clothes— clothes Dave had looked at all day—appeared different on this woman.

He cleared his throat, but before he could say anything, Karin gave him her most wicked grin, the one he'd never

OFFICIAL OPINION POLL

ANSWER 3 QUESTIONS AND WE'LL SEND YOU
2 FREE BOOKS AND A FREE GIFT!

`0074823` IIII█IIII█IIII IIIII█III IIIII█III   FREE GIFT CLAIM # **3953**

DETACH AND MAIL CARD TODAY!

YOUR OPINION COUNTS!

Please check TRUE or FALSE below to express your opinion about the following statements:

Q1 Do you believe in "true love"?

"TRUE LOVE HAPPENS ONLY ONCE IN A LIFETIME."
○ TRUE
○ FALSE

Q2 Do you think marriage has any value in today's world?

"YOU CAN BE TOTALLY COMMITTED TO SOMEONE WITHOUT BEING MARRIED."
○ TRUE
○ FALSE

Q3 What kind of books do you enjoy?

"A GREAT NOVEL MUST HAVE A HAPPY ENDING."
○ TRUE
○ FALSE

YES, I have scratched the area below.

Please send me the 2 **FREE BOOKS** and **FREE GIFT** for which I qualify. I understand I am under no obligation to purchase any books, as explained on the back of this card.

300 SDL EFVK   200 SDL EFZK

FIRST NAME   LAST NAME

(STF-B-04/06)

ADDRESS

APT.#   CITY

www.eHarlequin.com

STATE/PROV.   ZIP/POSTAL CODE

Offer limited to one per household and not valid to current Silhouette Bombshell® subscribers. All orders subject to approval. Credit or debit balances in a customer's account(s) may be offset by any other outstanding balance owed by or to the customer. Please allow 4 to 6 weeks for delivery.

seen until she'd completely dropped her Ellen persona. "Now," she said. "Shopping."

Dave swallowed hard.

Shopping with a vengeance. Karin seemed to know just what she wanted and just where to find it. They walked out of Royal Quality with two mix-and-match business outfits, trendy wide-cuff trousers, a slim-line skirt, a tailored jacket that highlighted her athletic form. A couple of colorful camisoles. On top of that, a sleek evening dress that Dave vaguely remembered as deep blue and sparkly, but his mind's eye couldn't much get past the way it turned that athletic form into something just-right curvy.

From there they hit Cato, where she picked out clothes for the casual side of this new self he was watching her create. Someone who looked enough like Ellen to get Longsford's attention, but not so similar that he'd even consider it might be her look-alike sister. Features obscured by the new coloring and makeup, body a stronger, more capable form than Ellen's and covered in clothes Ellen wouldn't even have considered. "My new name is Brooke," she informed him, standing over the chair provided for weary Significant Others to gesture at his laptop. "Brooke Ellington. Two *l*'s." And she waited for him to pull up a new document in OneNote. Pointedly. So she'd already caught on to his compulsive note-taking nature.

"Hey," he said. "It works for me." He meant the note taking, but if she took it to mean the name, that was fine, too.

He had the feeling she knew exactly what he meant.

He dropped her off at the Woodward House, disappearing inside only long enough to help carry her haul, including the small suitcase he'd purchased to carry it all. She'd insisted on something pricey for the suitcase, reminding him that she needed to play her role on all levels. The implication that Longsford might be in her hotel room made his voice rough and Karin looked at him in surprise as she picked out the tapestry carry-on case.

He kept his mouth shut for a while after that. Long enough to drop her off and run out to grab a couple of subs, lingering in the room only long enough to leave her food, grab his brief-case and head for the veranda. Before they'd left the farm, Karin had offered him another small box—the things she'd taken from Ellen's desk. In light of the newly discovered photo, she thought they might have meaning to him. It was time to take a look. He shuffled through the contents, skimming at first, and then making notes. Checking his old records.

And then he sat and looked out at dusk over Front Royal. The bed-and-breakfast sat above the village, offering a clear view of a vista framed by layered ridges on the distant edges. Another couple came out to cuddle in a wicker love seat, leaving him to his scowls.

There was plenty to scowl about. All the dark thoughts and doubts of the day might plague him, but they wouldn't sway him. Not after what his briefcase had spilled out for him.

Ellen had dated Longsford for several years; Dave had known that. Always a decorous, low-key relationship. She appeared on his arm in public at decent intervals, and she had a variety of keepsakes from those events. Museum brochures, benefit programs, a few matchbooks from clubs most people couldn't get into.

And then there were the travel brochures. Not faraway exotic places, but national parks within a day's drive of Alexandria. Special nature programs, traveling historical displays, modest day hikes…

Dave recognized those places. Places where children had disappeared, never to surface again. Not all cases that he'd worked, but cases he'd looked into while he was hunting Terry Williams. Hunting patterns, just in case.

Well, now he had it. Longsford was a park predator. Neighborhood park, national park…he liked variety.

Ellen must have picked up on it. When she came across that photo after he'd interviewed her…she must have realized what she'd been dating all that time.

Right through the shopping, Dave hadn't been sure if he would let Karin go through with her plans. Right up until the moment she made contact with Longsford, he'd left himself the option to change his mind.

Not any longer.

Ellen had discovered a monster. Karin would unmask him.

And Dave wasn't about to stop her.

When he returned to the room, the misty scent of shampoo and soap lingered on the air and the room was empty. He stared around at the heavily decorated room—log-cabin quilt over a queen bed, heavy antique bed frame offset by a flowery white pair of wing chairs. Visual overload for masculine eyes, but he'd have been happier to find one more thing in it.

Karin.

He squelched an impulse to go find her, suddenly suspicious of the entire day. She had a whole new look, a new wardrobe. She could well have gone on the run again.

He didn't like himself for thinking it.

He didn't like himself much for the thought that came next, either.

The one that wondered just what lurked in her past. The one that noted the ease with which she'd transformed herself. The one that urged him to check up on her.

First he took his own shower. He pulled on a clean pair of jeans and a Bully Hill T-shirt. Not all that far from Hunter's Full Cry Winery, the family business that had once supported the development of the agency. Now it supported itself…and then some.

Owen could have gotten him answers about Karin Sommers's secrets. But the safe house was already one favor too many.

Still damp, Dave sat in one of the wing chairs, pulling the other chair over for a footrest. He fired up his laptop for a quick e-mail check—there was one from Owen, with the safe-house details—and then found the e-mail for a good feeb friend in California. That much he knew: Karin had come from California. Those old notes were occasionally good for something after all.

He made the query vague, protecting the lie about Karin's death.

For now.

And when he'd written the e-mail, he stared at it a moment. He rubbed his hands down his face and scruffed his wet hair and wondered if he truly wanted to know.

And then he hit Send.

That was when she returned, of course. He heard the key in the lock and flipped the lid down on the laptop. It beeped plaintively and went into hibernation, hiding only his innocuous e-mail inbox. *Guilty conscience, Hunter?*

Hey. He wasn't the one with all the lies layered around him. The one pretending to be dead. The one who had spent his life scamming people out of their savings.

She slipped inside the door, closed it and leaned against it to regard him. The silence stretched between them.

She looked tired. No little wonder, after their nonstop day. And she looked thoughtful, regarding him with her blue-gray eyes, her head ducked as it often was. This time those spiky new bangs swept to the side, partially obscuring her gaze. The expression did what it always did to him, waking parts he'd thought weren't paying any attention. Reminding him how this conflict-of-interest situation had become quite tangled indeed.

None of his parts cared about that. Not the slowly stirring erection, not the tingle down his lower spine. Not the tightening along the backs of his thighs. At least he had the laptop, already casually positioned to keep his reaction from becoming a topic of conversation. It wasn't the kind of mixed message he wanted to send.

He wasn't quite ready when she sighed and said, "Had time to think about it, haven't you?"

Wary caution filled his reply. "Think about—"

"*It,*" she said, and gestured at herself—dressed in her own jeans and one of the new tops, wearing her new hair—everything but the colored contacts. For that moment she somehow drew herself up to stand differently, becoming not a tired fugitive planning a scam but someone cool, aware of her own classy nature, and just a little bit flirty around the edges. "What I've done."

Dave swallowed, hunting a truth that wouldn't sound harsh. Problem was, the truth *was* harsh.

"Watching you today…" He shook his head. "You're good,

aren't you? It wasn't just your stepfather kicking you into compliance. You did it and you were good at it."

She inclined her head just so, a refined gesture that suited Brooke quite perfectly, and said, "We've only just started. Tomorrow it's your turn."

Instant denial seized him, but he barely got his mouth open before she laughed, a pealing laugh he hadn't heard before. "Don't worry, dearling. A few key outfits and some temporary dye should do it. With those skin tones, we can't pull off anything darker than a medium brown."

He muttered his words. All of them. The laptop as camouflage suddenly didn't seem quite so necessary as before.

But when he looked back at her, she'd dropped the pose. She ran her hands through her hair, scrubbing her scalp as she stretched. The shirt—a fine, slippery cloth the color of a blush—rose to show even more of her tight belly. Dave inhaled sharp and quick.

Not a man who knew what he wanted, one way or the other; his body and mind danced around in opposition, flip-flopping positions.

And it wasn't that she couldn't tell, laptop or not. She moved into the room, perching a hip on the rounded lip of the footboard. Totally Karin. "Hey," she said, waiting for him to focus on her again. When he did, she gestured at herself once more—and then at him. "This is it, you know. This situation… my past, your future. It's not perfect…but it's what we have. It might be *all* we have. This *now* of ours."

He didn't have a ready answer. He didn't have any answer at all.

She didn't wait long. She came to his two-chair perch and picked up the laptop, setting it on the side table. Then she slung a leg over his knees and straddled the space she'd just cleared. Sat…right…*there.* Dave froze, letting his breath ease out through his teeth to stop himself from instantly thrusting up into her, clothes and all. He somehow managed not to garble his words. "Pretty confident, aren't you?"

"That's what I am," she told him. "A confident woman. I know what I want."

He reached for her waist, couldn't quite stop himself from caressing the sleek, warm sides beneath the drape of her shirt. After a moment he moved her against him. Just enough so her inner thighs quivered. He murmured, "And tomorrow? Or the next day? Or the day we're finished in Alexandria?"

"Or the day you decide you can't live with who I am?" Hard words, but she said them softly. Matter-of-factly. "Days like that happen. I think it's better when nights like this happen in between them." Then she cocked her head and said in bright, normal tones, "Of course, that's up to you," and shifted to get her feet under her so she could abandon him there.

Oh, no. He caught her, snagging her jeans pockets, and pulled her back down close and tight. The renewed contact scrambled his brains and he reached up, cupping her neck to pull her down for an unexpectedly slow kiss, with his mouth moving against hers in gentle, deliberate care, nibbling and flirting and courting—and building into a connection deeper than he'd ever intended.

Decision made. Regrets later. He put his glasses aside and tended to the side of her neck, her cheek, the corner of her mouth…he kissed the spot just beneath her earlobe and waited for her gasp to fade before murmuring, "I'll take our *now.*"

Chapter 14

Karin woke tangled in sheets. Alone.

From the *now* to the morning after. Nice letdown.

Didn't matter. She still owned the memory. Her skin still tingled from his touch, and his scent still lingered in her hair. She spent a moment savoring the sensations, and then she flipped back the sheets and headed for the bathroom.

Today was Dave's turn to be outfitted. Karin put her hair back in a high ponytail and dug into her courier bag, into the depths of the pocket that wasn't quite a bona fide hidden compartment. She flipped through the Brooke Ellington ID, satisfied that she'd grabbed everything, including alternative IDs. If Dave thought she'd made up the name on the spur of the moment, he was in for a surprise. Brooke was an old standby who "lived" in Florida but who'd done a lot of traveling for Karin.

She patted the paperwork and plastic and tucked it back

away, then packed her new belongings in the new suitcase, ready to go. She reached the dining room just in time for the second serving, and she was spreading chunky spiced apples over her French toast—thick bakery bread, oh yum—when Dave arrived.

She thought he looked tired. It gave her some satisfaction; she had a pretty good idea how he'd gotten that way. He pulled out one of the wooden tapestry-backed chairs and sat down.

"Fruit?" she said, offering him her bowl of melon cubes.

"Ate at the early serving," he told her, and then popped one of the juicy orange chunks into his mouth anyway. He wore jeans and that Red Wings sweatshirt this morning, though he still carried himself as if they were designer duds. His expression was far more pensive than melon-chewing could account for, and more remote than a man greeting his lover ought to be.

"Second thoughts?" she asked him. She forked the toast and apple mixture into her mouth and then had to close her eyes so she could absorb the wonderfulness of the combination.

When she opened them, there he was. Waiting. He nodded. "Second and third. But no better ideas. And Rashawn…" He scruffed up his hair. It didn't look as if this was the first time, and the day was young. "They found him under a water tower across the tracks from North Glendale. Just dumped. Just like an—" He stopped himself, shaking his head. The words were there; Karin could all but see them. He just couldn't bring himself to say them or perhaps to trust himself to stay calm about it. Instead he said, "No, I don't like it. But I want to stop this bastard. If this is what it takes…"

There was no need to say that Karin's scam was Dave's only way in. Officially, he wasn't even here anymore.

Karin said, "Hey." She waited for him to meet her gaze and then she said, "I want to do something about it, too."

He stole another piece of melon. "I'd feel better if I understood why."

Clink. She put her fork down too hard; the couple seated a table away glanced over in surprise. Karin said drily, bitterly, "You mean because I'm such a soul-sucking money-grubbing thief, why would I do a decent thing?"

He winced. "I would have used different words, thanks. And the offer of the safe house is open regardless—I'm the one who got you into this mess. I'm not going to leave you hanging."

She chewed another piece of her sublime concoction, but this time she didn't really taste it. "How about, if it wasn't for me, Ellen might have stopped this guy a year ago. Maybe I owe her this. Maybe I owe it to Rashawn and all the others who are still in danger. Maybe I just *care*." *Maybe I owe it to who I was as a child, needing my own rescue.* But she didn't say that one out loud. She waited for him to digest her words and said, still bitter, "Guess you never thought of that."

He didn't respond right away. Then he shook his head. "Caring," he said distinctly, "is a lot different than actually putting yourself on the line."

She snorted. A nice emphatic noise, not meant for the breakfast table in the cosy dining nook of the Woodward House. "Hey," she said. "If there's one thing I know, it's how to walk that line. This guy is ripe for the scam, and in the end I don't even have to pull it off."

"And how many times in the course of your…*career*…have you been investigating and poking around in well-protected places where you don't belong? It's not the same, Karin."

"And it's not so different." Okay, she wasn't so sure of that.

She was just mad. First the insult for who she was…and then to imply she wasn't even good at it? "This started out as a tasty little breakfast," she told him, and pulled back her melon bowl. "Get your own."

He was silent, one of those moments at which he seemed to be so good. He said, "I didn't mean to turn this conversation into *this* conversation. I just need to understand."

Still grumpy, thank you very much. "And if you've listened, then you do." But he wasn't the only one who'd been thinking about it all, and she was ready enough to move on. "Here's what *I* don't understand—none of the others were found."

Not a new thought to him. He tipped his head in affirmation. "Only Rashawn."

"So Longsfo—" She broke off, glanced around and decided not to finish the name out loud. "He's really spooked, then. He wasn't done…or ready. He got sloppy. Now's the time, Dave. Now's *exactly* the time."

He regarded her with skepticism. "When he's all stirred up and unhappy?"

"Yes." She leaned forward, pushing her plate aside. "Think of who he is. *What* he is. You've worked with enough profilers, right? Well, profiling is just a fancy name for assessing your mark. I bet your people have said he's taking these boys—building some kind of strange relationship with them—to create a situation where he's in complete control. Over his young self—that's the boy—and even his mother. Don't even try to tell me she's not overbearing."

Bemused, Dave admitted, "She's a strong woman."

"She'd have to be, to reach the Senate. So he's creating situations in which he has complete control. When the rush grows old, then the relationship changes…it escalates. The boys are molested, killed and discarded. But this time, he lost control. He wasn't able to complete his little ritual. He must be furious and confused. So here I come, offering him a way to make money and build face at the same time. To regain *control*. He's going to grab it."

Dave drummed his fingers on the table. He checked around the room—no one was paying attention to them now. "You're not so bad at this profiling thing."

She sat back in her chair, crossing her arms in a dare-you gesture. "I'm a people watcher."

She saw it instantly; he wasn't going to take that dare. The subject of her past was, for the moment, closed. "What I'd like to know," he said, "is how you're going to layer in this extra irresistible face-building opportunity."

Karin was suddenly hungry again. She pulled the plate over, stabbing up a chunk of toast and apples. "Okay," she said, hesitating with the fork halfway to her mouth. "But I get to finish this first. I'll tell you on the way to the thrift store."

"To—" Dave started, but stopped himself to cover his face and emit a reluctant groan. "This is going to be a nightmare, isn't it?"

"Oh, I don't know," Karin said cheerfully. "I'm looking forward to it." And she tackled her breakfast with renewed anticipation.

Dave walked away from the tiny thrift store with beat-up black jeans, a variety of tight, dark T-shirts and a stonewashed denim jacket with enough styling to give it interest if not class. His gratitude when she declared them ready for checkout was short-lived, for then she declared her intention to drag him into the Fairfax Fair Oaks Mall—and after an hour on the road, she did just that.

The Polo suit fit him right off the Macy's rack. She frowned at the price tag—normally a scam this big would pay for itself, but this one would never get that far—and smoothed the fit of the material over his shoulders. "I hope you need a new suit."

"Your farm took care of my last one," he said. "Now talk. Details, I mean."

He'd been patient at that, and she didn't hesitate. "Simple," she said. "There's some land in Florida, owned by developers. Let's call it Ranchwood Acres."

"Florida? You must be kidding."

She grinned. "That's the beauty of it. I'm not. It's an actual property in Palm Beach County—truly gorgeous—but it's surrounded by swampland. Perfectly usable, if you don't mind mosquitoes the size of pterodactyls or boating in and out during heavy rains. Five hundred acres, cypress trees, sweet gum, slash pine, palmetto…can't get any greener than that."

He looked at her askance and unbuttoned the three suit buttons, checking the fit of the low-rise slacks. "When did you check this out?"

"Just old habits," she told him. Not to mention the need to keep an eye on what might be of interest to Rumsey. "And trust me. The pants fit perfectly." *Trust me,* it turned out, weren't the best words she could have used. But she ignored his expression and said, "It's a million-dollar parcel. And the Florida Conservation Coalition is itching to get their hands on it to establish more territory for the Florida panther."

He slipped out of the jacket and vest, then headed for the changing room. Karin, jacket and vest slung over her arm, followed him right up to the open entranceway.

"I'm not getting it yet," he said from the changing booth. Keys and change jingled in his jeans pockets as he pulled the pants up, snapped, and zipped.

"I'm the roper," she said. "I approach our guy with this deal, playing middleman for the development company that hasn't been able to unload it. They're tired of the bugs, the snakes, the gators. So they—meaning I—present it in a single parcel for less than the valued price of the combined individual parcels, but at a decent profit for our developers. Once Longsford's got the property, he can sell off lots of small parcels at actual market price to recoup his investment, and then sell the rest of it to the coalition cheap. Guaranteed buyers. He more than makes his money back, and he gets great PR points while thumbing his nose at the development company."

"How's that?" Dave emerged, now wearing his newly acquired denim jacket and the black jeans. It seemed to Karin that he handed over the suit pants with some regret. Definitely not a boy used to dressing down on the job.

"The developers—and this is for real—have been refusing to deal with the coalition for years. They're all full of manifest destiny, and anything else that might want to live in that area— the panthers, the Indians, the snakes—is unfortunate inconvenience. So our guy gets his profit, gets his conservationist karma, and shows the developers that he makes his own decisions. Which, as we've established, is important to Longsford."

She let him ponder it as he put the suit on AmEx. Once they were out of earshot of the clerk, he moved in for a more confidential conversation, bumping shoulders as they headed for the mall exit.

She bumped against him on purpose, just to do it. If it

puzzled him, he didn't dwell on it. He asked, "Exactly what else are you going to need to pull this off?"

Didn't even take a second thought. She held out her hand, ticking off items on her fingers. "Hotel with suite amenities— not five-star. Three or four will do. It's okay if I give the impression of being careful with money—we want him to trust me with *his* money. I've got to set up a phone number, and someone to be the inside man, because he's going to check with the development company, and we'll have to intercept that call. But most of the work with this one is up-front. I need a good printer—the *right* printer—to work up the real-estate documentation. Finding that printer and getting the information we need…those will be the hardest parts. But I do believe I intend to be invited to a party." She paused, tapping her lower lip. "Could mean more party clothes." And then she laughed at the noise Dave made deep in his chest, snatching her elbow as if she might turn around on the spot and head back for Macy's.

They made it to the car in a silence that Karin didn't mind at all. Not on a beautiful spring day with the zing of job planning rushing through her body. In the real grift, Longsford would purchase land that Karin had no right to sell, and his deed would be worthless. And even though this one wouldn't get that far…

Yeah, there it was again.

She could still feel it.

Karin easily spotted Dave's Maxima and pulled out to reach it before he did, waiting for him to pop the trunk with his remote. The car beeped in response, and Karin quickly rearranged their purchases so they could smooth the suit along the top of the rest of it. Dave straightened, one hand on the lid and ready to push it back down, hesitating long enough to say, "I'm not sure where I fit in that plan. Or do I?"

Karin grinned, and he gave her a wary look. He'd figured out that grin already, had he? "Plenty for you to do," she assured him. "For starters, I need you to find someone we can trust for the inside man. And I need to know Longsford's friends, his party circle, his hangouts. I especially need to know which of those friends is close enough to see that I get a special invitation to one of his parties, but it's got to be someone who's also conveniently off on a cruise somewhere. And that's just for starters. I've got legwork to do, and I want you there for most of it." She caught the question in his eyes, and said, "I don't know this city well enough. It'll go faster if I have help from someone who does, and backup along the way. I'm going to be poking my nose into nastyville in order to get some of this stuff set up."

He shut the lid. "And you're sure—"

"I've been to nastyville before, Dave." She gave him her flattest voice, the one that meant this conversation had been over the last time she ended it.

He shrugged and let it go, coming around to open her car door out of what seemed to be undeniable force of habit. "Okay, then. We'll start with the safe house. We've got maps and phone books there, and you can scope out the city while I see about your inside man. As for the rest of it…I'll follow your lead."

Yes, she thought. *That you will. Let's just hope I don't take you too close to what I really am.*

Late afternoon found them at the safe house, tucked into a little neighborhood of cul-de-sacs on the southern edge of

Alexandria. Total urban-suburbia, with minivans, cultivated landscaping and a high school behind them. The house itself was a modest Victorian with a corner turret and an unusually open first-story floor plan. The upstairs held three bedrooms and a huge bathroom, but Karin dumped her stuff in the smaller middle room, deliberately avoiding the master bedroom, a room that pushed into the turret space and boasted three large windows.

Dave tossed his stuff into the third bedroom in the back corner, then came to her door.

Karin looked up from where she tested the twin bed. She sat on the edge of it. "I won't share my closet, but I never did need much space in a bed."

He didn't say anything, but she saw his eyes change. A smile hinted in the corners, and she thought he might come to her then and there. Eventually he said, "Good." And then he glanced over his shoulder toward his bedroom. "Done booting up. I can start in on that research for you right away. There are take-out lists in the kitchen if you want to pick your favorite."

"Humph." Karin leaned back on her arms, sinking into the bed. "And what do your neighbors think of this little house? Occupied by a stream of different people, sometimes vacant, and lots of takeout. Doesn't exactly fit into the neighborhood."

He shrugged. "Ostensibly, this place serves as temporary dwelling for travelers coming in for training and special projects out of D.C. It works. By the way, you're a civilian worker with the Army Corps of Engineers, contracting on a land-assessment project. I thought it might fit your sense of irony."

"Yes indeed." Smart-ass. She gestured him away. "Go play with your notes. I'm going to take a shower, and then I'll order something pizza-ish. I'd like to get an early start tomorrow."

If she could locate the right printers…if Dave could locate the information to put the finishing touches on her approach…

By all rights she should have had weeks to gain Longsford's interest and his confidence. But this was the time to strike. Longsford was at his most reactive, his most vulnerable. And she had an ace she could play any time she wanted.

Ellen.

With this new makeover she didn't truly resemble Ellen anymore; he'd probably see nothing in her but a puzzling familiarity. But that didn't mean she couldn't let Ellen's mannerisms peek out. Puzzling him. Enticing him. Reeling him in.

Now *that* was a line she didn't intend to tell Dave she'd walk.

She waved him out, then dumped her purchases from the morning—underwear, a slew of casual shirts, a lightweight hooded jacket. She plucked up a few items and headed for the shower. She could hear Dave tapping away, but when she looked inside his room she found he'd forgone the small desk to sit on the floor, his back to the wall and his feet braced high against the side of the bed. Total guy mode. He'd pulled the pillow from the bed for a lap desk and now was frowning in concentration over the laptop display. Upset about something, she would have said.

Longsford, no doubt. But this research was the one thing he could do, quickly and extensively, better than she could. And it left her free to concentrate on her own role. She walked Brooke's walk down the hall to the bathroom. A saucier walk than her own, yet not slutty. No, not at all. More a runway walk than a street walk.

She showered as Brooke would do…as Karin herself might have chosen, before a year of living on a farm where the well water sometimes ran low. Luxuriating in the halfway decent hand lotion, using the provided blades and shaving cream on her legs. She let her hair air-dry in a tousled bed-head look and left the Brooke makeup unused on the sink counter, ready for the morning.

She emerged from the steamy room to the enticing odor of pizza and followed her nose down the stairs. The formal dining area had been converted to a small but completely functional office, and the desktop computer now hummed to itself along with the printer. Dave and his notes had been busy.

She found them all—Dave, the notes, the pizza—at the back of the house in the kitchen breakfast nook. A pizza slice hung crookedly in his grip, looking forgotten. The papers spread out over the small table, pushing the box into a precarious position at the edge. When he saw her, he dropped his piece back into the box and pulled it to a safer spot, making way for her to sit opposite him. "Sorry," he said. "I didn't wait. But you said pizza-ish, so I hope this is okay. It's their meaty version."

All perfectly normal. Dave, deep in thought, surrounded by his notes in hard copy, ordering the pizza he thought— rightly so—that she'd like.

Then why had something inside her stumbled when he looked up at her? Why did she have that little warning trill in her head, the one that always told her when a scam was going off course? The difference being, this time she didn't try to hide it. She didn't try to smooth things over or retreat to reassess. She didn't try to pretend nothing was wrong at all. She asked, "What's up?"

He didn't quite look at her. "Just wishing I could have caught this bastard years ago. Looking at him in the society pages, living his privileged life..." He shook his head. "There's nothing right about any of it."

Uh-huh. Very true. But not the reason for his change in demeanor. She told him, "Well, we're here to change that," and slipped into a chair to help herself to a couple of pieces of pizza. He nudged the notes her way and she glanced at them with approval. Just what she needed—a neat list of contacts with details. Dave had highlighted two couples who were currently out of town, but who usually appeared in Longsford's personal orbit. She ran her finger over the green highlighter. "You're such a nerd," she said. "This is great."

"Good," he said, but his voice was studiously neutral.

She looked up at him, eyes narrowed. This was more than anger at Longsford. Definitely more. "If you're thinking I can't carry this off—"

He shook his head before she even finished. "I have no doubt you can do this," he told her. "I'm not so sure *I* can do it." He scraped his chair back and took the pizza box, stuffing the leftovers into the fridge.

He's not just talking about the scam.

She couldn't even remember a moment when there hadn't been some sort of spark between them, from the first moment she'd watched him deal with Ellen's dog. Sometimes it flared to rocket-fuel intensity, sometimes it merely glimmered. But it had always been there.

Not now.

"You'll do fine," she said. Lame, so lame.

"I'm headed up for bed." He gestured toward the front of the house. "We're all locked up and the alarm system is engaged, so don't go for any midnight walks if you have trouble sleeping."

"You're—" she started, and again he didn't let her finish.

"Early day tomorrow, you said. Let's be ready for it."

"Okay. Sure. That makes good sense." Lame and lamer. She should have been demanding to know the problem, digging away at it.

But she wasn't sure she wanted to know the answer.

Chapter 15

*S*on *of a bitch.*

Dave looked at himself in the mirror over the small dresser in his bedroom. His hair was gold-bright even in the low-wattage light, and the shadow of his eyes looked more haunted in contrast. *I'm talking about you, Hunter.*

Back at that farmhouse, he'd talked himself out of believing that his response to "Ellen" held no conflict of interest. That he could make love to her right on the floor of her office. *Make love, hell. More like wild sex. Great wild sex.*

Turned out there was a conflict of interest after all.

He hadn't expected these knotted results. Knots that blurred the lines between right and wrong and for the first time in his life left him unable to see where one turned into the other. Left him with a big bewildered empty spot where she'd so quickly made herself a part of him.

But then, that was what she was good at, wasn't it?

It hadn't taken his L.A. friend long to get him background on Karin Sommers. Her stepfather, Gregg Rumsey, had had early arrests and then seemed to have cleaned up his act. Dave knew he'd only hidden himself behind a little girl. No doubt he'd also finally gotten some good fixes in the local law agencies. Either way, he and his stepdaughter had kept a low profile until just over a year ago.

Until the elderly Vasilkovs. Irene and Earl. Shortly before their deaths, their retirement savings had dwindled significantly. Friends, interviewed after their deaths, were certain they'd been investing in some secret scheme. They'd left a joint suicide note, but nothing that convinced the M.E. to ignore the evidence of homicide. They'd closed in on Rumsey.

But Rumsey, with much beating of breast and teary regret, had provided an alibi and pointed the finger at his missing stepdaughter.

Karin Sommers.

Evidence was forthcoming. A warrant issued.

A warrant Dave would honor, as soon as he was done here. So what did that make him?

A son of a bitch.

And what did it make her? The woman he'd come to know and admire in these past intense days, so composed that she could make up her absurd Mad Sheep disease while clinging to the side of a mountain? She'd meant to run, sure, but she'd also changed her mind when she'd realized she could help.

Or maybe she simply planned to complete the scam to finance another run for it. Because she was far deeper underground than she'd let on. Not just running from her nasty stepfather, oh no.

Running from a murder conviction.

He snorted at the man in the mirror. The Hunter family's fair-haired boy, the youngest brother with so much potential who'd never lived up to expectations. No, he was too tied to his own goals, too attached to an honor that was more about helping the helpless and hopeless than hitting the international scene for the high-concept spy gigs. Satisfied to get his criminology degree and his investigator's license and to poke around in the bones of tragic cases, trying—and often succeeding—to make everything turn out right for that one child, that one family.

He had no excuse for leaving Karin free to run this scam. No excuse for hiding his knowledge from her, except that he wanted to use her before he turned her in. He'd finally become willing to trade his pristine honor intact for results. *I want Longsford.* And to get the man, Dave was scamming a scammer.

At least he was fully aware of his own price.

And, thinking of Karin's quietly stricken expression, her tacit acknowledgment of the change between them...of that bittersweet empty spot among the knots in his stomach...

He also knew the cost.

Karin woke to an unfamiliar ceiling, a tingling undercurrent touching her thoughts. Familiar enough, but not something she'd felt for a while. Mixed in was a sadness, and though she'd felt plenty of that since Ellen's death, this was different. More sorrow and regret than outright grief.

She stared at the ceiling fan until the details trickled in. She was building a scam, that was what. She was in Alexandria, in Dave Hunter's borrowed safe house, and she was building a scam. The jazz. *Oh yeahhh.* She'd learned to embrace it—to focus on it, so she wouldn't focus on the other aspects of her work. Just as she'd learned to embrace the complicated scams, to bury herself in the challenge.

Rumsey was the one who worked the easy marks. The elderly, who were often gullible and just a little confused, and who could be beguiled by the thought of leaving a fortune to their children. There was no jazz in that. There hadn't been for a long, long time.

But those who were rich and in the prime of their lives, they made their own choices. Like Longsford, their greed was their weak spot. And constructing a deeply layered scam that could hit that weak spot dead on...

That was Karin's weak spot.

But now there was sadness weighing against the building thrill of this scam.

Dave.

He'd figured her out, it seemed. Seen too much.

So she stared at the ceiling fan, and she realized the most important thing: he hadn't changed his mind. He might not like what he saw anymore, but he would still work with her. They'd still go after Longsford. Ellen's revenge.

Yes.

And the second important thing: she could deal with his change of heart. She'd expected it. She knew better than most not to take anything for granted. And what they'd experienced together...

She'd miss it, be sad for it...but never regret it.

Do what you have to do. Take what you can get.

It had worked before. She'd make it work now.

She breezed down into the kitchen to nab leftover pizza for breakfast. A glass of orange juice washed the pepperoni down with a nice zing. Dave appeared not long afterward, fresh from the shower in the worn black jeans and a charcoal tee and looking wary. Wary of her, wary of himself…even in her regret, she felt a little sorry for him. Of the two of them, she'd known what she was doing when she reached for him in the tiny dormer office of Ellen's house. He hadn't a clue.

Still wouldn't have a clue, if she hadn't done a true confessions on him.

She pulled the sadness inside and covered it up with the jazz. "Ready to get started?" she asked him, leaning back against the counter to watch him take out three eggs and a bowl, cracking the eggs with practiced efficiency.

His glance turned into something longer, a hesitation as he searched her face—long enough so she wondered just what he was looking for. He nodded abruptly and took a fork to the eggs, whipping them with vigor. "What's on the schedule?"

"Depends how much we get done, how fast." She squelched the urge to wipe away the tiny dab of shaving cream by his ear and held out a closed hand, unfolding her index finger as she spoke. "One, we get me into a hotel. Something truly nice but still practical."

"I know a place on King Street near the river," Dave interrupted, then softened—or tried to—the words by adding, "I've gotten to know this place pretty well in the past couple of years."

"Good." Dammit. Maybe this wouldn't be quite as easy as she thought, the pretending it didn't matter. "Then you know where to look for good printers. *Expensive* printers who think much of themselves and their clientele. And also the pawnshops. Skanky ones."

He poured a dollop of milk in with the eggs and briefly whipped them together, then went hunting for a frying pan. "Interesting combination."

"We'll be changing roles on the fly. You're my driver and my boy toy. You'll handle my suitcase and open my door, and when I'm dealing with business transactions, you'll stand decorously in the background. If you cast an admiring look at my ass now and then, that would be good, too."

He fumbled the frying pan on the way to the stove, caught it, and turned to give her a skeptical look.

"We're playing my game," she said. "Trust me to do it right. I retired free and clear, after all."

"Did you?" he murmured, as if that was supposed to mean something.

Impatience flashed through her. "Are we doing this, or not?" she asked. "Because I'm good to stay here until Longsford forgets about Ellen. But I won't run this con if you're going in half-assed. It's all or nothing."

He stood in front of the stove for a long moment, his back turned to her. His long, deep breath showed clearly in the rise and fall of his shoulders. Abruptly, he flicked the gas burner on. "Yeah," he said. "We're doing this."

She didn't respond right away. She let him dump a pat of butter into the pan and push it around the bottom, and meanwhile she weighed the risks. The long con…all in the details. And like it or not, he was an important detail. His demeanor could make or break this game. "You'd better mean it," she said. "If we're blown, I'm the one who's going to pay." She'd be revealed to the authorities. She'd end up back in California, vulnerable to her stepfather's legal contacts, charged with whatever bogus crimes he'd had pinned on her.

"That'd be a change, wouldn't it?" He looked at her then, a meaningful side glance as he reached for the eggs.

Flash point. "You let me know when you're done being a

bastard," she told him, cold anger spilling into temper. "And while you're at it, you might think about who *you* would be if you'd had my stepfather controlling your life. If *you'd* gone to your first-grade teacher for help and been scolded for lying. If your teacher had gone to your stepfather about it. What do you think happened then, Mr. Perfect-Family Hunter? Do you think you might possibly have discovered the best way to survive was to play the game? Do you think you might have decided the best way to avoid collecting more scars was to be *good* at it?"

The eggs sizzled quietly in an otherwise quiet kitchen. Eventually, he said, "I don't know."

"You just think about it," she told him, anger still hard in her chest. "I'll be upstairs. I picked up a good paperback yesterday and it's fine with me if I spend the day in bed reading."

She left him there and went upstairs, the jazz gone and the sadness twisted into hurt. *I don't know.*

She thought it was probably as good as she'd get.

She didn't head for the bed. Or at least, not for long. She picked up the book, she sat down…and she stood right back up again. Then she sat one more time, forcing herself to think through the impulse that gripped her.

I can do this alone. I should do this alone.

She'd be better off doing it alone than doing it with someone who wouldn't trust her. Someone who questioned her. Not about whether she could do it, but about whether he wanted to be part of it. Not a courage issue…an honor issue. He had courage to spare, she'd no doubt of that. Problem was, he had honor to spare, too.

That kind of hesitation could break a long con. Especially

a rushed job like this, when the mark had to have no doubt at all. And she could all too easily imagine Dave balking at a crucial moment.

She could do it alone. And it still had to be done. For Ellen, for Terry Williams, for Rashawn...

It had to be done.

And that left the details, all of which needed quick revisions. It'd be more money, of which she had not nearly enough. And she'd be on her own...no backup. She could hire someone, but that would be hit or miss in this area in which she had no connections. Nor did she have a fix in with any of the local cops.

Yeah, she'd have to be careful.

But she could do it.

This time when she stood up, she went into action. She dug into her courier bag and pulled out the leather wallet that held Brooke Ellington's ID. Brooke would have been best for this, but Dave already knew about her. So she'd use Maia Brenner. Maia had been created to live in Nebraska but traveled often for her bank job. It wouldn't be too much of a stretch.

And then there was the money. She could pull easy con games along the way—Rock in a Box, the Ketchup Squirt, phoney C.O.D. scams—but she didn't want to increase her chances of getting caught. Not when Dave would already be on her tail the whole time. Picking pockets or trading briefcases was as far as she wanted to go.

Do what you have to do.

Except this past year, *do what you have to do* had turned into getting up early for chores, harvesting food she'd grown herself, trading the excess for the venison that filled the freezer she'd left behind, and shearing her own damned sheep.

It had meant a different kind of jazz…a quiet jazz. Sitting up in the dormer office writing to Ellen, letting her know how things were going.

Stop it. She'd sabotage herself if she wasn't careful. If she was going to do this, she'd have to focus on her needs and her solutions. Need: money. Solution?

She stood in the doorway to her bedroom and cocked an ear at the stairs. The splash of water came to her ear; the clatter of the fry pan in the sink. *As good as it gets.*

She moved swiftly to Dave's room, bypassing the closed laptop to reach for his overnight bag. She knew much of the contents were in the bathroom, but she was willing to bet—

Ah, yes. Her hand closed around cold metal. His Ruger DAO. Very nice. It wasn't what she'd come for, but she didn't hesitate to take it or his extra magazines. She rifled his laptop case and headed for the small dresser.

Oh yeah.

His wallet looked back up at her from the top drawer, ripe for the taking. And she might have done it, had she not wanted to keep him off balance. She wanted him wondering what she was up to and wondering what he should do about it, not raging after her in a fury. So she grabbed a few twenties to help cover immediate cash expenses and then hesitated over his credit cards. *Yes. It's what you came for.* No time to get flinchy about it. She pulled them out of their little card slots, assessing them, knowing which company was more likely to call immediately about what they felt were unusual purchases and which wasn't. Karin tapped a finger on the one he'd used to buy their clothes the previous day and almost plucked it from the batch.

And then she saw the card behind it. *Oh ho!* This time, she didn't hesitate. The card bore not only Dave's name, but the imprint of the Hunter Agency. The family business credit card. She'd bet anything he hardly ever used it; he might not miss it at all. And an agency like Hunter had expenses pouring in all the time. A few more would hardly be noticed—at least, not until it was too late.

She pulled the card, tucked it away in her jeans pocket and replaced it with another of his second-layer cards. He might not notice if a different card sat behind his preferred AmEx, but he'd sure notice if there wasn't anything there at all.

That done, she gave the room a quick look to make sure she hadn't left anything out of place, and returned to her bedroom with silent steps.

It could have been nice, the two of them working this job together. She already knew they partnered well; she'd been looking forward to riding the jazz with him beside her. And all for a good cause—the *best* of causes. No beating that.

But looking back meant she wasn't looking ahead. Karin dumped her thoughts at the threshold to her room and quickly packed what little she'd pulled from her snazzy von Furstenberg carry-on. She wasn't quite through when she heard bumping-around noises that could only mean Dave was on his way up. She stashed the case and sat on the bed, pulling out her journal as she followed his progress.

By the time he made it upstairs, she was writing to her sister. *Dear Ellen, you're gonna love this…*

I'm sorry. Dave said the words in his head one more time. He hoped they sounded better out loud. The truth was, learning about Karin's life…about her stepfather…about her *warrant*…

It had done a number on his head.

He told himself—again—that a warrant wasn't the same as a conviction. He told himself she'd come here to help. That she'd started a new life in her sister's name, working that little homestead with dedication. He reminded himself how he had been the one to shove her back into the middle of things, and of how he'd admired her grit the night she'd gone over the cliff. He recalled the shivery feeling of locking gazes with her, from his nape all the way down his spine to tingle through his—

Halfway up the stairs he stopped short, closed his eyes to tell himself what an idiot he was and moved forward with a determination to forget that part.

No, not to forget it. Some things…you couldn't. But to put it aside long enough to get through the next moments, the next days.

To catch Longsford.

He found her sitting cross-legged on the bed, writing in her leather-bound journal. Small, precise writing. "Still more than just a diary," he commented, leaning in the doorway.

"Letters to my sister." She spoke without looking up, her tone so matter-of-fact that Dave was taken aback. She'd been so private about it before….

Of course, at that point she'd been calling herself Ellen.

Karin straightened her shoulders, still looking down at the book. "Dear Ellen," she read. "You won't believe where I am. Or what I'm about to do." She looked up at him for the first time since his arrival in her space and he blinked at what he saw in her eyes. He couldn't quite name it, but it struck him deeply. Those smoky gray eyes had a confident intensity that momentarily left him without words.

"What would she say?" he asked her.

"She'd worry. She'd say to tell her about it when it was over. But she'd be glad I was doing it," Karin answered easily, and then laughed a little at his surprise. "I've been having daily conversations with her for over a year. You think I don't give her a chance to talk back?"

Not much to say about that. But plenty left to say. "About what happened downstairs—"

She looked straight at him. "You mean, when you were snide and rude to me?"

Ouch. "I'm sorry," he said. "Things have gotten…complicated."

"You don't say." She didn't seem in the mood to be forgiving. He supposed things had gotten complicated for her since he'd arrived in her driveway. But there was no anger in her voice, seemed to be none on her face. Just determination.

"We okay?" he asked.

She shrugged. "Sure."

He didn't quite believe it. But he figured he'd pushed her as far as she'd go for one day. "I'll go change. You wanted the suit?"

"What I'd really like are the codes you use to get outside."

That took him by surprise. "The point is that you don't go outside. It's a safe house."

"Right," she said. "But if someone's out there watching us, we're blown either way, don't you think? And I'd rather not feel like a prisoner. Unless maybe I am?"

"If you wanted to get out," he told her drily, "I'm sure you'd find a way."

"Ah. Another dig?"

"I just meant you don't give up easily. And I'm doubly sorry about this morning if it means you'll hear everything I say to you through a snide filter."

She was quiet on the bed. Quiet in body, quiet in voice. "It's easier to put that particular filter on than it is to take it off. And I'd really rather just use the alarm code."

So he gave it to her, and she closed the book and set it aside. "I'll get dressed," she said. "Go do something with your hair." And as his hand went up to check his hair, she grinned. A small grin, but better than no grin at all, and much better than a snide filter. "It's fine," she told him. "It just needs to be a little more conservative for the morning's work."

"Can do," he said, and went off to see to it. Her door was shut as he passed by on the way back, and he went on to his own room to dress the part of the boy-toy chauffeur. When he came back out the door was still shut and he knocked; no answer.

The knob turned under his hand, and the door opened wide to an empty room.

Chapter 16

Karin moved quickly, cutting through a manicured yard to reach the next street over, heading south to reach Duke Street and then west toward the small business center. There she found a public phone, a phone book from which to tear a few key Yellow Pages and a place to lurk out of sight until the taxi she'd called arrived. Dave's unmistakable Maxima drove by twice.

Too bad it worked out this way. I'd have liked to see you in that suit again.

But she'd done the right thing. He was too conflicted to pull off this scam. When she'd gathered enough information to sink Longsford, then maybe she'd see Dave again.

Or maybe not. Maybe she'd take her new nest egg and head off to Alaska. Or maybe to one of the little Caribbean islands that didn't have extradition. They had plenty of jobs for a woman who knew how to work people, how to keep them happy. For that was what it was all about—that was what a good long con did. Kept the mark happy. Some of them never did realize they'd been taken at all…just chalked it up to bad luck when their big opportunity didn't come through.

This was one opportunity that Karin would *make* come through. *Look out, Longsford.*

When the taxi arrived she directed it to her new destination, the Embassy Suites in Old Town. Maia Brenner checked into a room on the first floor at the end of the hall. Easy to come and go unseen. The place had everything she needed—the fridge, the microwave, the coffeemaker, a complimentary breakfast.

And the phones. She hadn't had a chance to check in with Amy Lynn since leaving home the second time. Later she'd get herself a prepaid cell phone, but for now she'd eat the hotel long-distance charges. She flopped onto the suite's sofa and pulled the phone close, dialing Amy Lynn's number from memory.

"Be there," she said to the phone after it rang three times. "Just *be there.*"

She was composing a voice-mail message in her head when the phone was snatched up, fumbled, and finally made it to someone's ear. Amy Lynn's breathless voice said, "Hello?"

"Thought I was going to miss you," Karin told her.

"Ellen! Thank goodness. Are you okay?"

The question surprised her. She'd been okay when she left; Amy Lynn hadn't known a thing about the night on the cliff. "I'm fine," she said. "Is everything okay there?"

Amy Lynn hastened to reassure her with the understanding of a woman who also owned a bevy of farm animals. "The animals are fine," she said. "Agatha's milk is wonderful—you really should have me start it on cheese."

"Drink it or sell it," Karin said. No need to think twice about that one. Amy Lynn might think Karin was off wrapping up old business from before her move with plans to return imminently, but Karin herself no longer assumed she could pick up where she'd left off. "What about Dewey?"

"He's fine." Amy Lynn had caught her breath; her voice sounded more casual. "I adore him, as ever."

Good thing. Karin knew he'd have a good home if she couldn't get back to him. But she suddenly missed him, a great big unexpected wave of longing for a canine friend who'd at first been wary of her but now watched over her as if he'd always been hers, his tail wagging at every glance she gave him.

It wasn't enough to deter her from what she'd first heard in her friend's voice. "Something's up," she said. "Out with it."

"Never could hide anything from you," Amy Lynn grumbled. "Look, I don't know what's going on. First you leave, then you're back and you've hurt your wrist, and then you're off again. And I saw that car in your driveway."

They'd had this talk before. The one where Karin made it clear that "Ellen" would gently decline to talk about the past she was trying to leave behind. "Amy Lynn—"

"Okay, okay. I'm not asking. I'm just telling you I'm not blind. Anyhow, this morning I went in to water plants and your answering machine had a message. I checked it—I thought it might be important."

Sudden dread replaced the lingering homesickness. "Who was it?"

"Really weird, that's what it was. Some guy named Gregg. Said he'd had some inquiries about you, and the attention would be a problem for him, and if it didn't stop he'd come out to talk about it in person."

Karin's hand clenched on the phone. *Cree-ap.* Rumsey.

Longsford must have dug into Ellen's past, probably even while they were dating. Might even have been why he stayed with her. Not only was she a nonconfrontational and unwitting ally in his disgusting personal pursuits, he probably felt he had the means to control her if she got out of hand. He probably didn't realize that Ellen was the only one with nothing hanging over her head.

And now Longsford was looking for Ellen, so he'd gone to Rumsey. Karin could only imagine Rumsey's rage—no con man wanted a spotlight shining his way. And the man was perfectly capable of turning down a finder's fee if it meant he might gain that unwanted attention in the local community, just as he was perfectly capable of showing up at Ellen's farm if he thought it would put an end to the inquiries.

"Ellen?" Amy Lynn sounded worried again. "Does the message mean anything to you? Do you know who it was?"

She kept her voice casual. "Just a strange little man from too many years ago," she said. "No telling what got into his head. Don't worry about it. He lives on the West Coast. There's no chance he'll just show up at your place."

"Hmm," Amy Lynn said. Then she offered, "That was my unconvinced noise. But the animals are all fine and the weather here is perfect. You're gonna be sorry you missed it."

"I'm already sorry I'm missing it," Karin told her, somewhat more fervently than she'd planned. "I'll be back as soon as I can. No doubt after I miss most of the spring planting." She glanced at her watch and winced. The day would get away from her if she wasn't careful. "Look, I've got to go. I'll check in again as soon as I can. I should have a cell number for you the next time."

"Alrighty. You're gonna owe me for this one, you know."

"Already do," Karin said. "Tell your hubby 'hey' for me."

"Will do. And Ellen…whatever's going on, be careful, okay?"

"Nothing like that," Karin said, putting the breeze back in her voice. "But I will."

But when she hung up the phone she found herself staring at it balefully, as if it was at fault.

Rumsey, back in her life. Rumsey, the man who'd rigged those felony charges against her. Rumsey, the single person who could take one look at her and know exactly who she was.

Crap.

She changed into one of the suit outfits—the short skirt, barely there camisole and tailored jacket. It was a lean combination and it made her legs look impossibly long; the unusual chocolate brown shade brought out her contact-colored eyes. From her room she called a limo service and hired them for the day on Hunter's credit card, requesting a luxury sedan and a driver who knew how to keep appearances.

She had the limo pick her up at a nearby flower shop, where she acquired several small daisies that she tucked into her hair above her ear. Put-together and yet confidently carefree, that was Maia Brenner. She leaned forward to hand the driver one of her Yellow Pages. "I need to visit some printers."

"All of them?" he said in doubt. He was as advertised—trim and neatly dressed, one of those spare men who would never flesh out, his hair silvered at the edges of its conservative cut, his tie precisely knotted and his currently wrinkled brow holding just the right amount of deference for the question.

"That depends on how fast we find the right printer," she

said. "I'm looking for someone with high standards and creative, impeccable work on invitations and announcements."

He gave a decisive nod. "That's better, then. I can narrow that down for you."

"That would be wonderful," she said, using her warm Maia voice. "Also, I'll need a driver frequently during my visits here. Would it be all right to ask for you?"

"It would be a pleasure, ma'am. You can ask for Bill Chantrey." He put aside the Yellow Pages, checked his side view mirror and pulled smoothly into traffic.

"Please, Bill—may I call you Bill?—I'd feel much better if you called me Maia."

"Miss Maia," Bill allowed in a broad Coastal accent, unwittingly becoming part of her deliberate trail through town. Before she was done, she'd have him convinced she was throwing her own party, complete with the implication that the occasion would offer a select group of people an opportunity of some sort.

If Longsford checked her out—and he should—he'd learn just what she wanted him to. Maia Brenner was in town to do business, and if Longsford wanted in on it, he'd get the distinct impression he'd have to move fast.

The first printer was a bust; she knew as soon as she entered the shop that they weren't of the caliber Longsford would use. In these high-tech days where genteel formality often fell by the wayside, he always sent beautifully printed invitations. One of the national entertainment magazines had gone so far as to print a photo of one in their piece on a recent party.

Dave had been thorough in his research, she'd say that for him.

At the second printer's she walked in and caught the proprietor's eye in an instant. Maia was a woman with class, someone used to buying what she wanted and used to making things happen. She said nothing, nodding a fractional greeting before she put the printout on the counter and pushed it toward him.

He put a finger on it, pulling it closer, and pretended to examine it before he nodded. "This is one of ours," he said, and pushed it back to her.

She smiled, guileless and relieved. "I'm so pleased to have finally found you," she said. "I love the look of the invitation, and would like something similar for an upcoming event. I'd choose my own font, of course—this has a lovely bold, masculine look, but that's not quite me."

"Not quite," he said, somewhat bemused at her take-charge approach. Good. The less time he had to think, the better.

"But if we could use the same paper, and that ink—the embossing is perfect, and I love the matte surface—I'd be delighted. Do you have a font book I could look through? And I'd love to see that paper." She dug through her fashionably petite purse and pulled out a folded piece of paper. "This isn't so much an invitation as it is an announcement, but I think it'll look wonderful in a small fold-over version, don't you?"

He traded his font sample book for her carefully printed words about a cocktail party at a swanky hotel. Peering at them through the glasses sitting near the end of his nose, he gave a little nod at the simple lines of invitation, but then looked up at her in question. "That's it?"

She smiled as if quite delighted with herself. "It's enough. They're going out by hand." She pushed the font book back at him. "This one. What do you think?" Also a bold font, but arguably feminine. Perfectly appropriate, even though the

cards would never be distributed. She couldn't come in asking
for the details of Longsford's invitations without a good backstory, and she had to support the backstory with action.

Not to mention that should Longsford hear about it, he'd
only be more convinced that she intended to follow through
with her efforts to sell the Ranchwood property. Her proposal
would suit anyone on the hunt for charitable donations and
eventual profit on the side, and he'd know it. *Opportunity
knocks once, and then moves on....*

The printer was nodding at her choice. Karin pulled out a
tiny notebook and flipped it open, also producing a classy, expensive pen that Dave might or might not have missed by now.
"And what's the name of that paper...and the ink?"

"Arches Cover, slate," he murmured, making his own
notes. "How many of these would you like printed?"

"Two hundred," she said. "I know it's not much...I could
do the same on almost any desktop these days. But the quality...the impression the invitations give...it just wouldn't be
the same, don't you agree?"

"A rhetorical question, I assume," he said. "And do four-
by-five-inch cards suit you?"

"Perfect. What was that ink again?"

And he told her as he finished writing up her order, even
making sure she had spelled it right. He promised the results
within a week, and he gladly took her credit card number
for a deposit.

Her own credit card this time; this was an expense likely
to stand out to any Hunter accountant's eye, especially should
the sudden activity on the card bring the account to anyone's
attention. She'd already transferred most of her Ellen accounts
into Maia's holdings, but she didn't have nearly enough to

finance this gig and then still move on. She might well have to pay herself back by completing the scam.

She waited for the thrill at the thought, but it didn't come. She still managed to smile at the nice man behind the counter, and she left the printer with the information she'd come to get. It was as she was leaving that she suddenly understood. She'd planned to have someone at her side for this job...and she didn't.

Bill the driver didn't open the shop door for her, but he did spring from the car to open the back passenger door. "You stayed a few moments, Miss Maia," he offered, as he slid back behind the wheel. "Was that the jackpot?"

Karin smiled. "That was indeed the jackpot. Now...I have a little shopping to do. Women's accessories, that sort of thing. Can you recommend a spot?"

"Just leave the driving up to me," he promised, and deftly navigated the thickening traffic.

Karin lost herself in the details, staring at the note in her hand. Now she needed an entirely different sort of printer to forge an invitation for Longsford's party two evenings from now.

After that it was just a matter of wooing him, and the wooing wouldn't be hard. Not with an investment tailor-made to suit both his greed and his need to establish control. It might take a week or so...and she certainly still had details to sort out. People to hire as extras, a few more technical things to sort out. If she'd been on her home turf, she'd have known exactly who to go to. Here...

She'd know more before the evening was over, one way or the other.

She parted ways with Bill in the late afternoon, peeling off a generous tip for his day's work and reserving his time for

Longsford's party. It was getting a step or two ahead of herself, as she had yet to acquire the invitation—but then, that was what she was about to start working on.

She'd given herself five long blocks to walk before she reached the hotel, here in the middle of rush hour. The streets were jammed with traffic and the sidewalks likewise, making it difficult for a woman with a handful of shopping bags to make any graceful progress. Karin sidestepped several near-collisions until she found the older man who suited her needs. For him, she contrived to trip into his path.

Her shopping bags went flying; she bumped into him and he into her during their efforts to recover her belongings— the scanty panties and lacy bras she'd bought just for him. And he didn't have the slightest clue when she lifted his watch.

After that she sorted out the lacy things with efficient cheer, stuffing them back into random bags and making apologies and calling him a gentleman. For a moment she was worried—it had been a while since she'd seen a man's face so red—but he went on his way with swift, stable strides and she decided maybe he wouldn't have a stroke after all.

She didn't look at the watch until she was back in the hotel room, a smooth journey with no more bumps or jostles. There, she dumped the lingerie on the middle of her big queen bed and pulled the watch out from the tangle.

Oh, yeah. A large Tiffany Mark bracelet watch. Self-winding, in stainless steel. Well over two thou retail.

This would get someone's attention.

She pulled off the Maia clothes, hanging them with neat precision. She'd need to grab some food, but first of all she had to get out of here unseen. She wasn't leaving this place as Maia. She pulled on a pair of tight, worn jeans, not espe-

cially stylish but attention-getting all the same. A black tur-
tleneck, taken from Dave's thrift-store purchases. Her own
worn army surplus field jacket over it all…and Dave's Ruger
stuck into the deep pocket of that jacket. She slicked her hair
back tight, turning the blond society coif into a mean ponytail, and pulled out the brown contacts. She scrubbed her face
of its gentle makeup and applied mascara and a hard eyeliner,
leaving the rest alone. A few things in her back jeans pockets,
the watch in an inside jacket pocket, a Baltimore Orioles
baseball cap on her head with the ponytail sticking out the
back…

Ready to go. She checked the hall and she slipped out the
door and into the stairwell; half a flight of stairs down got her
to the main exit door. She hesitated there long enough to insert
her door key into a planter of early annuals. Tonight would be
the riskiest part of this whole operation, and if she happened
to get searched by the people she hoped to find, she didn't
want to give up anything but the watch. No ID, no key card,
no credit cards. Just some cash, a watch and a lot of attitude.

On the other hand, with the Ruger in her pocket, she hoped
to avoid anything that up close and personal.

She walked a few blocks away from the hotel and picked up
a battered taxi, waving it down in the dark. When she told the
driver she wanted to check out the southeast pawnshops, he
turned to look at her askance, assessing her expression. Then he
turned back to the road with a shrug, and accelerated into traffic.

She paid him to wait at the first place, where she idly
played with the watch and asked questions about special-
interest printers. The man behind the counter turned impatient
fast and bitched at her for wasting his time.

The second store visit netted her the grudging suggestion

that she try Freddie's. The cabbie rolled his eyes when he heard their new destination, and this time he opened his mouth. Karin cut him off. "I know," she said. "But it's where I need to go. And I'm a big tipper."

Another eye roll, but he took them there. A tight little storefront with a darkened shoe-repair place on one side and a dimly lit sex-toy shop on the other. Bars across all the windows, of course. Looked just about right.

Karin leaned forward to catch the cabbie's attention. "Wait for me."

He gave her a dour look behind an overgrown mustache. She slid out of the car, striding confidently for the pawnshop door, one hand on the Ruger in her pocket and the other already holding the watch. She pushed inside to the inevitable jingle of bells and quickly spotted the security cameras. Three of them. This guy wasn't taking any chances. A few more steps of the crowded store revealed that the cash register was behind security glass.

Yup. This looked like the place.

"We're closing!" a man called from the back, bored with her already.

Karin held the watch up in clear view of at least two of the security cameras, dangling it enticingly from her fingers.

Yup. Here he came. She heard footsteps with a limp. When the man came into sight from the back room—grizzled, beefy and clearly a candidate for hip replacement—she lowered the watch but kept it in sight. "It's yours, if you can give me the right information."

He grunted. "And just how hot is it?"

She didn't pretend otherwise. "You've got a day or two."

"Whatta you want?"

"I'm looking for a printer."

He grunted again. "Try the phone book."

She sighed loudly, and stuffed the watch into her coat pocket. "Oh, *please*."

A shrug. He eyed the pocket where the watch now resided.

"Look. I give you the watch, you've got something over me if you want it. Meanwhile, I've got a special print job to run. It's a one-time job, then I'll be out of here. I'm not moving in on anyone's turf." She cocked her head. "Though I could, if I wanted to. Just in case you think I might blunder around leaving tracks to this place. Not gonna happen."

"I should think that?" The very picture of innocence. Deeply sarcastic innocence at that.

"A name," she said. "The go-to guy. Where I can find him. That's all." She withdrew the watch but kept it close to her body this time.

"Tiffany's?" he asked, not quite believing it.

"Just something I bumped into." She smiled at him, knowing he'd catch her meaning just fine.

Someone else came into the store; she stepped aside so she could keep them both in view at the same time. This fellow was scruffy—way beyond fashionably scruffy—and he had a mean, leering look. At least ten years older than Karin, he'd gone far past *youthful indiscretions* and straight to *loser*.

He said, "Hey, Freddie, you got nice company." He turned to Karin. "Don't suppose that's your cab what just took off?"

Karin glared at him. "What'd you say to him?"

He grinned. "Just my natural charm."

She looked him up and down with distaste. "I can imagine." And then, when he took a few steps toward her, she shook her head sharply. "I can imagine quite well from here, thanks."

He stopped, but she didn't like the looks of him. Too confident, too anticipatory. He was playing with her, and didn't think she'd know it. He said, "Nice watch," and couldn't quite hide the greed in his voice.

"Yes," she said shortly. "That's why I took it." She angled her head back at Freddie, but kept a close eye on the unwelcome newcomer. "Just write it down, Freddie. We'll make the swap. I'll handle my business and be out of this area for good."

Freddie exchanged glances with the man—he'd inched a little closer to Karin and clearly thought himself sly for it—and shrugged, a gesture limited by Freddie's own beefy nature.

Karin almost tsked out loud at the obvious nature of his underlying decision. Write the stuff down, then have the scruffy guy pounce on her for the watch without ever giving anything away. But she wanted the information, so she kept her tsking to herself until Freddie was done, holding the paper up for her inspection from a distance.

She was supposed to reach for it, to be distracted and off balance, not noticing the other man. And she did reach for it, snatching it out of Freddie's thick-fingered grip even as she drew the Ruger and jammed it into the belly of the other man, stopping his sly move short.

"Whoa," he said, and his hands shot up, surrender and denial both. He backed away in slow motion, casting meaningful glances at Freddie. Appeal. He expected the man to do something, and no doubt there was a sawed-off behind the counter somewhere.

But Freddie didn't look like a fast man, and he looked like he knew his limits. "You got what you came for. Now what about that watch?"

She could have snorted and left, but she didn't. He'd been

right to be concerned about her credentials and the effect of her activity on his turf. And she had indeed gotten what she'd come for. *Don't cross the local players unless you want them popping up to jam up the con.*

Karin watched them both as she pulled out the watch and tossed it underhand at Freddie. "All yours," she said. "Of course, if you've scribbled up some nonsense here, the cops will know where to look for that watch."

He waved her off with such disinterest that she knew he'd stopped toying with her. She'd earned her way to the local printing expert—a woman she would visit the next day—and with any luck she'd never see Freddie or his friend again.

Said friend was easing toward the door. Karin stopped him merely by aiming the gun not at him, but at the spot just ahead of him. To continue, he'd have to walk right into her sights. "Hey," he said. "I'm not part of this."

"Keys," she told him.

"Whatta you—"

"*Keys.*"

In the background, Freddie grunted. "You scared off her ride, dope. Next time maybe you'll check things out before you try weaseling in."

But the man sulked. "It's a motorcycle."

She only smiled at him. "It's a beautiful night for a ride." It wasn't; it was chilly and she wasn't dressed for the wind of a motorcycle ride. But she wasn't going to wait for another cab. She held out her hand, twitching her fingers in a little come-hither gesture meant for the keys. "Toss 'em."

He fished on his belt for the release to the big jangle of keys by his side, a sullen eye on the Ruger. When he freed the key, he tossed it just to the side—an invitation to reach out and become off balance, or to miss the key altogether.

Karin snatched it out of the air with satisfaction, and then gestured with the pistol, suggesting that the sullen man join up with Freddie. "You'll find the bike in Old Town, a couple of blocks from the flower shop."

The man snorted. "What do I know about Old Town?"

"Not my problem. You shouldn't have interfered with my business. And oh—they use parking meters on that part of the street, so I wouldn't dawdle. I'm really low on change right now."

Freddie grunted again, but this time with amusement at the man's expense. When he turned to Karin he said, "Go on. He won't try to stop you. You played this clean…come back if you need to." He ran a meaty thumb over the watch face and added, "Bring another nice gift if you do."

Karin grinned. "Always do." She pulled the door open just enough to slip through, and found the motorcycle half a block down, up against the curb. A big solid Kawasaki Vulcan—no wonder the guy was anxious about it. Well, he'd have it back by morning.

She hopped on the bike, started it up and slowly released the hand clutch to pull out into the thinning traffic of late evening, reveling in the trickle of excitement that told her *well done*. Tomorrow she'd meet with the printer and see if they could pull off the invitation.

Just like old times. From the bump-and-snatch on the street to her ability to handle Freddie to keeping on track in spite of the complications caused by the bike's owner. It might have been easier with Dave at her side, but—

The excitement took a strange dive as she realized how he

would have reacted to the watch, how he would have reacted to her casual use of the gun. To how easily she'd performed the little dance of acceptance with Freddie.

No, it wouldn't have been easier with Dave after all. She'd made the right decision, going solo.

But her excitement had disappeared, to be replaced by an unexpected, sullen fatigue. She rode the motorcycle north, winding her way through unfamiliar streets until she found a good spot, and left the bike by the curb. She dropped a few coins in the meter, and then wondered if she'd have done the same had she not been thinking about Dave and his damnable honor.

Damnable was right. "It was good work," she told the bike in defiance, and then left it there, walking the blocks to the hotel. She plucked up her room key card out of the potted plant, buffed it clean against her thigh and went to her room. She needed a good night's sleep, and then she'd head off into tomorrow.

And this time she'd be sure to leave the anchor of Dave's conscience behind.

Chapter 17

She was still here somewhere. Dave propped his forehead in his hands and muttered a sound of pure frustration.

She just wasn't here as Ellen Sommers, Karin Sommers or Brooke Ellington. Big surprise, she'd had another identity to fall back on.

But she was out there. She'd taken the list of links, the society page printouts, the pages of notes about the people who ran in Barret Longsford's circles…everything she needed to continue the scam.

And she'd taken his gun. That irritated him the most. It seemed…*personal*. He'd already replaced the Ruger, although not before he'd spent the morning alternating between fury and pain as he unsuccessfully hunted Karin.

He hadn't expected her to leave.

And exactly what, his almost-buried common sense asked

him, had he thought she *would* do? He'd given her plenty of reason to doubt him. She'd broken her cover to offer him her expertise, and he'd given her grief.

Even now, unease made his stomach do a slow roll. Her skills were built on a lifetime of theft and deception, and it wasn't a morality he could accept. Nor was the California warrant something he could ignore, even if he hoped the charges weren't true.

But leaving her out there to carry this off on her own wasn't an option, either.

He looked at the thick Yellow Pages spread open before him—all the hotels he'd called marked off with neat *X*'s. "Where are you, dammit?"

But she wasn't going to be easily found. He shut the phone book with a thump and turned his thoughts to Longsford, reaching for the thick sheaf of notes he'd collected on the man so far.

That was when it hit him.

He didn't have to find Karin. He knew what she was after. If he put himself in the right spot at the right time, she'd find *him*.

And meanwhile, he had work to do. One way or the other, Longsford was going down.

Dave wished he didn't think Karin would go down with him.

Karin walked out into the crisp morning, depositing her key card into its damp hiding spot with no more hesitation than a woman recovering from a slight misstep. She had the Ruger in the field jacket, but she didn't expect to use it. Today the printer might decide to work for her or he might not, but either way it would be a genteel encounter as compared to the gauntlet she'd run to get this far.

And if the printer refused to work with her, she'd find

another. Definitely not an optimal plan; her timetable depended on this step. And on Longsford's next big social whirl—cocktails at an environmental benefit event held in his own home.

Too perfect, really.

She walked past where she'd parked the motorcycle the night before; the bike had been reclaimed. She smiled to herself. She hadn't really wanted him to lose the thing. Be it on his head that he'd walked into the wrong shop at the wrong time and acted like a jerk.

Well, she'd done what she had to. And she'd made it back to the hotel safely, and here she was in the same clothes—her laid-back tough-girl outfit—ready to take the next step.

Today's destination wasn't far from the pawnshop, but it nonetheless crossed one of those invisible lines between neighborhoods. The new neighborhood upgraded from scum-of-the-earth sordidness to merely plain, old and crowded. Touches of leftover class peeked out through the architecture, the occasional Victorian paint job and the windowsill plantings. The cabbie took her through a business strip and into a small warren of streets, and when he pulled to the curb, it was at a pleasant little house with a Big Wheels out front and toys scattered near the sidewalk leading to the front door. Barbie, baby, G.I. Joe—they all met the same naked fate. The tiny clothesline strung between two azalea bushes went a long way toward explaining that one.

Had she been anyone else, Karin might have hesitated, assuming she had the wrong address. But she had reason enough to know that scammers had family, too.

The woman who opened the door was plump with rich brown skin, marked with random ink stains on the old men's shirt she wore. She took one look at Karin and said, "Ah. The Tiffany watch and the big black gun."

"It's a Ruger," Karin told her. "Can I come in?"

"Do you have it with you now?"

She didn't answer directly, just gave the smallest of shrugs—a little bit apology, a little bit matter-of-fact. "After my reception at Freddie's?"

"Yeah, I guess so." But when she stepped back so Karin could enter the foyer, she pointed at a high shelf over the door. "Put it there. My kid's in the house."

Karin complied, though not without a quick assessment of the woman, who gave her a scornful look. "No, I don't have a gun. What did I just say about my kid being in the house? Besides, people here know better than to harass me. I'm the best this city has, and we do look after our own." She glanced back at Karin as she led the way to the basement, a stairwell and low-ceilinged area so well lit that it might as well have been daylight down there. "You'll learn that fast enough, if you're looking to move into this area."

"I told Freddie I wasn't."

No doubt she knew that, too. No doubt she was leaving Karin room to tie her cover story into knots.

"Doesn't matter," Karin added. "I know the score. I'm not part of this community. That makes me expendable. So I'm looking after myself, and that means not messing with you."

The woman gave a short laugh and gestured at a long work-table with high-backed stools. "Have a seat." The table itself was covered with evidence of previous jobs—stains and smears and lumps of dried ink—but no sign of current work. Karin hoped it meant she was in between jobs, and not merely playing it safe after she got Freddie's heads-up.

Karin didn't waste any time. She pulled out the picture of the invitation, and then the sheet with the printer specs on it. "Can you make me one of these? Thirty-six hours?"

The woman snorted at her bluntness but didn't dismiss the idea. "This is pricey stuff. Looks like Houghlin's work." She glanced up long enough to receive Karin's nod of affirmation and then looked at the invitation again, this time biting her lower lip. From above them came a thump and a flurry of giggles; without looking up, the woman called up the stairs, "I'm watching you!" and then, finally, returned the picture.

"I need it to look just like that, but made out to Maia Brenner, for this event." She handed over the card on which she'd written Maia's name, and the name of Longsford's benefit event.

"They're just going to ask for your money." She tapped the picture a few times in thought, and then shook her head. "It's specialty paper. I can't get it that fast."

"It's not about money at all," Karin said, dropping her voice just in case the words might carry upstairs. "I'm looking to reel in bigger fish. Someone who takes children. He does unspeakable things to them, and then he kills them. He'll be at this function. I need to meet him there."

The woman paled slightly. "The water-tower boy?"

Karin gave a succinct nod. "Exactly."

"Whatever it's about, I need to get paid. And I don't take Tiffany's."

"Cash for you," Karin said. "Where it comes from isn't your problem." She still hoped to complete the scam and get herself a new start, but nothing was going according to plan for this one. Especially not the man who was meant to be her partner and who was instead now probably trying to do his best to stop her. "Charge for the fast turnaround. Whatever."

Finally the woman sighed. "No promises," she said. "The ink's no problem, but I might not be able to get the paper. Let me know where I can reach you."

Karin gave her the number, assuring her it was a prepaid cell phone purchased only the day before. "I'm Maia," she said, and then grinned. "Well, as long as I'm *here,* I'm Maia."

"You can call me anything you like," the woman said absently; her thoughts already seemed caught up in the challenge of the job. "Just don't try to get in touch. I'll make contact."

Sensing her dismissal, Karin pulled out the material for Ranchwood Acres and slapped it on the table. "Now that we've got that out of the way, I also need this material prepared in slicks. The URLs to the Web site pages are included, and there's a PDF download. Very thoughtful of them. I just need a few pertinent details changed. I'll get back to you on those when you call about the invitation. Can you do it?"

She snorted. "This one's hardly worth coming to me."

"Except for your reputation for quality," Karin said. "I'm pushing this one. There can't be so much as a smudge out of place. He's got to take the bait hard and fast."

"And you're sure—"

"Oh, this is him." She smiled thinly. "And I'm going to stop him."

The woman looked at her with dark humor that seemed out of place on her otherwise urban young mother face. "Not exactly something I'd expect from someone in your line of work."

"No," Karin admitted, her voice tinged with her own surprise. "I don't suppose it is."

* * *

Karin Sommers's Journal: On the Make Again

Dear Ellen,
Believe it or not, here we go. I was so glad to get away
from Rumsey, so eager to start my new life. Now it
looks like I'm starting my old life instead.
    But one of these days when I pick up this journal, it'll
be to tell you that Longsford is behind bars. I just hope
I'm not behind bars right along with him.

Dave took a giant swig of spring water and tossed his
apple core into the garbage. He patted the Maxima's dash.
"I know, baby. You weren't meant to be a surveillance car."
Not that the car wasn't comfortable, but blending in wasn't
one of its virtues. Especially in this high-class Old Town
neighborhood.
    At least it wasn't red.
    He'd been here since midafternoon, not far from the
Potomac waterfront—outside Longsford's redbrick home,
waiting for the cocktail benefit to start. Like many homes in
Old Town, the house was tall and narrow and beautifully
landscaped. The neighbors were close on either side of the
tight property, and those attending knew better than to expect
parking in the tiny driveway.
    Then again, few of those attending did their own driving.
    The day was gorgeously springlike, over seventy degrees and
already humid. No doubt the event would spill into the backyard, a considerable stretch of land in this tightly developed
area. The first hour or so Dave had slouched to observe arriving
caterers, florists, the environmental beneficiaries with their *give
me money* materials and the event coordinator who fluttered out

to hurry the worker bees along. Now the guests were arriving, and Dave straightened to see who'd come to the party.

And if Karin was among them. Or if he was wrong, and she'd just plain skipped out on him.

Sunshine splashed down through the long, narrow sunroof; Dave shifted to keep the glare of it from sneaking in behind his sunglasses, and almost missed her.

She'd found a driver—one who hopped out from behind the wheel to open the back door of the dark blue Cadillac Catera and offer her formal-looking assistance as she disembarked. They'd pulled over behind several other cars, and she had half a block to walk before reaching the house.

Dave could intercept her, and he did. He slipped out of his sedan and jogged across the street, into the shade of the giant maple in the lawn adjoining Longsford's.

If he hadn't been looking for her…if he hadn't seen this dress when she first tried it on…

She was all class this afternoon, the cocktail dress short and swingy and just the right combination of traditional and original. Midnight blue cut a diagonal swath across the skirt and bodice; she'd covered the spaghetti straps with a light, sparkly shawl she wouldn't need once she hit the sunlight. Her hair was gathered in a perfect updo with just the right amount of loose fringe at her nape to make it look casually chic; her earrings dangled just so. Even the wrist cast was covered with a gauzy scarf.

She was Karin, and yet not Karin at all.

She stopped short when she saw him, her hand clutching down on a fashionably small purse. And then, by apparent sheer strength of will, she relaxed. "Took you long enough."

"Took me way too long," he said shortly. And told himself, *don't be an asshole.*

He just hadn't expected to be affected by the sight of her. Or the sound of her. Or even the awareness that snapped into place between them. Fool, to have forgotten the strength of it, in defiance of all that had now separated them.

She cocked her head. "You here to stop me?"

"Stop you? I said I'd *help* you."

"You did," she agreed. A slight breeze shifted the sunshine-blond wisps of hair over her forehead—not enough there to be called bangs, but they softened her hairline and in some strange way brought out the fullness of her lower lip, made the unusual straightness of her upper lip into something sexy. He felt suddenly as though he didn't know her at all, and at the same time as though she'd become part of his life. But she brought him down to earth quickly enough, and so did the quick flash of hurt in her eyes. "You offered to help, and then something changed. *You* changed. You didn't really know what you wanted, I think. Do you now?"

"No," he told her. *You, but…not what you are.* "And yes. I want Longsford."

"Any way you can get him?" She gave him that look, the one from beneath her lashes, the gray of her eyes still piercing even through that veil.

He couldn't bend that far. "Within the limits of what we talked about earlier, yes."

Sudden frustration crept into her voice. "Then why the hell are you blowing my cover?"

He smiled back at her. Grinned, actually, freed up from the personal byplay to attend the practical. "I'm not. I'm observing his guests, and you're a new face to me. I've accosted you so we can talk. And by the way, I've got someone to play the role of the developer. You want the phone number? It's a Florida cell. I had it shipped to her just for you."

She blinked. "Who?"

"Her name is Kimmer Reed. She works for Owen, but she owes me a favor or two right now. She can play him any way you like—and she's got an incredible ability to read people, even over the phone. She can tell you what he's really thinking."

"Maybe you should talk to her, then. Maybe she can tell you what *you're* really thinking."

"Ow." Dave mimed taking a blow to the heart. "Nice hit."

"Far from a killing blow. Give me the number."

He pulled out his notepad, and she shook her head. "That's just plain evidence, and I'm headed for the lion's den. I'll memorize it." And she did. When he gave it to her, slowly, she immediately rattled it back off at him. Then she gave him her own number—a new cell, apparently—and said, "Go ahead. Write it down. You'll feel better, you and your notes."

Flushing slightly, he did, then tucked the notebook back inside his suit. The one that dressed him up too finely for his cop role, but would have been perfect for the chauffeur boy-toy role she'd had sketched out for him. "And now? You really got an invitation to this thing?"

"I really do. And now that we've been standing here for so long, I need you to grab me."

"You—what?"

Her face flashed impatience. "We've been here too long. We've been noticed. I'm going to walk past you, and I want you to grab me—like you mean it, too. And you should know I'm gonna slap you."

"You've been planning this?" While they stood there and talked, she'd choreographed interpersonal mayhem?

"Make it up as I go along," she said tartly, shifting the shawl over her shoulders as she straightened in offense at some imaginary thing he'd said, raised her chin, and stalked past him.

But two could play that game. He dug into his pocket, searching for the tiny device there even as he turned on her, grabbing her arm. She tugged away, hissing through her teeth, "Make it real!" and he latched on to her with the other hand, planting the device on the soft skin beneath her upper arm.

"Real enough?" he asked, as they struggled on the sidewalk in incongruous contrast to the continuing arrival of the beautiful people.

"Not quite," she said, and yanked one arm free to deal him a resounding slap. A slap hard enough to stagger him, and she sprang away, readjusting her shawl and stalking down the sidewalk as though she owned it.

Had to hand it to her. For that moment, she did.

Karin's hand still stung with the impact of the slap she'd dealt Dave; anger and chagrin warred for dominance within, somehow settling into a churning stomach. *Get it together, Karin.*

She followed another couple up the impeccably maintained walk surrounded by a colorful splash of iris and forsythia. Tulips lined the stairs; clumps of hyacinths clustered beside them. Two hanging pots flanked the doorway, spilling over with bright fuchsia blossoms. The beautiful life, with the beautiful people.

Things change, Longsford.

She smiled at the perky young thing who served as door greeter, and knew enough to flash her invitation at just the right moment so as not to create an embarrassing hesitation.

And then she was in.

Her goal for the day? Just to catch Longsford's attention. No pushing, no sales talk. To judge by the sound of things, the main activity would be out back, taking advantage of the huge, long backyard and the weather. But no rush. There was a small number of people circulating in what was once a parlor, and Karin folded her shawl over her arm and went to introduce herself as a friend of the Braddocks'—one of the two traveling couples from Dave's notes. By the end of the party they'd all know that the gregarious couple had wielded influence to get her the invitation. A kindness to someone from out of town, with just enough implication that they thought the introduction could be beneficial to Longsford, too.

Except she'd only taken one step into the parlor when a hand fell on her shoulder. A heavy hand, full of authority. In some ways, a hand she'd been expecting since she was eight years old. She turned, a smile ready on her face.

At the sight of Longsford, she faltered momentarily. His pictures hadn't conveyed the impact of his presence, not one bit. Not just because his features were attractive, if flawed enough to keep him real, or that he was a large man. More that he was a man used to exerting power and influence; that confidence radiated from his very core. If there was some part of him still frustrated with the struggle to take control from his domineering mother, it didn't so much as peek through. For the first time, Karin felt a trickle of doubt. *What if it's not him?*

Then no harm done. She'd run her scam without finding evidence, she'd relieve him of a little extra cash and she'd be on her way. His reputation would be unsullied, and Dave Hunter would have to get used to being wrong. He'd have to find a new suspect. Meanwhile Karin would start her new life—again. As fast as the thoughts flickered through her mind, Karin recovered her smile. "Mr. Longsford," she said warmly. "I'm so pleased to meet you. Lily and Kent have told me so much about you."

"And they've told me nothing of you," he said. "I frankly can't imagine how you made it on the guest list." But when she opened her mouth to explain, he cut her off. "We'll deal with that later. Right now I want to know what that was all about."

She discovered he had a hand on her arm, and that he'd drawn her aside—still in the parlor, but just barely. Those who had recently occupied the space drifted oh-so-casually away, their perfume and their alcohol fumes still on the air. "I'm not sure—"

He jerked his head toward the front windows. "There's a good view of the street from there. I saw you talking with that man. Do you know who he is?"

No lying here. The tone behind his question gave away the fact that Longsford had recognized Dave. Not a big surprise.

"I know he's arrogant, rude and pushy. I know he's investigating something." She smiled. "If you saw the conversation, I expect you also saw how it ended."

Longsford smiled, too. "In fact, I did. But I still need to know what you told him."

Time to take a little control. No one had the right to interrogate her like this, and if she allowed it she'd give the wrong impression of Maia. Longsford wouldn't trust her to represent his interests if she was easy to push around. She held out her hand. "I'm Maia Brenner," she said. "I saw the Braddocks in Florida before they left for their cruise. They were interested in some land I'm representing. They learned I was coming north on business, and said they'd arrange for us to meet. When I received this invitation, I assumed that's what they meant."

His expression remained thoughtful—absorbing the implications, pondering the explanation. Probably pondering her vague familiarity, too. Not pleased.

It was time to give him back control. "You look unhappy. I'm sorry. If this was a mistake, I'll be glad to leave."

"I'm not sure that's the answer," he said, and glanced at a door. Karin thought it would probably lead to just a little bit too much privacy.

Then again, what would he do? In his own home, in the middle of a charity benefit?

Don't be naive, Karin. He'll do anything he wants to. It sounded like Ellen's voice in her head. Ellen, the cautious one. Karin listened but didn't back down. "He asked me questions about you. I don't know a thing, so in the end we didn't talk about much at all. I had nothing to tell him."

And still he studied her.

"Here," she said. "I've got my cell phone. I don't think the Braddocks' secretary will give out their number—they really wanted to get away from it all. But maybe since it's you—?" Flattery never hurt, oh no.

But he wasn't going for it. She saw it in the set of his jaw. He might not truly disbelieve her, but he didn't want to deal with her.

So. Fight vulnerability with vulnerability. She was still reaching for her cell phone; she deliberately fumbled her purse. It fell to the gorgeous parquet, spilling the contents everywhere. "Oh, my," she said, inane but for the embarrassment in her voice as she crouched to scoop up the phone, the lipstick, the little canister of pepper spray.

And the invitation. That, she carefully nudged farther away as she picked up the rest of it.

Someone came up behind Longsford. "Barry, your guests out back…" The event coordinator. "These benefits are so much more successful when you circulate."

Crap! Go away. Go. Away.

Karin held her breath with anticipation as well as intent, and gave Longsford just enough time to pick up the invitation—to get a good look at her name, and at the apparent authenticity of the thing. Just enough time, but not any more. Then she stood up, knowing her face was now flushed, knowing just how convincing she'd look when her eyes rolled back and she crumpled gracefully to the floor.

She couldn't have planned it better. Those clustered on the other side of the room gasped in dismay; the conversation level rose dramatically. Rather like the stiff material of her skirt, which ended up indecently high on her thigh.

"What the hell?" Longsford grunted, bending over her.

"I'll call 911—"

"Don't be an old woman. She's probably just fainted. You want a successful event? Let's keep the paramedics out of it." An instant later, he easily lifted her in his arms. Her head rolled; she let her eyes flutter. "Be still," he told her, his voice more brusque than compassionate. And to his companion, "The sitting room. I'd like a private chat with her in any event."

Maybe not such a great idea after all.

Then again, he didn't still seem to be thinking about having her escorted out.

Karin kept herself limp in the man's arms—feeling the strength of them, trying not to imagine what it would be like to be a child on the other end of that strength.

"Bring some water," Longsford commanded to someone on the way to the sitting room. Karin had slitted her eyes open, but saw nothing she could make sense of—bobbing faces and swooping architecture, and then her dangling ankles bumped a door frame. Within moments she'd been carefully deposited on a couch.

People pressed in around the doorway with curiosity and questions. "Do you know her?" "What happened?" "Did you see her go down?" And another, more directed; a woman's voice. "Mr. Longsford? A cool cloth for the young lady?"

"Yes, get that." His big hand grasped her jaw for a good look, then gave the side of her face a pat. "Miss Brenner?"

"See if she's got a Medic Alert bracelet." Someone checked her wrists—smaller hands than Longsford. Sweaty hands. *Yuck.*

Karin let herself make a little noise of surprise. That, too, got a crowd reaction, and a reaction from Longsford. "Enough, people. She's fine. I'll see you out back in a few moments, where our beneficiaries for the afternoon have materials for your attention."

When he turned back to her she met his gaze. "I'm sorry," she said softly, and rearranged herself to sit up a little straighter. "I'll be fine. Low blood pressure…I should know not to stand up so quickly."

Longsford grunted. It was a noncommittal sound. He sat down across from her in a lightly stuffed wing chair. One of the caterers entered with a glass of ice water and a cool wet cloth. Karin accepted both with gratitude, and hesitated over her next step.

Longsford took it for her. He gestured at the small coffee table between them, and she found her purse there; the invitation still stuck out the top. "Maia Brenner," he said. "I don't know you. I have my doubts about your connection to the Braddocks." He stopped long enough to catch her eye, and his

own were dark and flat and offered no quarter. She wasn't expecting the jolt they gave her, the stab of unexpected fear.

"Why are you really here?"

Chapter 18

How can he possibly know?

Karin took a deep breath and slid back into her game face. Of course he didn't know. He'd merely twigged that Maia Brenner's true purpose wasn't to mingle with the Braddocks' friends. She could work with that. In fact, it might well move things along a little faster.

So she let herself look abashed. "I was hoping it wouldn't be quite so obvious. I suppose that man outside didn't help."

"He brought you to my attention," Longsford agreed. "Miss Brenner, I'm a busy man. I don't like to play games."

Actually, yes, you do. You just like to make the rules.

But this was Karin's game. Her rules. He just didn't know it yet.

She sat up a little straighter, making sure her hem hadn't ridden too high, one hand checking the state of her hair. Not her own first concern, but Maia would care. Finding herself moderately presentable, she said, "I met Lily and Kent at a pitch reception before the cruise. You know the type—cocktails, their fanciest hors d'oeuvres, a big come-on for the next cruise. I find it's a good place to feel people out for the opportunities I broker, and—"

"I see." His interruption was brusque; he shifted his weight in preparation to stand.

"Mr. Longsford," she said firmly. "I already have my own reception planned, and a list of exclusive clients who are interested in my presentation. I wouldn't have gone to the effort of arranging this invitation if I wasn't convinced you were a perfect match for this particular investment."

He rose to his feet anyway, but he hesitated, regarding her silently for a long moment. Finally he said, "And why is that?"

"Because of just this." She gestured out the door at the gathering, the environmental charity. "It's an opportunity to invest in high-value property, recoup that investment and at the same time earn some spotlight publicity for your support of the environment."

Skepticism laced his words. "And why do I think that sounds too good to be true?"

Time for frank honesty. "Because it almost is. For anyone else, it's just an investment opportunity. Only for someone in your position does the environmental aspect of it kick in."

He regarded her another long moment and gave a dismissive shake of his head. "You've wasted your time."

She lifted one shoulder, let it fall. "Not really. I'm here to arrange my own reception—I just wanted to speak to you first. I hope you'll tell the Braddocks that I did follow through on their generosity. They were so pleased to think they'd helped, especially with your recently announced candidacy for the Senate." She stood, making it an impulsive gesture, and watched the weight of her words sink in.

Longsford said, "Wait," and then just looked at her, a hard assessment.

"I know your time is valuable," she said, and stepped into the opening he'd left. "Please, let me take you to lunch. I have a complete package of information, including financial details. Bring your accountant—bring whomever you'd like. If you're still not interested, then I'll move ahead with the reception."

He didn't respond right away, visibly weighing the decision. One last nudge… She smiled at him. "Your choice of restaurant, of course. You call the shots, all the way."

His nod came abruptly. "As long as you understand that."

"It would never work any other way," she assured him. "I'm a facilitator, not a manager."

He withdrew a business card from his inside jacket pocket and handed it over to her. "Call my secretary."

Crap. It would have been much better if she'd been able to pin him down on a day and time—

"I'd love to make sure you have first crack at this," she said, even as she took the card. "I'm seeing my printer—you know Houghlin's?—tomorrow at eleven to make final arrangements for the reception materials. I'd be happy to hold off my approval on the print job until after lunch."

Longsford's frown gave her a glimpse of the man he could be. The man who was capable of snatching young boys from their families and locking them away for his own use…then killing them when he was through. She hid her shiver, wishing her shawl was still draped over her shoulders. She met his eyes, pretended she couldn't see behind them and smiled.

"Please," she said. "Whatever restaurant is most convenient for you."

He eyed her in an almost proprietary way, as though he expected to acquire her right along with the property. "Call in the morning for place and time," he said. "Now. I have my own guests to attend to. Please feel free to make a contribution to the cause. And Maia—" He waited for her to meet his gaze, her expression attentive, before adding, "If you drop something, do let someone else pick it up."

It sounded like a warning.

Karin put a modest donation to Keep It Green on a credit card and ate enough of the gourmet finger food to satisfy her stomach for the rest of the day. She exchanged dignified and appropriate conversation with the other guests and didn't overstay her welcome.

It was as she was climbing into the car that her thoughts returned to her encounter with Dave. Her wary, suspicious mind had had time to mull it over—to realize the significance of their encounter. Of just how hard he'd held her arms.

And she thought of the first time he'd held her that tightly, and what he'd really been doing.

"Miss?" Bill paused with his hand on the door.

She smiled at him. "Sorry. It was an interesting event…it left me with a lot to think about."

"It's not many find themselves invited here," he agreed, and gently pushed the door closed.

By the time he settled into the front seat, Karin had found the bug. *Son of a—*

No, don't jump to conclusions. Just because he'd put another of those bugs on her—and damned clever about it, too—didn't mean he intended to track her down and reel her in. Maybe he'd just wanted to keep his hand in the game.

But she couldn't be sure.

She leaned forward as Bill put the car in gear. He glanced at her in the rearview mirror. "Ma'am?"

"I find myself in need of a nightcap, but not company. And I have a particular fondness for single-malt whiskey."

"There's no place in this city I don't know," he told her, and grinned. "We'll get you that nightcap, miss."

Karin smiled her thanks and leaned back into the luxurious seat, content to pass the time by peeling the tracker patch off the back of her arm, gentle with it as she placed it inside her powder compact. When Bill pulled the car to the curb outside one of the charming little stores near the waterfront—Thomas P.'s, it said, with a window display of lovingly arranged bottles on half casks and velvet—she had the compact palmed and ready to go. It was a simple matter to drop her purse and, upon recovering it, to hide the compact behind the planter along the storefront. *Thank goodness for old ploys.* And for a community determined to decorate itself with flowering plants.

Maybe Dave would find it. Maybe he wouldn't. But he certainly wasn't going to find *her.*

God, she's good.

Dave sat in the Maxima outside the recently closed liquor store and couldn't help the little tingle of admiration, not even as it warred with annoyance. That would teach him to assume anything about Karin Sommers. When the tracker had stopped moving, he'd been certain he'd pinned down her hotel, that from here on out he'd be able to keep a decent surveillance on her.

But no, she'd found the little bug. Found it and stashed it.

That she'd led him to the area's best fine-liquor store while she was at it…

Okay, that was the part that made him smile.

Made him remember, too, their scotch tasting—his surprise that she knew the formal details, his response to the sensual nature of her delight in the taste of it.

Maybe she'd meant to evoke those memories…maybe not. No assumptions either way.

And he had no idea where she'd take the scam from here. He was within yards of the bug, but couldn't find it without engaging in some decidedly suspicious activity outside a liquor store in one of the better parts of town.

He'd given her his number. He'd have to hope she used it.

And that was the part that annoyed him.

Or maybe it just frightened him.

He thought about it another moment. Karin on her own against Longsford plying a scam was one thing, but this time the scam was only the means to an end. She was two layers undercover, and she was up against a high-profile player who'd been preying on little boys for years—and a man who killed children wouldn't stop at killing a woman. Not even the most clever, determined woman with whom Dave had ever butted heads.

Yeah. It definitely frightened him.

Regardless of what she'd told Longsford, Karin had no appointment with the printer the next morning. She called Longsford's secretary and set up lunch, and then spent her time at the Kate Waller Barrett Branch Library, saving photos off the Ranchwood Web site and pulling the information together in a rough flyer that included the number for the Florida cell phone Dave had sent to Kimmer Reed.

And then she found herself a park bench out in an overcast, rain-spitting day and called the Florida number herself.

The woman who answered the phone was breathless, enough so Karin paused a moment before asking to speak to Kimmer Reed. And then, before the woman could tell her it was a wrong number, Karin quickly added, "This is Karin, Dave's friend. I've got some background info you'll need to hold your cover."

Kimmer's breathing was already settling down. She said, "Don't mind me, I was on the treadmill. Why did you call the dedicated phone?"

Karin winced. This one was on top of things, all right. She decided then and there that the only way to go was the truth; gut instinct honed by a lifetime of practice told her she couldn't play this woman. "I don't have your number," she said. "Dave and I are still working separately. He probably mentioned that."

"Not in detail. I know he's worried sick about you. From the sounds of it, I understand why."

If he didn't want it this way, he shouldn't have made it impossible to trust him.

Totally ironic, considering he was the honor-bound rescuer and she was the one who so comfortably hovered around the line between wrong and right and, by his definition, probably crossed it on a regular basis.

But Kimmer was waiting, and Karin said, "I know what I'm doing."

Only the faintest of hesitations, and Kimmer said, "Yes, I see that you do." Before Karin could make sense of that, Kimmer added, "Okay, I've got something to scribble with."

"You're representing Ranchwood Acres," Karin told her. "You've got three hundred acres of prime land southeast of Okeechobee, and you want a million dollars for it. That's well under the going rate for one-acre parcels. You're willing to do private financing with a thirty percent down payment— and if you can sneak in a snide remark about keeping it out of the hands of the Florida Conservation Coalition, that would be perfect. The land has limited access due to the whole swamp thing, but play that up as a plus—it's exclusive, private property. You acquired it with the idea of selling it off into ranch-size estates, but one of your other projects in development has run into a cash-flow problem and when I said I'd hunt up an investment buyer for a piece of the pie, you went for it. A note of desperation—but like you're trying to hide it—would be good there."

"I can do that," Kimmer said, so matter-of-factly that Karin immediately believed her. Unlike Dave, here was someone who could spin a convincing story.

Good. Karin found herself relaxing. "If he pushes beyond that, I think you should contrive for an interruption of your choice. I'm going to try to nudge him into calling during our lunch meeting today, so I should be there to pick up wherever you leave off."

"I can do that, too," Kimmer agreed. "You have timing on this lunch?"

"One o'clock." Karin checked her watch, alas, not a Tiffany's. "Will that work for you?"

"My flight's not till later in the day," Kimmer said. "We should be good."

Flight?

"But what if—"

"Once I'm back on the ground, I'm fair game. Multitasking is no biggie." Kimmer's shrug all but came through on the line. "Listen, don't worry about it. It'll work. And I owe this one to Dave. He really came through for me last year."

Great. Mr. Rescue, coming through for everyone but himself. Because in the end, he was the one who'd made this harder. But Karin cleared her throat, expressed her thanks, left her cell number with Kimmer and hung up to head back to the hotel to put on her Maia Brenner suit.

Once she'd gotten back to the hotel room she decided to check in with Amy Lynn, but no one picked up. Not unusual. But given their last conversation…

She dialed her own number and punched in the answering-machine code, then hit the option for new messages only.

Gregg Rumsey's voice blasted out at her loud and clear; she had to fight to keep from pulling the phone away from her face in pure revulsion. "Dammit to hell, Ellen, you'd better fucking call me before this day is out! I know those busy-bodies came here by way of Barret Longsford, and they're in the way of my work. You find a way to call them off, or I'm heading east my own damn self to take care of things. This isn't the way things work in this family!"

Sure they do, stepdaddy dearest. He just wasn't used to being on the receiving end of the inconvenience.

"Call me!" he barked, and slammed the phone down.

Karin did the same, flinging the cell phone into the bed pillows hard enough that it bounced high and came to a spinning halt in the middle of the bed. "Stay out of it!" she snarled at him.

For she had no answers that would satisfy him, and he was the only person in her life who had a chance of fingering her for Karin even over the phone. He'd wait not even a moment before calling the police to let them know she was still alive and ripe for their attention to the warrant. He wasn't a man to forgive a grudge; he hadn't even made contact with "Ellen" at Karin's apparent death.

And still…it had to be done.

In spite of what she'd recently told Amy Lynn, Karin knew well enough that Rumsey wouldn't hesitate to show up on Ellen's doorstep. Then he would scam Amy Lynn—honest, gullible Amy Lynn—into offering up all the information he needed, things she'd think insignificant. Enough to let him know that something wasn't quite right with Ellen. That his phone call verifying his dead daughter's identity after the crash hadn't quite been enough.

She couldn't have that. Not now, not ever.

And that meant pulling off the biggest scam of her life. *For* her life. Calling Gregg Rumsey and convincing him she was Ellen.

Too damned bad she had such a distinctive voice. Nothing like Ellen's.

Saint Gelasinus, let this be the best acting I've ever done….

She didn't have to look up his cell number. She'd had it memorized since he got it, burned into her brain and not likely ever to go away. She took a deep breath, putting herself into an Ellen frame of mind. Those final days in the car…it was all she had to go on. In truth, it was enough. Rumsey didn't know just who Ellen was; they hadn't spoken in years. He just had to believe she wasn't Karin.

She punched in the number and scowled at her shaking finger. *Get over it!*

"Rumsey!" He answered short and sharp, and she knew

she'd interrupted the middle of some early-morning wheeling-dealing. Probably something to do with stolen goods; he never showed that sharp side of himself to his marks.

She made herself hesitate. And then she offered, "It's Ellen."

"Ellen! What the hell are you doing, sending trouble my way? You weren't worth shit in the family business, but you damn sure ought to know better than that."

Hello to you, too, Rumsey. "I'm sorry," she said, and kept her voice soft. If he could hear her tension, maybe he'd interpret it as anxiety. "It's a misunderstanding. I just called because…I wanted you to know. I'm taking care of it, really." She couldn't remember using more restraint, keeping the crack of assertiveness from her normally husky tones. *Back off, Rumsey. I'm dealing with it.*

"You damned well better be dealing with it. If I have to come straighten things out…"

More restraint, letting him trail off unchallenged instead of interrupting his last word. "Please," she said, and made her voice worried like Ellen's had so often been. *Work it all the way through…he'll hear a scowl in an instant.* "You know I don't want that. Please don't go to that trouble."

"What's this asshole got on you, anyway?"

"On me?" She pretended confusion, even as she realized… *he's buying it. He's actually buying it.* Somehow it made her pulse pound even faster. "Nothing. He's just a guy who doesn't want to admit we're not dating any longer. That's all there is to it."

Rumsey's voice turned solicitous. "You want some help? I can deal with this for you. In fact, I like the sound of that. It'd damn sure get him off my turf sooner than if you handle it."

The sly bastard. He wanted nothing more than to get Ellen

under his thumb again and maybe scam Longsford while he was at it, dumping the mess on Ellen's head on his way out. But she made herself pause once more, as if she was considering it. Then she said, "He's loud, Gregg. He doesn't like to be pushed. He's just as likely to switch his attention from me to you."

Magic words, that threat to Rumsey's little world. And words that would ring true. She had no doubt he'd checked into Longsford's background and already knew just the kind of man Longsford was. If he was smart, he'd hear the unspoken possibility—that she would be unable to keep Rumsey's secrets once her stepfather came to Longsford's focused attention.

Solicitousness gone, Rumsey turned brusque again. "Deal with it, then," he said. "Deal with it *now*. Or I'll have to buy myself a plane ticket and deal with it in person, and I don't think things will turn out well for you if that happens."

Karin took a deep breath. She managed to make herself sound tremulous near the end, knowing he'd hear it. "I will," she said, and if her voice was shaky, it was through the effort of holding herself in check. *Keep it together, Karin. You're almost there.* "I promise," she told him, and shifted to a pleading note. "Taking care of this is the most important thing in my life right now. I can do it. Okay?"

Swallow it...swallow it...

"You'd better," he said, and hung up.

Karin scowled at the phone again. A good, hard scowl, one that made her face hurt. A sudden tremble made her sit down, and in the next moment she pondered a dash to the bathroom, not even sure she could make it in time to suit her roiling stomach. She wanted to bail out here and now. If Rumsey truly became involved, she'd not only lose the chance at Longsford and her own second start—third start, this time—she'd likely lose her freedom altogether.

But the reasons she was doing this…they all still mattered.

So she kicked a pillow around the room, uttered an explosive curse at it, and turned away to prepare for the day. Right now that meant getting ready for lunch at the Med Grille, Longsford's restaurant of choice.

Karin threw on the jacket-and-slacks outfit. Because she wanted Longsford to see that she had her mind on practical matters, she made no effort to dress up her cast.

She made it to the flower shop as Bill arrived with the classy Caddy, but when she opened the door she found herself near to gaping at the large wicker basket on the seat. A spray of fuchsia orchids leaned over the end, and flawless pears and apples were tucked in among chocolate-covered nuts, assorted cheeses—and a familiar-looking flask.

She guessed that Dave had found the tracker.

"I wish I could take credit, miss, but this fellow came into the office this morning and—"

"That's fine," Karin murmured, reaching for the note taped to the back of the flask. "I know who sent them."

As Bill closed the door behind her, she unfolded the note to find a few words in Dave's slanted, spiky script. *If you need me…* She leaned back in the seat with a sigh, not sure what the warm spot in her chest was all about. *If you need me…*

He had to know she'd ditched his bug, whether or not he'd actually recovered it. And if he'd tracked her down enough to get this basket in place…

She checked the basket over for one of the little tracers. Finding nothing, she looked out the back window, hunting for any sight of his distinctive sedan. That she saw nothing gave her little comfort. If he'd tracked down the limo service from their encounter the previous afternoon, he could easily have followed the Caddy from a safe distance and Bill, the dear man, wouldn't have had a clue.

She resigned herself to the possibility. As long as he didn't interfere. As long as he didn't spook Longsford.

Bill knew the Med Grille as well as he knew the rest of the town, and at ten minutes before the hour Karin found herself standing just inside the door, looking around with surprise. She'd expected Longsford to go for something posh and impressive—something on the ostentatious side. She hadn't expected this airy interior with well-spaced tables, their black marble surfaces gleaming. A bar lined the back of the room and old movie posters dotted otherwise stark walls. At this time of day the light was mostly natural, pouring in from huge banks of windows along the south wall. At a table near those windows, a man stood, so strongly backlit that his features were obscured. But Karin already had a bead on the formal manner in which Longsford held himself, and she headed in that direction. It wasn't difficult to thread her way through the tables to reach him, and by the time she sat down she'd been able to assess his company. *Dave's notes pay off....*

The slight man who sat with his back to the window—strong nose, weak chin, losing the battle of the hair—was a man who'd been with Longsford for years. Not his official financial advisor—more like a jester in the king's court. A man Friday who considered meeting Longsford's need his priority, and not necessarily constrained by petty rules, morals or expectations. She got the impression the man probably knew just about everything of Longsford's business over the years…if not anything about his unsavory obsession.

At least, that was what she'd gotten of him from Dave's notes. Scribbled slashes of words, strong with his personality.

Another man stood as she approached, hovering behind Longsford's shoulder. Karin's casual smile of greeting froze for an instant; her stomach felt as if she'd just walked off the edge of a cliff and stood waiting for the solidity beneath her feet to dissolve as she plunged a thousand feet to her death.

It was one of the goons from her very first encounter, before she even knew who Longsford was or what he'd done or that he'd dated her sister. The ex-boxer. The one whose face she'd ripped open only a few days earlier.

It hadn't been nearly long enough for his healing to begin. His eye socket hid behind a plain black patch; his nose and the features on the left side of his face were stitched, distorted and swollen. Even the right side of his face had swollen in sympathy, especially around the eye; she'd be surprised if he had a full field of view. *He's only got one eye,* she told herself. *Probably can't see really well out of it. And you don't look anything like you did.*

Her fingers, lightly grasping the portfolio she'd brought along, subtly crossed one over the other. *Saint Dismas, keep me safe….*

But she was still smiling, and she held out her hand to shake Longsford's even as she looked around the table to include the others in her greeting. "Gentlemen. Nice to be here."

"How'd you hurt your hand?" the ex-boxer said bluntly, drawing surprise from Longsford. He squinted his one eye at her, confirming his visual difficulties. If he wore contacts, he couldn't wear them right now, and there was no way glasses would fit on that swollen face.

Karin breathed a little more easily, and was able to keep her answer light in spite of his rude tone. "It's a long story," she said. "And an embarrassing one. Let's just say it involves some stealth skinny-dipping, a slippery surface and towels that got blown away by the wind."

For an instant, all three men froze. Karin kept her smile inward, knowing that they were visualizing the situation.

But the ex-boxer shook his head, almost defiantly. "I could swear I know her—"

"Yes," Longsford agreed. "She looks like someone we both knew."

"Not much," snorted the man who hadn't bothered to get up. "There is more to any woman than a mere general cast of feature."

The ex-boxer snorted back at him. "Think you got a fancy turn of phrase, don't you?"

Longsford spoke, short and sharp. "That's enough. Diffie, I'll catch up with you later. Let Landry know."

Unhappy but accepting, the ex-boxer nodded, gave Karin another squinty look, and left without further comment. Longsford turned to her. "Please sit," he said. "I'm sorry for the delay."

"I'm Carl Rucsher," the smaller man said as Karin sat, fending for her own chair. Their server had been hovering invisibly in the background, but now correctly assessed the situation as ripe for intrusion. She brought out a pitcher of ice water and left behind a basket of butter herb bread sticks, murmuring about returning shortly to take their orders.

"Carl is my long-term financial advisor," Longsford told

Karin as she picked up a menu. "Sometimes I think he knows more than I do about my business."

Oh, I doubt that. But Karin only smiled. And then, with the menu open but not yet perused, she asked, "Do you gentlemen prefer to separate the dining and the business, or would you prefer that I dive right in?"

Longsford spread his hands in a magnanimous gesture. "Any time you'd like. It is, I believe, your treat."

"Definitely my treat," she told him cheerfully. "Give me a moment with this menu…the food looks too delightful to shortchange my selection."

"It's all good," Longsford said, implying he wouldn't be here if it weren't.

Karin didn't need long. Seasonal greens with Manchego cheese and walnuts, glazed chicken Dijonnaise, and then just maybe that crema cotta for dessert. Mmm. But when the salad came, she made herself eat it in a purposeful way, not lingering over the mix of flavors or the way the strong nutty flavor of the sheep cheese hit her tongue.

Maybe it had come from a Mad Sheep.

And before she was done, she started talking. She told them of the real-estate situation—of their need to sell it fast and sell it all. She told them the area was zoned for several-acre parcels, and how much he could expect to get for each. She told them about the political spin, and the opportunity to make his money back while still acquiring feel-good vibes for his support of the environment.

And then she told him of that extra satisfaction—that the development company for Ranchwood Acres had long ago declared their philosophical opposition to environmentalist buyers. Their vision was of a manifest destiny for Florida—

a tamed land. No more gators, no more panthers—no more territory for either.

"I've noticed that the environment is important to you," Karin finished, about halfway through her chicken and now surrounded by the fruits of her morning's labor—the photos, the pitches, the developer's vision as stolen from the Web site and massaged to suit Karin. "But I've also noticed that you seem to enjoy letting the smug and self-assured—such as our developers—know they aren't quite as important as they think they are."

Longsford gave her a tight smile over an empty plate that had recently held a pasta dish. "I see."

She shrugged. "It was forward of me to say so. But I did think you might find this deal particularly satisfying."

Until this point, Carl Rucsher had done little more than catch Longsford's eye in a way that Karin interpreted as surreptitious approval. All she knew for sure was that neither of them had cut her short, and they'd both finished their meals and had moved on with coffee. But now Rucsher offered, "With an investment like this, you could dump that old factory on North West."

Longsford frowned, lifting his chin in a defiant gesture that Karin hadn't expected. When did this man need to feel defiant? "It's not in my name, so it has no effect on my public image. But it will when that area revitalizes and I'm one of the first to support it."

"It's been years," Rucsher observed. Karin took the opportunity to focus on what remained of her meal, turning herself into another fixture of the table as Rucsher continued. "Just because it's by a metro station…it's also stuck in behind that new office complex."

"Speculative investment demands patience." Longsford made a dismissive gesture, tension in his voice. "In any event, it's irrelevant to this discussion."

"I'd be pleased if you would discuss whatever you feel is necessary," Karin said. She eyed her empty plate, visibly pondering dessert, and then made a point to pull her attention back to the men. Even without glancing at her watch, she knew they were pushing the front edge of Kimmer's phone blackout. "Also, you've probably noticed that I've listed a contact for the Ranchwood development company. She's made a point to be available this afternoon, in the event that you'd like to speak directly to a Ranchwood representative."

He raised an eyebrow, favoring her with a pointed expression. "Not concerned we'll dispense with the middleman and you'll lose your cut of the proceeds?"

She laughed. "I'm covered," she said, still smiling. "I've already done enough to earn my cut." She tapped the paper where Kimmer's number was located. "I'm thinking hard about that crema cotta, so take your time."

Rucsher caught Longsford's eye for another meaningful look, one that Karin knew well. One of them, at least, had taken the bait already. "Everything's checked out so far," he reminded Longsford, letting Karin know that they'd investigated her back trail. The print job for sure, possibly the hotel.

"It'll all check out," she said. "And the Ranchwood rep will be disappointed if you don't ask the hard questions. It only means you're serious." She turned in her chair, looking for their server. By the time she'd ordered her dessert and an espresso, Longsford had his phone out. She plucked a piece of crispy flatbread from the bread basket and kept herself busy by applying the lightest possible film of butter before she started to nibble, hiding her anxiety that they'd missed Kimmer. But Longsford tensed slightly only a moment after dialing, taking a breath to start the conversation. *Thank God.*

Longsford glanced at her frequently as he spoke to Kimmer, confirming the details Karin had already told him, asking leading questions and letting Kimmer fill in the blanks to his satisfaction.

And then he did what she'd been hoping for. He said, so casually, "I understand the Florida Conservation Coalition has an interest in this land."

And Kimmer, primed and ready, apparently offered just the right response. For Longsford smiled that tight little smile of his and locked gazes with Rucsher, and Karin felt the thrill of the bait taken. The jazz.

She had him. Oh, there were details to attend to, conversations to have, more questions to answer. But deep down, he'd already made up his mind. And she had him.

Chapter 19

Karin felt as if she were two different people during the remainder of lunch. Part of her ate her white-chocolate custard dessert, chatting pleasantly with her tablemates, confident that the scam was moving forward.

Another part of her sat back and tried to put things into perspective, reminding herself that this scam wasn't about bringing it home. It was about putting Longsford away for the rest of his life, and that meant drawing the process out in a way she would never normally consider.

Except that in the background of it all, her life had still been wrecked. Rumsey teetered on exposing her. And Dave knew she was still alive. Knew her history. The havoc he could wreak if he chose...

She needed to get out of here as quickly as possible, money in hand.

And yet she still needed to linger, to soak up Longsford's habits, find ways to use whatever advantage her resemblance to Ellen gave her. He'd obviously seen the resemblance even if he didn't assign any particular meaning to it, and that meant she was likely to be his type. Physically, at least.

You'd think differently if I weren't all made over as Maia Brenner. If I was still wearing Ellen's clothes. You'd figure out the meaning to it then.

The resentment startled her, resentment that Longsford had failed to recognize a woman who could literally pass for Ellen's twin. That he hadn't paid enough attention to Ellen to see what was before his eyes, even though that failure kept Karin safe. *Yes, resentment.* Because Longsford had used her sister. Never truly respected her, merely acquired and controlled her just enough to establish a public perception of the couple.

And now I'm using you.

But not without conflict.

For Ellen's sake, for Rashawn's and Terry's sakes, Karin had to prolong her time here, exposed to this monster hidden in a politician's clothes, the scam a distant second priority.

But for Karin's sake, she had to close down this con as soon as possible, grab the money and run. Literally. Away from here, maybe out of the country. With Ellen gone and her life on the farm blown, there was nothing keeping her here.

France, maybe. Switzerland.

"Miss Brenner?"

Karin looked down at the tiny espresso cup in her hand and the empty dessert plate before her. She tried to recapture the taste of the custard on her tongue and couldn't. But she smiled at Rucsher and said, "Please. Call me Maia."

"We seem to have lost your attention," Longsford said drily.

"Actually, I was pondering what to do about the reception. I don't have much time to decide whether I should cancel."

Longsford's face turned dark. "That's not terribly subtle."

Karin laughed. "Subtle? I was clear about the situation when I spoke to you yesterday. Anyway, it's my problem. You make whatever decision you think is best for you. Honestly, gentlemen, although I do consider you a very good match for this investment, I'm quite sure I can walk away from that reception with a handful of potential buyers. This is how I make my living and, as it happens, I make a very nice living indeed."

Or she once had. The real question was whether she'd be doing it again—or what she'd be doing at all.

The only thing not in question was the need to stop this man.

Her thoughts caught on the one moment in which Longsford had broken character during lunch, when Rucher had mentioned the building on North West. Only an instant of defensiveness, but significant. Perhaps a weakness she could exploit later.

Yeah. Something to investigate.

Karin licked the last taste from her dessert spoon, watching her mark with a guileless and steady gaze. "Tell you what," she said. "Think about it. Check out what you've learned today, and let's touch base tomorrow. After that, you lose your exclusive, but you're certainly still welcome to bid against the others."

And either way, you're mine.

Karin sweated out some of her conflicting emotions in the hotel gym, working a stair stepper and cooling down on a treadmill. The shower afterward felt blissful, and she emerged from the hotel dressed down, heading to catch a bus to the library. At the library she went to work narrowing down the building question. *North West Street, near the tracks, near an office complex.* The city maps gave her the general area, but not potential buildings. Not until a nearby librarian saw her tapping her fingers on the map, pondering her next move, and drew her over to one of the computers.

There, she showed Karin the new Alexandria parcel viewer online. Karin quickly zoomed in on the street in question, enabling the photographic overlay that painted in satellite photography around the big pale brick blocks of buildings. Navigation was a little tricky, but she was able to survey the buildings along the street in question. She hunted for a confluence of railroad tracks, a stand-alone building, and an office-building complex—and when she spotted it, there was no question that she'd found the correct building. Literally jammed in behind a long, complex conglomeration of offices and the railroad tracks, the small factory sat on a tiny lot of scraggly grasses, and had a hard-to-access parking area tucked in behind it. The whole parcel sat plopped on the north end of North West Street.

When queried, the parcel viewer data bank—so eager to give out detailed information about the ownership, various sales prices, taxable value and exact address—told her merely *no parcels found.* Experimentation with other buildings and even empty lots gave her, at minimum, the current owner and property type. Even if it was *vacant land, commercial.*

But not this one.

Interesting.

She played with the interface a bit, getting an idea of the area. The offices looked like they'd be nice, and the land just beyond that was in development. Not a bad area at all. She thought Longsford had a good point, that the building would become worth more in the near future. So what was the deal with his defensive behavior?

Or maybe Karin had just misinterpreted his reaction. Maybe he'd just been impatient; Rucsher had obviously lobbied to get rid of the building before. She panned north, hunting an alternate approach by car, and stopped short at the sight of what appeared to be a giant white marshmallow squatting on many legs half a mile from the factory. A giant white—

Water tower.

"Cree-*ap*," she breathed. She scrambled in her notes—in *Dave's* notes—and confirmed what memory had told her. Rashawn had been found under a water tower. North Payne Street said the notes, and there it was on the map beside the squatting marshmallow. *N. PAYNE ST.*

She closed the folder, abruptly enough to make the stiff paper slap together. Ignoring the looks she got, she leaned back in her chair and stared blindly at the screen, not seeing the interactive parcel map at all. Seeing Dave's face when he'd heard about Rashawn. Seeing the inexplicable expression on Longsford's face when the factory had come up in conversation.

Seeing what she thought could be the answer.

"Hey," said a guy's voice from behind her, a challenging greeting. "You done with that or what?"

Done with—? Oh. The computer. "Sure," she said. She flushed the browser cache and closed out the window, pulling her things together with her thoughts still fogged by what she'd seen. The young man who'd been hovering behind her plopped himself gracelessly in the chair almost before Karin had completely vacated it, but she didn't offer him so much as the glare he deserved.

Surely it couldn't be that easy. Surely Dave would have figured it out by now—

Except Dave hadn't known about the factory. *No one* had known about the factory. If Karin headed to the courthouse, she had no doubt she'd find the trail that would eventually lead back to Longsford, but until now, no one had known there was any reason even to look.

It might be nothing. It might be absolutely nothing at all.

As Karin passed the front desk on the way out, the librarian smiled at her and asked, "Find what you were looking for?"

Karin didn't think twice. "*Oh,* yeah," she said. Words that had come from that gut instinct of hers. Words that superceded her doubt and told her exactly what she'd be doing the next morning, exactly where she'd be.

Now *this* was being on the jazz.

She should have been exhausted. She should have been asleep as soon as she turned out the light in her hotel room. There was no way she should be staring at the ceiling in the dark, listening to her neighbors play bump-the-headboard and pondering *what next.*

It's not rocket science.

She could tell Dave what she knew and leave it up to him. *I don't know anything. I'm guessing.* Not to mention that she wasn't ready to call him. Not to talk to him, not to leave him a message. Definitely not to bring him into this game of hers.

She could check out the factory herself, and—if she found anything—delay acting on it until she'd finished out the scam. It was a beautiful scam, fully operational and well on the way to closure. Once she had funds, she'd be out of here. On her way to something new.

No downside there. Bad guy gets caught, smart girl gets away clean....

She could check out the factory, and—if she found any-thing—give Dave a heads-up on her way out of Alexandria. Shuffle her remaining funds into an account for another persona and start again on a shoestring. Or—and Karin winced, finally facing the inevitability of it—she'd have to sell Ellen's farm. Start her life again just as she'd always intended, with a new career. Clean.

Too bad there aren't any more aliases left in the goody bag. But she bet pawn-shop Freddie could help with that. For a price.

"Or," she told herself out loud, "wait until you reach the factory and see what you find. Might be a big fat zero. Make your decisions then." *Be ready for anything.* Motto of all good Boy Scouts and con artists alike.

That sounded like a plan. Karin closed her eyes, deter-mined to sleep. It took her somewhat by surprise when she found them open again mere moments later, staring at that same old ceiling.

Because it didn't really matter if she felt like calling Dave. She was a con artist, not a skulk, a thief or an officer of the law. The factory lead had too much potential to mess up…and if there was one thing she did know from her lifetime under Rumsey's guidance, it was not to let pride or ego get in the way of a successful finish. And that meant Door Number One: the phone.

Smothering darkness turned to flashing lights, the back-ground full of grief and wailing, the rural ground uneven beneath his feet. Curiosity foremost, overlaid with a child's naive certainty that everything will turn out all right—

*Nom de Dieu de bordel de merde! The words cut through
the night, unfamiliar and yet shattering his naiveté to inspire
the first shard of trepidation. Endless barking, then, and the
lights and noise and emotions turned to a smear of sensation.
Irresistible, it drew him onward—and suddenly resolved in a
crystal-clear image, a battered face, a shock of curly red hair,
a stench of corruption—*

Dave pulled himself from the dream with a grunt. Only a
grunt, because he'd had so much opportunity to train himself
to deal with it. So many deaths…so many dreams. If only he
hadn't been half asleep by the time his father pulled into the
dump site. If only he hadn't foolishly run toward the solemn
cluster of adults and the excited police dog. If only he hadn't
tripped upon reaching them, sliding forward with momentum
until he met the dead boy face-to-face.

Yeah, right. What if. *Whatever.* He scrubbed his hands over
his face and sat up in bed, surprised when a farsighted glance
at the clock told him it was only a little past midnight. Great.
Could be a long night.

Especially after a day in which the feebs had tracked him
down and told him to go home. No uncertain terms there. And
Dave had told them he was here with a friend and he'd
damned well show her the sights if he wanted to.

He hadn't fooled them.

Then again, he hadn't expected to. But he didn't intend to
be chased away, either. Not with Rashawn's death dogging
him. Not with Karin still out there, a killer hunting a killer.

It occurred to him then that she'd had Gregg Rumsey
hanging over her head for every bit as long as he'd had his
own nightmare.

It wasn't a thought he knew what to do with. It made him

suddenly hurt for her in a way he hadn't done before, empathizing with the child she'd been, understanding how her young life had been changed. And yet she was wanted for killing an elderly couple who had recently emptied their savings accounts. Didn't take a lot of dots to connect that line. If she'd done that…

It didn't matter what had been done to her as a child. What she'd lived with. Who had failed her. She was still responsible for crossing that line.

For killing.

He headed for his laptop on the dresser. His OneNote files about Longsford were displayed in LCD glory. Dead children in a newly extended list, based on Ellen's photos. Dated photos. How had Longsford ever let her take them?

Because he thought he had her under control.

His cell phone rang, echoing in the silent room. He jumped, snarled at himself for being so reactive and flipped it open to discover an unfamiliar number on the caller ID.

No. Not unfamiliar. Recently learned. He thumbed the on button, still torn over who she was and what she'd done. And dammit, still eager to hear her voice. "Karin."

"Tell me you're not tracing this," she said warily.

He gave a short laugh. "The tracker is my only big toy."

This time she was the one to laugh. "It most certainly isn't." A palpable flush of emotion filled the silence between them, and her next words came out chagrined. "I'm sorry. That wasn't… I shouldn't have…"

He couldn't remember hearing her at a loss for words before. "It's okay," he said. "And no, you didn't wake me. What's up?" Because there was no point pretending this was just a casual call.

She said, "I think he's going to go for it. Which is kind of a problem. I really thought I'd have to woo him longer. I think your Kimmer could have been a great con artist—"

"No," he said bluntly. "She couldn't. She's about helping people." *Not ripping them off.* He didn't have to say it out loud.

"The point is," Karin said, her voice gone cool, "that I've got some decisions to make, earlier than I thought I'd have to make them. And I need to know—if I drop out of sight, are you going to let me go?"

He sat heavily on the edge of the rumpled bed. How could she even think—? "Karin," he asked, "why didn't you tell me about the warrant?"

"Oh, *crap.*" And then she didn't speak for a moment, long enough that he almost checked to see if she was still on the line. She said, "How long have you—? No, wait. I know. Since that first night at the safe house. When you got strange over pizza."

"Since that night," he agreed.

"Fine. Now you've had it confirmed that I'm a bad egg, which I'd pretty much told you already. That doesn't answer my question. I've gone out on a limb here. I've set up this scam and I'm already pulling in information. If I get you enough to come down on Longsford and then quit the area, are you going to come after me?" He didn't hear any worry in her voice, no implications that he would actually catch her. Just that he could complicate her life.

The casual nature of her response floored him. "You must be kidding," he said, and couldn't keep the dismay from his voice. "Do you really think I'm the kind of person who can ignore a murder warrant?"

"A murder—!" Her speechless pause didn't last long. "That

giant bag of frog pus! That scum-sucking son of a bitch!" Her voice came from afar, as though she'd moved the phone away from her mouth. Then she said, "No. I don't think you are."

And she hung up.

Dave stared at the cell-phone display, trying to parse all the things that had just happened in that single short phone call. The reappearance of their unmistakable connection…it was still there. But her casual initial response to the warrant, followed by that outburst and then…

He could only call it loss of hope.

He stared at the phone a moment longer, then dialed her number. Whatever she'd been going to tell him, she'd never gotten around to it. Nor, he realized with disgust as the phone flipped over to voice mail, was she likely to do so now. He was still out in the cold…and she was still in the thick of it.

Wait and see was getting old fast.

Murder. What the hell had Rumsey thought he could do? Palm that old couple off on Karin to keep his own prospects free and clear? *As if!*

Except, Karin realized grimly, he'd obviously gotten away with it. And she knew he'd done it well. No doubt there'd been plenty of evidence planted in her apartment, in the almost-empty bank account she hadn't tried to access since her "death," in numerous sly comments and with his fix in the local police department.

She also knew better than to think the police would listen to her if she told them the truth of it.

Ah, crap.

Which was about how she'd slept the night before. Now it was midmorning on North Payne Street and Karin shuffled her sneakered feet, hugging herself within the army surplus field jacket as she cast a wary eye at Longsford's old factory. The one he was so certain no one knew he owned.

She'd already walked up along First Street, the road that ran behind the factory. The water tower squatted just beyond its sharp turn, white and huge and looking like a marshmallow on legs even from this ground vantage point. The grass beneath it appeared damaged; around its perimeter, tire tracks skewed off the road and dug ruts into the soft spring ground. Crime scene tape still marked off one corner of the ground beneath the tower. She didn't have to imagine how the little body had looked. There had been pictures.

How could Longsford be so dumb? The man who'd been evading the authorities for years, dumping a body near his own building? Near the building Karin suspected served as his own private playground? It just didn't make sense.

And that was why she hesitated, hanging at the corner of the Metro maintenance station, fingering the fragile tracker she'd liberated from its hiding place and from her compact. Dave would get the idea if she tagged this building and walked away, but she had no idea if it would be enough. The feebs sure wouldn't get a warrant on her hunch.

But it would point them in the right direction. And by the time Longsford had a chance to snatch someone else, maybe Dave would have dug through the layers to understand the connection between Longsford and the building. He'd be in the position to act.

Or maybe not.

Crap.

Karin tugged at the billed cap she wore—one of Ellen's, with a sheep on the front and the words "Ewe Bet!" captioning it, a faded lilac thing that didn't go with her olive green jacket but did a decent job of fending off the intermittent drizzle. Strands of bright blond hair had escaped the ponytail she'd gathered out the back of the cap.

Look, Sommers. Just get yourself to the building and see what you see.

She really preferred to have a plan. And a fallback plan. All she had now was too many choices.

She took a single step away from the Metro building, crunching on the gravel footing, and then she eased back again. Not that she wasn't still visible, but as long as she stayed low and still, maybe the fellow who had just driven up to the building from the North West Street access wouldn't see her. He didn't bother to park properly; he just pulled off the road and made his own parking space on the small area of winter-bleached grass. "In a hurry?" Karin murmured. For there was a perfectly good if tiny parking area off First Street.

Yup, in a hurry. Only moments afterward, he came back out again. Karin squinted and wished for binoculars, but couldn't recognize the guy as anyone she'd seen around Longsford. "Just go away, then," she told him. "I've got things to do."

He obliged, spinning turf into mud as he reversed out of his parking spot and backed onto the street without even checking to see if it was already occupied. Definitely didn't want to be here.

Then what had brought him here?

Hmm.

Karin put her casual face on and headed for the building. Its dull red-brick color had intensified in the damp weather and her feet were soaked through. If nothing else it was time to get out of the rain. Too bad the doors to the building were locked down tight. The main door of cardboard-covered glass, the double doors of the loading area, the metal door to the side of the loading area…all of them. She saw enough battered old signage to realize this place had once manufactured dry ice. The area around the base of the building was clean, totally devoid of useful pry bars.

Doesn't matter. I never intended to go in. Just to look. She stood on her tiptoes to peek through the glass of the loading area door, shading it with her hand. Couldn't see a thing.

Well, then…things weren't going to be as easy as all that. She'd leave the tracker here to bring Dave this way, and then she'd go back to her scam. She'd invited Longsford to an ice-cream social at Jones Point Park in the late afternoon, an event complete with barbershop singing and a little petting zoo for the kids, and she bet they wouldn't call it off for a little drizzle like this. No big surprise he'd taken her up on the invitation—*petting zoo equals kids.* She hoped to finagle an invitation back to his home, drinks and discussion and a chance to look around.

Karin pondered the door a moment longer, and finally found a spot in the corner of the window where she could gently wedge the tracker into place. It would bring him here eventually. Whenever he bothered to check the tracker.

Hmm. On second thought, she'd have to call him once she was safely away.

After last night, she knew he'd never just let her go. Why should he? He thought she was a murderer. The best thing she could do for herself was to stay out of his sight and out of his range, and to beat feet out of this city the moment she was of no more use to him. Because that was all he was doing now… using her, just as Rumsey had done. He'd known about the warrant since before their encounter on the sidewalk, and he could have grabbed her there. But he hadn't, because he wanted her to bring him Longsford. To do what he hadn't been able to do.

She wondered how that fit into his little honor system.

Time to go. This place was neat, clean and impenetrable. Not a clue to be found.

From inside the building came a faint cry.

Karin froze. She tried to convince herself it had been a cat. She tried to convince herself that she hadn't heard it at all.

It turned out that this con girl wasn't so good at lying to herself.

She stood on her tiptoes and cupped her hands around her mouth to yell through the window. "Hello? Anyone in there?" And she instantly felt foolish, so she added, "Landshark!" just so she could feel like a smart-ass instead.

She didn't feel so smart when the cry repeated itself in a string of hysterically shrieked words. High-pitched words. A child's distant voice.

What the hell—? If any kids had gone missing, surely Dave would have known it? And how could Longsford have been so bold as to snatch another—to *keep* another—right here, a mile from the recent dump site?

Just as quickly as she asked herself, she knew the answer. His last little power-play game, his orchestrated scenario to exert complete control, had gone badly wrong. Now he was desperately trying to make his world right again.

No wonder he's been wound so tight.

She forced herself to step back and breathe deep, taken by surprise at her suddenly racing heart.

She thought she'd been jaded. She thought she'd faced so

many high-risk moments that they could no longer get the best of her.

She'd been wrong.

Don't be an idiot. Don't try to do this alone.

She pulled out her cell phone and dialed Dave's number. She had to do it twice, thanks to her shaking hands and the cast. She didn't worry about what she might say; the need to help this latest victim superceded whatever stood between them. The words gathered at the tip of her tongue, ready to burst out—*I found Longsford's playground there's a boy here I need help!*

She couldn't believe it when the ring rolled over to his voice mail. She pulled the phone away from her ear, glared at it and hung up with an angry stab at the off button.

Another deep breath. Okay, that was stupid. She'd leave a message. She dialed again and this time the words burst from her mouth as soon as he said, "This is Dave Hunter. Talk now." She added a hasty warning that she was turning her phone off so it wouldn't ring at the wrong moment and suggested he follow his tracker if he couldn't find exactly where she was.

Then she tucked the phone away and considered the situation, her fists jammed into her jacket pockets and the gun there suddenly feeling a lot more necessary than she'd ever expected. No more scam, no more games, no meeting Longsford in the park. Just an abandoned building and a terrified kid.

The place was locked up tighter than a fortress and B and E had never been her thing. She gazed at the window. Double-paned glass, but just glass. But she'd barely fit through the thing, supposing she could even climb high enough to do it.

She closed her eyes, all-too-easily imagining she could still hear the boy's cries for help. The helplessness of it triggered a swell of resentment…and of rebellion. She *would* climb high enough. And she would fit through the damn window, too.

Her hand tightened around Dave's Ruger, then released. She couldn't see through the window well enough to risk shooting through it—there was no telling exactly where the kid was located. Not to mention that the noise might get someone's attention. The *wrong* someone.

She remembered the parking lot on the other side of the building, full of chunky-edged asphalt. Keeping an eye out for unwanted visitors—with a kid here, who knew when Longsford or one of his minions might appear—she sprinted around the building to prowl the edges of the lot. She spotted a fist-size chunk of asphalt and pried it loose. "I'm coming, I'm coming," she muttered under her breath as she ran back to the door. With another quick glance to assure herself she was still alone, she smashed the man-made rock against the window, ducking away from the shards that fell outward.

Yeah, she was gonna be in big trouble if this was a cat after all.

But with the noise of breaking glass the cries renewed, and there was no mistaking that frantic if muffled howling for anything but a human child. Karin pulled her sleeve over her hand for protection as she scraped the asphalt chunk along the window frame, crushing the glass she couldn't knock out. If she got the kid loose she'd have to send him right back out through this window, and she didn't want him sliced and diced on the way.

Finally, swiping away glass dust with her protected hand and blowing off what she could, she tossed the asphalt inside the building. No telling how many doors she'd have to go through on her way to finding the kid.

For a moment, then, she stepped back to consider the window. *Leap, grab, shove*…she'd have to wiggle her way through and hope she had the momentum to do it.

She pictured it in her head, decided she was crazy, and reminded herself that she'd climbed a wall of kudzu not so long ago. Also not one of those things she had pictured herself able to do.

A few quick breaths, a glance around to make sure no one would see her ass disappearing through the window, and she went for it. Three steps, a leap, her casted wrist awkward enough to slip and skew her to the side—

She made it as far as her hips, folding over the window frame with half of herself on either side. But a curse and a wiggle and a shove and suddenly she was falling onto a short set of wooden steps. Karin tucked her shoulder and bumped down to the cement floor. The dingy old foot mat did nothing to soften her landing. She flopped over to her back and stared up through the dim interior to the high ceiling. "Aw, crap."

But she had no sense of any real injury, so she checked the door—yup, it needed a key on this side, too—and crawled to her feet to take her first good look around, scooping up her rock along the way. Lots of old pallets and a roller spool conveyer led back to the freezer units.

Surely not. Surely they wouldn't put a kid into such a dark, airless place. Not for any length of time.

But it was the first thing she checked anyway. She found the doors not even latched, the interior emitting permanent mustiness. Strike one, and glad of it.

She veered to the right and found an office. The customer

counter window had been boarded shut, and when she nudged the unlocked door open she found a surprising sight.

A child's bedroom. A *boy's* bedroom, all bold colors and little-boy images—race-car posters on the wall, a plastic toy box at the end of the bed. Longsford's little playroom.

But of course the boy wasn't here. A child left unsupervised might do something to mar this perfect little cubicle of *the way things were.* "I've got news for you," she muttered to Longsford, wherever he was. "Not even Beaver's room was this perfect."

She left the room as it was, knowing she had to do this as quickly as possible. "Where are you?" she called, aiming it at the high ceiling for lack of even a best guess.

The muffled cries of reply were no help. They echoed inside the building, leaving her as disoriented as she'd started. Somewhere back beyond the freezer units. She broke into a run, rounding the end of the giant freezer, and found herself confronted with a lineup of exotic machinery. Rows of it, painted a worn but cheery shade of blue. And beyond that, steel devices with tall aluminum columns, steel boxes with ominous silhouettes…

With a blink, it all came together. Dry-ice presses for the fifty-pound blocks, pelletizers, CO_2 gas recovery and recycling units.

"*¡Ayúdeme! ¡Ayúdeme!*" The voice was high and thin and much closer now.

And speaking Spanish.

Was that how Longsford had evaded the news of another kidnapping? Chosen a family who didn't speak English?

No, that didn't make sense. The family could have spoken Vulcan and there'd have been a way to handle it.

Unless…

"God, you're evil," Karin told the absent Longsford. "Not even Saint Fillan would deal with your brand of insanity."

Immigrants. Illegal immigrants. Afraid of the law, afraid of even those who would help them save their child. He'd had a child stolen off the streets, replacing his ideal park-snatched victim with one he knew would give him time to linger. *Bastard.*

"*¿Dónde está usted?*" she shouted, calling on marginal Spanish skills that had only ever been enough to get her by on southern California streets.

He responded even before her words died away. "*¡En la jaula!*"

In the…not jail. Cage. *Great.* To a kid locked up, anything could be a cage.

As if he sensed her urgency and frustration, he started screaming wordlessly at her. Or if there were words, she had no chance of deciphering them, even had they been in English. "*¡Calma!*" she shouted. "*¡Calma!*" As if that was going to do any good.

It didn't.

She gave an anxious glance over her shoulder, knowing she was moving ahead only on luck…and not believing in luck at all. If you did manage a little of it, someone like Longsford came along and took it. Or someone like Rumsey.

Or someone like Karin herself.

She threaded her way through the machines, beyond the tall columns and the plastic sheeting that had served as a back wall. There were a few stray carbon dioxide containers, big gray steel cylinders she assumed would be empty. There was a pile of junk under a tarp, and an odd, puzzling area of broken concrete flooring beyond it. And there, in the corner, was a maintenance area behind a steel-mesh cage. *Jaula.* He'd meant just that.

He saw her and flung himself against the mesh, fingers sticking through to reach out to her. She ran to him, forgetting her Spanish. "Hey, hey there. It's okay. It's gonna be okay. I'll get you out of there." He clutched at her through the mesh—skinny, dressed in clothes too big, as adorable as any kid with huge dark eyes and thick black hair could ever be. No visible signs of abuse. *Maybe it was too soon. God, please let it be too soon.* She twined her fingers through his as best she could. "I'm gonna get you out of there. No worries. It's gonna be okay."

He sobbed, his grip on her hands amazingly strong. Not fearful now, unless it was fear that she might give up. Just relieved. Just looking at her with those big dark eyes shining, innocent hope blazed across his features.

Karin's heart started racing again, catching her by surprise. Her throat seemed too big for itself and she suddenly felt strong enough to do anything. *Anything.*

She knew what it was like to be not-rescued. And since Dave's arrival in her life and that one sweet moment of safety on the cliff, she knew what being rescued felt like.

But she hadn't realized what it would feel like to be the one who came to the rescue.

She floundered for a moment. *The kid's not rescued yet, Sommers.* Not with that big fat padlock still hanging from the door. She scrambled for the asphalt rock she'd dropped when she'd rushed to the kid's side, slamming it against the stout padlock. Within a few blows the asphalt crumbled into pieces, leaving Karin with bleeding knuckles and not much else to

show for her efforts. She threw the remnants away and kicked
the door in disgust, if not hard enough to damage any toes.
She might need those toes to finish getting them out of here.

Karin eyed the door hinges, feeling her pockets for any
sign of a tool that might pry them free…racking her brains
for the memory of anything she might have glimpsed on her
way through the building. Her penknife would break at the
first application.

Doubt crept into the boy's expression.

"Hey," Karin said. "I'm Karin. What's your name, kid?"

The boy sniffled. His face was filthy from the standard mix
of kid tears, snot and grime. Karin had the sudden thought that
Longsford would have someone clean him up. He obviously
had a backup crew who knew about his recreational activities. And someone else had probably dumped that body so
carelessly, someone panicked by pressure from the feebs.
Longsford had been doing this for too many years to get such
a simple thing wrong.

It would explain why the ex-boxer and his pal had been so
insistent at their first meeting on Ellen's farm, and so persistent afterward. They hadn't just been sent on a blind errand;
they understood the stakes.

"Atilio," the boy said, prodding her from her thoughts.

"Okay, Atilio. Just hang tight. I'll think of something."

Yeah, like a call to 911. *I was just walking past, Officer,
and I heard someone crying inside. So I broke into the Fortress
of Solitude and I found this kid and oh, by the way, I'm outta
here! And say, can you delay your arrival till I can climb my
way back out of this building and make myself scarce?
Leaving this terrified kid by himself till you get here?*

And yet she'd already used too much time. Even if she had

no reason to believe anyone would arrive so soon after the last guy had been here, she'd just taken too much darned time.

"All right," she said out loud. "I've got one thing to try. If this doesn't work, kiddo, I'll make the call and take my chances." She pushed away from the mesh door and went to check out the CO_2 cylinders. Yep, the gauges all read empty. Just as well. She gave one an experimental heft and discovered it weighed half as much as she did. But she'd been hauling fifty-pound sacks of feed for a year now, and knew how to use leverage to her best advantage. She played with her grip on the awkward thing, knowing she'd have to rest it on her forearm behind the cast and knowing the whole exercise would be useless if she didn't get up enough speed.

Screw breaking the lock. She'd try to warp the door enough so that skinny little kid could wiggle his way out. *"¡Al revés!"* she said, hoping she was telling him to move back away from the door. She gestured wildly at his hesitation and he slowly complied, clearly not quite understanding her intent. She only hoped he'd get the idea once she came charging at him with her modern-day battering ram.

And then, suddenly inspired, she pulled out her cell phone. The photos it took might not be high quality, but they'd do the trick. She snapped several of Atilio huddled in his cage, a few of the equipment to help establish location, and stuffed the phone back into the breast pocket of her field jacket, making the mental note to take pics of the creepy boy's room on the way out.

Atilio said something querulous and Karin muttered, "Hold on, kid," as she bent over the cylinder.

Oh. My. Gawd. Her first effort to lift the thing garnered her nothing more than a grunt. "Okay, Florentius," she said, figuring the patron saint against ruptures was her best bet. "It's you and me…." And with a loud grunt of effort, she got the thing off the ground, staggering back and forth as she tried to find its balance point. Her cast scrabbled against cold gray steel and she shifted the cylinder onto her forearm with no little effort—and then it started to tip forward.

Rather than lose it and start all over again, Karin mustered a warrior's battle cry and staggered into a run. *The brief image of Atilio's startled face, the rush of looming mesh…stunning impact.* She immediately lost her grip on the cylinder and flung herself sideways, out from beneath it. Her head and ears rang and when she hit the floor it wasn't quite where she'd expected it to be.

And then, finally, silence.

She lay facedown on the cold, hard concrete, and when she opened her eyes she discovered just how dirty the floor was. *Gross.* Slowly, she pulled her knees beneath herself and climbed to her feet, patting herself for lumps and bumps. Everything seemed to be in its proper place. "Hey, Florentius! Way to go!" She straightened herself out and checked Atilio's cage.

She barely had time to register that the impact of her improvised self-powered missile had indeed warped the door when he slammed into her, wrapping his arms around her low waist with all the strength of a full-grown bear. "Hey, hey!" she said, delighted; she knelt to hug him in return. "Let's say we get the hell outta here, huh?" She stood, held out her hand to him and wasted no time navigating through the machinery and past the freezer. There she told him to wait and ducked inside Longsford's creepy playroom, snapping a few quick phone pics.

When she emerged, Atilio was gone.

"Hey," she said, trying not to raise her voice too loudly, or let the sudden tight anxiety come through in her voice. "C'mon, kid, where are you?"

He whimpered. She found him crouched behind the roller conveyer, and relief washed through her body in a startling wave of weakness. "Don't do that to me, kid," she told him, but froze as he pointed frantically at the door.

I am so not meant for slinking. She wasn't used to checking doors or keeping an eye out for sly intrusions. She was used to being on the front line, bold as brass and running the show. It hadn't occurred to her to check for movement at the window before emerging from the special little room.

And yeah. There it was. Movement. While she stood out in the open like a deer in the headlights. Too little too late...she dashed for the wall beside the stairs, where the angle was too sharp for anyone to see her through that window.

It occurred to her then that if Longsford's men had arrived, they ought to be fussing about that window. They ought to be putting their keys into the lock and bursting in to take charge instead of rattling around the door in an experimental way. Huh.

She glanced over to catch Atilio's eye and put her finger to her lips. He stared back, deer-in-the-headlights. He did, at least, stay put and stay quiet as she moved closer to the stairs...close enough to catch a muttered French phrase of badness.

She hadn't known she could grin quite so broadly until this moment. She leaned toward the door and said, "Pssst. Hey, little boy. You wanna cheap deal on some watches?"

The door noises stopped. "Karin?"

"You got my phone message?"

"Your what—?" She caught a glimpse of his head as he shook it. "No. I've been keeping an eye on the tracker, just in case you went back for it. I got back into the car at the gym and saw the thing was on the move…I just followed you here. What's going on? How the hell did you get in there?"

He'd kept an eye on the tracker. *Bless you.* "How about we get out of here first? I've got a friend with me. An unwilling young visitor, let's say." She paused long enough for him to work through his favorite phrase all over again, then said, "I came in through that window. I'm sure we can get Atilio out that way, but there are stairs on this side of the door…I'm not so sure I can get up to the window."

"We'll figure it out," he said, his words determined. The voice of a man who truly believed he could make things work if only he tried hard enough. "Did you try kicking it in?"

"I thought a little quiet glass-breaking would draw less attention," she said, not mentioning that she didn't think for a minute she'd get through that sturdy metal door and wasn't so certain he could, either. "But heck, now that you're here—have at it." She turned back to Atilio. "It's okay, kid. He's our amigo."

Atilio probably took in one word of ten from the conversation he'd heard, but her tone and manner did the trick. His frightened features relaxed, and if his eyes didn't shine with hope, they once again showed some spark.

Wham. The impact of foot against door shook the frame, but nothing seemed inclined to break.

"Hit it at the lock," Karin suggested, knowing just how well such suggestions were likely to go over.

"Oh, right. Hit it at the lock," Dave said, breathless. "Hadn't thought of that." *Wham!*

"Hit it *hard*," Karin offered.

"You just think if you make me mad enough, I'll turn into the Hulk and rip it off the hinges." *Wham!*

"You never know." She waited for his response. She only got his grunt of effort, an oddly surprised sound. "C'mon," she said after a moment. "I think it's working. The frame is starting to crack at the—"

At the lock. Which was now turning. As in, someone on the other side was using a key.

She didn't hesitate. She whirled around to the boy. "Atilio! *¡Oculta!*" She stabbed a finger at the freezer, around and beyond, and kept her voice low. Whisper-low. "Use the *manta azul*—that tarp! Go! *¡Vaya, vaya!*"

He scampered away and she didn't dare follow to make sure he fully concealed himself. She reached for the big Ruger, clutching it awkwardly. At least she knew it was a double-action only. A long, steady pull on the trigger would do it. No safeties, no cocking, no nothing. She pressed herself up against the rough cement brick wall. *Be wrong, self. Be oh so very wrong about who's coming through that door....*

She wasn't wrong.

First came one of Longsford's men, his gun out but not pointing in any useful direction unless he intended toe target practice. And Longsford himself. And someone behind him, but by then Karin thought it'd be a good idea to introduce herself. She stepped away from the wall slightly and pointed the gun at them in a two-fisted hold. "How'd you know?"

Longsford and friend stopped short, assessing her stance with the gun, the confidence on her face—and slowly coming to recognize her without her Maia wardrobe, makeup and comportment. And the eyes—light again, like Ellen's. Surprise flickered across his features but quickly faded to cold annoyance. "Exactly who are you?"

"Did you want to guess Ellen? You can sit on that a

moment, until we get ourselves sorted out. My vote is that you all drop your various little guns and back yourselves into that corner on the other side of the stairs. You can hold hands if you're frightened."

Longsford looked back at her with those small, flat eyes and Karin's heart suddenly did triple beat. It could be tricky, playing layered personalities. Longsford was just the man she'd have avoided for a real scam, and this moment was the perfect illustration of why. His expression teetered on the edge of something nasty before he gave her a cold smile from that almost-handsome face with its close-set eyes. He tipped his head at the figures behind him, and they moved forward.

The ex-boxer, Diffie, had Dave's arm slung over his shoulder, a careless support that was nonetheless the only thing still holding him up. Dave's head lolled back, his mouth slack and his eyes rolled out of sight; blood streamed down the side of his neck.

Yet another new feeling roared through Karin's body, rushing through her ears to drown out all other noise. Help-lessness. But not for herself this time. For someone she knew. For someone she—

It wasn't at all the same feeling. And to judge by the watery nature of her knees, not nearly as easy to fake her way through.

Diffie looked at her and grunted in satisfaction, recogniz-ing her. With her hair hidden, her eyes their normal color and her grubby state, she probably didn't look much different than she had at the farm. But the grunt was the closest thing to an I-told-you-so that he'd probably dare.

"This is a fine and interesting tangle," Longsford said. "I think we'll talk about it until I understand what's going on." At his infinitesimal nod, Diffie dropped his burden. Dave tumbled down the steps and sprawled there, jeans and sweat-shirt picking up the dirt that Karin had already disturbed.

She almost went for him. She almost lost her advantage, lowering the gun to rush to his side. But no. *I might be stupid, but I have no intention of being predictable.* So she kept the gun where it was and asked, all in annoyance, "How the hell did you know I was here?"

Longsford nodded at the door. "How stupid do you think I am? This place is wired. You triggered motion detectors as soon as you came through that window."

Karin swore resoundingly. *Of course he protected this place.*

Longsford's eyes narrowed at her reaction. "You look like Ellen," he said, scanning her up and down. "But Ellen couldn't have hidden herself from me as you did. She wouldn't have the nerve to have done any of this."

"She wouldn't," Karin agreed. "Not to mention holding you at gunpoint."

He responded without concern. "My men have guns trained on your friend. I don't get the connection between you yet, but I will." He turned to the man who'd come down the stairs first. "Make sure the boy is secure."

"No!" Karin fine-tuned her aim at the man. "You don't come inside any farther than this. In fact, I think you should all leave. Go away. Run. I'll bet you've got a nice nest egg set up somewhere. Now's the time to take advantage of it. Forget about disappointing Mummy and *run*."

Longsford shook his head in a patronizing gesture. "We're nowhere near that point yet. I can clean up all my problems within a few moments." To the errand boy, he said, "Go."

Karin took aim and pulled the trigger. Or rather, she took aim and she pulled and *pulled* the heavy trigger, and by the time the big gun fired her aim had shifted and the man in her sights was no longer in her sights. He leaped at her, smashing his own gun across the injured wrist.

Karin howled, a sound she'd never heard from the inside out, and her legs crumpled. She curled up around the newly injured wrist with pain roaring through her mind as loudly as the helplessness. But she still had the gun and like an animal she struck out, snarling and leaping up with her finger already on the trigger.

The man met her movement with a dead-center kick to her chest, knocking her flat backward and on top of Dave. Dave grunted at the impact but made no effort to shove her off, no attempt to mutter his smarmy French curse phrases. The gun went flying somewhere; Karin had no idea where. She coughed, hunting air, and by the time she'd gotten to her knees, Longsford had taken over. "Brad, secure the boy. Diffie, stand at the door and keep these two in and everyone else out."

Okay, fine. They weren't going anywhere. Not just this moment. But the game wasn't over yet.

And Karin knew how to play it better than anyone.

First she took the time to do that which she hadn't allowed herself to think about. *Dave, limp and injured and bleeding.* He was scary-still, his breathing uneven and riding the edge of a groan, but even in his motionlessness he still gave the impression that he was trying, trying *hard*, to leap to his feet and save the day. *You would.* Karin rolled him over just enough to check his head. Glass crunched just to the side of her leg— old window glass, some of it now under her shin. She found an ugly wound, split and puffy and pumping a steady stream of blood, and glared up at Longsford. "You didn't have to hit him so hard."

Longsford just shrugged. "I owe this man, after his many attempts to interfere with my life."

"I don't think he gave a damn about *your* life," Karin said. She let Dave settle back into place and as clichéd as it was, put his head on her knees rather than see it rest on the hard, dirty floor. The immediate warmth of his blood soaked her jeans; her fingers, as she withdrew them, gleamed wetly. She wiped them on her jacket and glared up at Longsford. "If you hit him hard enough to kill him, the authorities won't ever leave you alone. His brother Owen won't leave you alone. But you probably don't know about Owen, do you? Runs an international investigative agency? Plays with all the big boys? The feebs might be limited to pursuing you in the States, but Owen will find you wherever you go."

Longsford appeared unimpressed. "I believe we were discussing your identity."

Karin stared down at Dave's golden hair, now smeared with clotty blood. She trailed her fingers down his cheek, and his eyes finally fluttered open. They weren't anywhere near focused, and whatever he'd intended to say came out in an unintelligible grunt. "It's okay," she told him, though she could see he knew it wasn't even close. She told Longsford, "Ellen was my sister. She died a year ago and I've been living in her name. And you can blame yourself for all this. If you hadn't sent your errand boys down to fetch me no matter what, I'd have shrugged off Dave's visit. But instead…" She paused, looked down to find Dave listening, struggling but understanding. He'd hear everything she had to say, as long as he didn't pass out again. She said it anyway. "Instead, you intrigued me, and I came with him."

The slightest of frowns etched Dave's forehead. "Karin—"

"You should have known better," she told him, and leaned over to plant a gentle kiss on unresponsive lips. "You really should have."

Longsford drank it in, a control-freak alert to games of power. "You're Karin," he said. "You're the sister who stayed behind with Daddy Gregg."

"Not anymore. Dave thinks I came with him to help corner you—and in a way I did. But only because I think we can be of benefit to one another." Okay, so it wouldn't hold up under scrutiny. She was only buying time here. A little room to maneuver.

"Karin—" Dave again, and this time he made the effort to get up; she easily kept him down, just a hand on his chest. Still, she felt the tension in his body. Knew that he wanted to roll over, to claw his way to his feet and change everything he saw and heard.

Of course, he'd fall flat on his face if he tried.

Longsford snorted, but only to hide a sudden gleam of fascination, one that made Karin go cold and sick inside. She'd just pushed his buttons…she'd turned herself into an enigma. Into a challenge.

Into something worth controlling.

"Look," she said bluntly. "I came for the boy so I could get your attention. Really get your attention. I've done that, don't you think? And what you need to know now is that we're both killers. You and I."

He laughed outright. "You couldn't even pull the trigger on that gun."

She scowled. "It's not *my* gun." Where was the damned thing, anyway? She spotted it, finally, under the wooden stairs. Well out of her reach. "Lady scammers don't use guns, Longsford. We're better than that. When I killed that old couple, I did it with gas. Uncoupled their gas dryer when they thought I was in the bathroom, left a pretty scented candle burning as a gift. They just got too curious about exactly when their investments would find a return."

"And mine?" Longsford asked, taking the news about the elderly couple in stride. "Would it ever have found a return?"

Karin shrugged. "That's something you might learn if you decide to take me on. It was meant to bring me to your attention, and it did."

"Take you on." Longsford's eyes suddenly looked flat and mean again.

"You put me in charge of your investments and I'll make you more money than you ever dreamed. We've already got each other's fail-safe, don't we? You have your secrets, I have mine. It makes this a no-risk situation."

"There's the money," he pointed out.

She grinned, all cocky confidence and ignoring the buildup of bruises and battering and the throbbing shriek of her wrist. "No risk there. Not if it's in my hands. I don't lose money— I make and take it."

He snorted.

But he was intrigued. She'd seen the quick gleam of interest at the challenge of keeping her close by and under control. The thrill of doing it. The ability to thumb his nose at his mother… and all the while continue his own personal hobby.

Not that Karin had any illusions about the ultimate outcome. He'd play the game for a short while, just as he did with the boys. And when he failed to find that perfect, ultimate control, he'd kill her.

Supposing she gave him the chance.

Longsford nodded. "All right. Maybe we have a thing or two in common after all." He looked up at the guy in the doorway. "All clear?"

"Yes, sir," the errand boy said smartly.

"Fine. Kill Hunter, bring the boy, and we'll go."

"Uh-uh," Karin told him. "He's got nothing. He's not going to remember this, he won't have the boy or any evidence, and the feebs have already told him to take a hike. Just dump him somewhere. He's already lost, Longsford. He's not in your league."

"And you are?" Amusement colored Longsford's tone. His eyes had never looked more closely set.

Karin laughed. "You'll have to find out, won't you?" And she didn't look down. She didn't look to where Dave's dazed expression broke through with hurt and betrayal, those piercing blue eyes still unable to focus but somehow perfectly able to convey his feelings.

He said, "God, Karin. This is what it was about? *This?*"

"You were the one who brought a wrecking ball through my life," she told him, but she turned her face away from Longsford to hide the sudden shimmer of tears in her eyes. "I'm just doing what I have to. Always have, always will."

This was a day in which he already believed she'd killed two old people. And if he believed that, it couldn't be such a leap to believe she'd been using him all along.

All of it.

It wasn't, she whispered silently to him. *Don't you even think it.*

But Dave, concussed and bleeding and shocky, was in no shape to hear it.

She bent over him again, offering up a goodbye kiss. Even

with his stubborn unresponsiveness, she imbued their contact with silent intent—lingering, persistent, adding a gentle touch of her tongue to his bottom lip. *Trust me. Just this once. Trust me utterly.* Until finally—*finally*—he kissed her back. Just a hint of response, still not quite believing her but at least aware something had gone unspoken. She drew back and rested her bloody finger on his lower lip, giving no sign she saw the new clarity in his gaze, not with Longsford's eyes riveted upon the scene she created. "Fun while it lasted."

"Take what you can get," he said, his voice rough. But he was no longer merely a barely conscious body under her hand. Not vibrant, not unhurt…but not a limp rag doll, either. She chanced the very smallest lift of her chin, knowing it would tell him nothing but hoping to confirm the presence of those things unspoken.

Because she had no intention of going anywhere with the subhuman son of a bitch Longsford.

She removed Dave's head from her lap, wincing when he set his mouth against pain. "You'll be okay," she said, as if she could feel so casual about his fate, and she tried to catch his gaze again but found he wasn't focusing any longer.

But Longsford shifted impatiently, and something crashed beyond the freezers as the search for Atilio continued. No more time to send silent messages to a barely conscious man who wasn't even certain of their alliance.

Now it starts. She made a show of wiping her hands free of Dave's blood, and in the process pulled her jacket cuff over her good hand to protect it as she palmed glass onto the heavily cracked cast. Swift, decisive, no lingering. She stood, shook her shoulders out, and joined Longsford with a matter-of-fact demeanor, cocking her head to say *your ball game…now what?*

Interruption, that's what. The errand boy came around the freezer and said with irritation, "There's no sign of him."

Longsford sent Karin a swift glare of impatience…possibly even disappointment. "I thought we were through playing games. Where is he?"

Karin applied a contemplative expression. "We-ell," she said, drawing out the word until she gave a decisive shake of her head. She let him wait a moment longer, and said, "Nope. You can't have him."

His surprise was beauteous. It left him open to her attack, and she held nothing back as she shoved her handful of glass shards and splinters into his face, grinding her cast against his skin and crying out from the pain of her wrist, pushing until her hand skidded up over his eye and brow and then she wasn't the only one bellowing.

Longsford's hands clapped to his face as he whirled away from her, and Karin didn't linger, didn't cradle her wrist to her chest or bend over it to curse her own pain. She dove for the stairs, reaching between the plain wooden steps to snag her gun—*Dave's* gun—already knowing she'd have to choose between Diffie above her in the doorway and the guy at the freezer. Both were armed; neither would hesitate to shoot. Stretching, she fumbled her grip on the pistol, tugged it out by a fingerhold and scrambled for the wall beside the stairs to make herself an awkward target for Diffie. *Damn fool woman. What made you think you could handle a gun?*

Braced against the wall, she flinched at the impact of a bullet into the drywall beside her head. But she took a breath, held the Ruger out and sighted it as though it were a rifle, and reminded herself about that long trigger pull. Something plucked at her sleeve; she ignored that, too. She aimed low and took the shot.

The Ruger discharged with a strange double explosion, and her target flinched. The gun rose with the kickback and the second time she pulled the trigger, the sights rested on the man's breastbone.

The second time she pulled the trigger, the man went down.

She whirled to take aim at the doorway, but only in time for her target to tumble down beside her, yet another body taking a fall on those stairs. A startled glance showed her Dave propped on his side and already sagging, eyes rolling back in his head. She leaped for him, catching him before he could clonk his head on that concrete. "Some guys are so predictable," she told him tenderly, but there was none of it on her face as she looked up at Longsford. She cradled Dave to her with her forearm while holding her gun steady. "Changed my mind, Longsford," she said, her voice loud enough to reach him over the sound of his own unending stream of curses. "Price was too high."

One hand still pressed to his bleeding face, Longsford finally groped for his own gun. Only belatedly did he realize she had him covered, and even then he hesitated, hand still halfway to his weapon.

"Nope. Sorry. You lose," she told him. "And let me tell you…you're just gonna love prison. Total loss of control." The guards would control every tiny little part of his life, and he would control…

Nothing.

Not even himself.

Most especially not himself.

She watched the realization cross his face. She watched as he took the full impact of the press, the courts…all before he even got to prison. He looked at her with his one working eye and he said, just as coldly as ever, "You're wrong. I can control it all."

She'd never seen that look before, but she knew it. Utterly calm, totally defiant…and totally in control. Ready to win by losing.

She knew, even as he snatched for the gun at his side, what he intended. But she couldn't take the chance he wouldn't change his mind—and change his aim. She pulled the trigger on a body shot even as he jammed the barrel of his little semiautomatic against his chin and blew off the top of his head.

The building stayed silent for a long moment, or maybe it was just the ringing of Karin's head, providing silence for her. She lowered the gun, then deliberately set it down on the floor. No one else moved. Longsford, most certainly dead…the two errand boys not likely to survive. Dave, pale and sweaty and his eyelids fluttering as he tried and failed to pull himself out of unconsciousness. Damned hard blow he'd taken, and she needed to get him help. She patted her jacket, hunting the cell phone, and discovered she'd ground a good deal of glass into her hand at the edge of the cast. "Crap," she muttered, but she found the phone and pulled it free. The call to 911 was short and sweet, and she ignored the operator's request that she stay on the line. She folded the phone up and tucked it into Dave's front jeans pocket, hooking a finger into his car keys while she was at it.

By then Atilio had crept out from hiding, and she gestured him over. She hated to leave him…but then, she hated to leave Dave, too.

It wasn't like she could stay. If she hadn't been a killer before, she could quite rightly carry that label now. She sat Atilio beside Dave and folded the kid's small hand over Dave's fingers. *"Ayuda viene,"* she told him. *"Espera."* And then, a little frantic, "Don't tell anyone I was here!"

She bent to kiss Dave again, willing him to remember the imprint of her lips.

And then she ran.

Karin took the Maxima. She hit a drugstore in the Freddie end of the city and picked up tweezers, a magnifying glass, a wrist brace, ibuprofen and first-aid supplies. Back at the hotel she cleaned herself up, popped four ibu, took a wistful sniff of Dave's Cardhu flask and gingerly lowered herself onto the bed to ponder her totally questionable future.

She fell asleep.

When she woke, she drove to the shore in early-evening darkness and pulled out the phone Dave had left in the Maxima. She'd turned it off as soon as she found it, figuring it would be the latest thing…figuring it would have a GPS. Its directory put her straight through to Owen Hunter, who answered the phone with startling directness. "This must be Ellen."

It gave Karin a pretty clear picture of just how much Dave hadn't told his brother. "More or less," she said, tired of games, not ready for explanations. "How's Dave?"

"Why don't you come and see?" Owen's voice had a dark edge to it.

She caught the implications immediately. The invitation to come forward, the threat of it—and the fact that he was here with Dave. "You came," she breathed. "God, is he okay?"

"I've got a lot of questions."

Karin took a deep breath, biting her lip on hasty words. She managed to say evenly, "Dave never mentioned that you were a cruel man."

Owen gave a short laugh. No humor there at all. "Hairline-skull fracture. His CAT scan was normal, but his neuro exam isn't and he sure as hell isn't all there. He'll be hospitalized for a few days at best."

Karin found she wasn't breathing; she struggled with herself. When she finally drew air it was in a hiccup of a gasp, and she moved the phone away from her mouth, tucking it against her neck. *That's not fair. It's not right. He was only ever trying to do his best to save those kids.* She heard Owen's voice only vaguely, but knew he wouldn't wait forever. She held the phone up and said, "I'll call back tomorrow."

And the next day, and the next day. However long it took.

Chapter 20

Owen drove his all-too-sensible rented sedan down the dead-end street to the safe house, letting Dave sit in grateful silence. Owen had finally acknowledged that Dave wouldn't discuss Karin's role in the Longsford case. Not the newly gathered evidence; not the man's death. None of it mattered so much anyway, given the small skeletons recovered from the grave-yard beneath the broken concrete. And the second Ruger at the scene had been wiped clean; as skeptical as the feebs were about Dave's claim to have had two guns, they couldn't prove he hadn't fired the weapon—not at the dead errand boy and not at Longsford.

He'd have to do something about Karin, but it wasn't a decision he wanted to make while he still sometimes saw double and when he still wasn't quite sure where his feet would end up at each step. Walking on land wasn't supposed to feel like navigating heavy seas. "Give it time," the doctors had all said. And meanwhile the world had gone on without him—tying up the legal ends to Longsford's activities, ignorant of Karin's role in the whole thing. Owen said the feebs had interviewed Dave. Evidently he'd said the right things.

"Earth to Dave." Owen's tone was light, but his hard-featured face was worried as he turned to Dave, the keys already out of the ignition and his seat belt released. Owen had gotten the Hunter nose, but little else of his features reflected those of his siblings. If Dave was the sleek potential clothes horse, Owen took up the other end of the spectrum. Fullback material. Always the responsible one, the compass for the Hunter world. Dave tried to remember when his older brother had given him that particular look, that worry.

"I'm here," Dave said. "I'm okay. The doctors said so, remember?"

"Just…" Owen paused, also not a common thing. "Reconsider my suggestion to stay at the home place for a while, okay?"

For once, Dave was able to hear the genuine concern behind one of Owen's *suggestions*. "I will," he said. "I just have a thing or two to get straight in my head first. If you can give me a day or two—"

Owen nodded. "I'll return the rental and we'll drive your car back home."

Dave snorted—carefully, because the dizziness still hit if he did anything too abruptly. "Which of us took that hit on the head? The car's AWOL."

In reply, Owen nodded toward the safe house.

Only then did Dave realize they were parked at the curb of the cul-de-sac. Only then did he realize there was already a car in the driveway. His car.

That someone sat on the porch, waiting.

Karin.

"What the…"

"Let's just say we've been in touch," Owen told him drily, then gave Dave a gentle push, unlatching his seat belt as though he were a child. "Go on. I'll talk to you later."

No more prodding necessary. Dave pushed the car door open and pulled himself out, still careful with uneven surfaces and still nearly overpowered by his light overnight bag. Owen's watchful gaze was nearly a palpable thing; Dave did his best to ignore it. He did his best to grapple with a sudden wash of mixed emotions as Karin waited, motionless on his steps. The one thing he suddenly understood very clearly was the overwhelming nature of his relief. Only then did he realize he had a stupid grin plastered on his face.

"Hey," she said, looking up at him with her chin in her hand. "You greet all your witnesses like this?"

"Only you." Damn, he was breathless already.

She looked little like she had a week ago, vibrant in her Maia persona. Her eyes were bruised and strained. Her newly blond hair was pulled back in a tight ponytail that should have been unflattering but instead drew his eyes right to her wide, unusual mouth, to the strong structure of her face. She kept her wrist cradled in her lap. Somewhere along the way she'd ended up in a flimsy drugstore brace. Her clothes looked familiar, though. Black jeans, newly stained with something that hadn't quite come out. Tight black T-shirt under a field jacket that had definitely seen better days and now bore something that looked suspiciously like a bullet hole.

In response to his inspection, she held out a credit card. "Here," she said. "I suppose Owen could have canceled it any time this last week. I probably owe him for that."

He turned the card over in his fingers. The Hunter credit card. "You took this when you left?"

"Mmm-hmm."

His balance faltered. "Okay. Sitting down now."

She took it as a response to her confession. "I know. I'll go—"

"No," he said, a *you're not getting it* voice. "I mean, I'm sitting down *now.*"

Enlightenment widened her eyes; she jumped to her feet and helped him make a graceful landing. "Owen said you still weren't right. I'm surprised he left you alone." The car, at some point, had disappeared.

Dave grinned. "I don't think he figured he *was* leaving me alone."

She gave him a squint. "I already ran out on you once. And I'm still wanted by the law, and my stepfather's all stirred up. It won't be long before the whole Ellen-Karin thing falls apart. I figure my best bet is to sell the farm as fast as possible and go deep. Unless, of course, you turn me in for the California warrant right now."

Dave hesitated so long that Karin thought maybe he'd already called the California cops. *Dear Ellen: no stupidity goes unpunished, right?*

But when he shook his head there was frustration in the gesture. "I don't have all the details about that day," he said. "But I have this distinct memory of being on a very hard floor with my head turning inside out, and hearing your voice talking about killing two old people, and thinking to myself, *I don't believe it.*"

"You don't?" Her mouth quirked rebelliously, unable to decide between a smile and a quiver of hope.

He shook his head. "No. Not you. I guess for a while I thought it was possible, but you can chalk that up to fear."

She blinked.

He reached over and took her good hand. "Yes. Big brave investigator. Scared of being involved with someone who doesn't live in his black-and-white world. Scared of someone who comes in infinite shades of gray." He took a deep breath. "I should have trusted you. I shouldn't have driven you away like that."

Another blink. Some hidden hurt place inside her filled with warmth.

He sighed. "I've spent my life holding on to what I do—having to be unreproachable just to defend my choice to break from the family business. I couldn't—"

"I get it," she said, and she did. Owen Hunter, so strong, so exacting. She'd felt the force of his personality this past week. She knew what it was like to live under someone's expectations...and what it was like to break away. And he'd been doing it for years.

"You did an amazing thing," he told her, and reached out to her cheek with an unsteady hand, rubbing his thumb across her cheek. "You did what I couldn't. Maybe it's time I learned there's merit to those infinite shades of gray."

Karin shook her head. "There is a line," she said. "Rumsey crossed it. That's why I left."

"Convenient for him, apparently. You made quite the scapegoat." He caught her gaze, watching her with one of those long, silent looks that always made the backs of her knees tingle. "We can fix that, you know."

She almost said, *My knees?* but at the last moment, understood. "Fix what? The warrant? It's already *fixed*. That's how Rumsey took care of things—he's got friends where he needs them. I learned a long time ago that the people who are supposed to come through for you, the people who are supposed to see justice done…don't."

He cleared his throat. Then, when she didn't respond, too lost in bitter thoughts of how futile it would be to buck the warrant, he did it again. More meaningfully. She looked at him in surprise. "I did," he said. "I pulled you off that mountain. I found you in that factory." Then he grimaced, and said, "Okay, maybe I didn't actually do much there after I found you. But I *meant* to."

She couldn't bring herself to speak for a long moment. The big damn fat lump in her throat might have had something to do with it. He waited, looking paler than anyone should, his hair in ultimate chic scruff mode and his thrift-store T-shirt tight enough to emphasize that gorgeous line of his shoulder. She couldn't look him in the eye any longer; she stared at the notch between his collarbones. Finally, she managed, "I've got to do more than fix the warrant. I've got to see Rumsey behind bars for killing those people."

He gave a minute shrug, a silent *and?*

"You really think—"

He put a finger to her lips. "Fixing things is what I do, right?"

She looked down the street. Owen had really gone. In spite of all his suspicion these past days, he'd left his vulnerable brother here in her company. In her care. "Hey," she said suddenly, more than ready for a change of subject. "How about Atilio?"

"Back with his family." Dave relaxed a little, as though the conversation had been a little intense for him, too. "They were recent immigrants, their papers still in transition. Longsford sent some men their way to suggest that under the circumstances, the authorities would take all their children away and reconsider their immigrant status." He snorted, shaking his head in a gingerly fashion. "But Atilio hadn't been at the dry-ice place for long. Longsford never had the chance to—"

"Good," Karin interrupted him. She added more pensively, "I saw the newspapers. That broken concrete...I should have known it meant something. They've found all the boys now?"

"All of them," Dave said, and closed his eyes, tightening his mouth on pain. His head or his heart, she wasn't sure. He opened them with obvious determination. In spite of his paleness, he gently bumped her shoulder with his own. "What's with your wrist?"

She looked down at it. "Longsford's guy smashed my cast. I didn't figure it was safe to go to any of the city hospitals. If you'd—well, if you'd told them—"

"Nothing," he said. "They don't even know you were there. Atilio kept your secret. But *I* know you were there. Among other things, I remember an excellent kiss. I remember screaming, and then this guy in the door was coming for you...." He shook his head, his gaze going vague as he hunted for more. "No, that's as good as it gets."

"You played the hero," she said, and laughed at his frankly skeptical look. "No, seriously. It's what you do, isn't it?"

"It could be what you do, too."

She laughed, loudly enough that he winced. "Sorry," she told him, shifting her aching wrist to a more protected position—a gesture that hid her sudden longing. The rush of being the rescuer had been so much more intense than the jazz of any scam. The rush of doing it with Dave...yow. But she shook her head. "You've forgotten which side of the law I'm on."

"Were on." He said it firmly. "We'll take care of the warrant. And after that, what's the problem? I liked working with you. I want to do it some more. I'm the black-and-white guy, you're the creative gray. We've got it all covered."

"Creative." She wrinkled her nose. "Not a term that's been applied to me before."

"Let's go inside. Talk about it."

"Trying to lure me into your lair?" she asked, but her words were teasing and her hand ached to hold his.

"My butt's cold," he said. "I'm wounded. I want the nice soft couch. I want you on the nice soft couch next to me, telling me that you'll think about it."

"I'll think about thinking about it," she corrected him. "There's a lot about my life to straighten out first." But she stood, and she extended her good hand to help him up. "Come on. Let's go sniff some Cardhu together."

He took her hand, but his lean face with its wide jaw and lurking early smile lines reflected nothing but confusion as she hauled him to his feet. "*Sniff* it? Is this something new we came up with that I don't remember, or—"

She held the screen door open so he could fumble with the key and unlock the front door, and gestured at him. "You, head injury. Me, not drinking without you. That leaves sniffing. I've actually gotten pretty good at it this last week."

"I'm touched. You waited." He opened the door and made it just exactly as far as the couch.

She shrugged, and gave him a wicked grin. "Or maybe I just wasn't sure you hadn't drugged it."

He regarded her with horror. "Drug my *Cardhu?*"

No. Not Dave. Not the Cardhu. Her grin turned genuine, enough so he realized he'd been had. She dropped his overnight bag at the side of the couch. "Hold on," she said. "I'll get the flask. We can sniff a toast."

He still looked bemused when she pulled the flask from her courier bag, uncapping it. "Sniffing requires a silent toast," she told him, sitting down beside him. "Like this." She closed her eyes, dared to hope that Dave was right about clearing her name, and toasted their chances. Then she moved the flask under her nose, breathing deeply of the peaty essence of scotch. When her sinuses reached the stinging point, she opened her eyes and passed the flask over. Dave imitated her thoughtful silence and was purely a natural at the scotch-sniffing.

And when he opened his eyes and caught her gaze, she had no question about his silent toast. About his beliefs…or about his wants.

Good thing the couch was comfortable.

* * * * *

*At Silhouette Bombshell,
you can always expect the unexpected!
Turn the page for an exciting sneak peek
at one of next month's releases,*

NO SAFE PLACE
by Judy Fitzwater

*Just when she thought her life had finally
reached normal, college professor Elizabeth Larocca's
world takes a dangerous turn when her secretive
husband's body turns up…again.*

Available May 2006 wherever Silhouette Books are sold.

"Why are you so certain we're in danger?"

"Things have happened."

"What sort of things?"

I'd never planned to tell Cara any of this. If she'd been younger, I might have gotten away with it, but now she gave me no choice.

"Do you remember when you were five and your father picked you up from kindergarten?"

"Yes. We met you at work and he took us on a surprise vacation to Disney World? Sure. Why?"

"He packed your clothes and he packed mine, and he ordered me into the car. I had no idea where we were going or why. I almost lost my job over it. But I saw the fear in his eyes and I dared not refuse.

"On the way to Florida, your dad told me a man had been

seen talking to you on the playground of your school. He had you by the hand when a teacher saw him. She got you inside the building and called your father as well as the police. But the man was gone by the time they got there."

She paled. "It was probably some random—"

"There was nothing random about it. It was a warning. I was furious with your father."

"But you went to Florida anyway."

"Yes. I went. I had no other options. We were gone two weeks, three days of which you and I were by ourselves. I have no idea where he was."

"He never offered you any further explanation?"

I shook my head. "Only that there'd been a security breach, and he'd taken care of it. He promised it would never happen again, and it didn't. At least not until now. It was after that incident that he started training me."

"Training you? What are you talking about?"

"He made sure I knew how to use a gun, showed me how to canvass a room, plan an escape, secure phony ID."

"Crap, Mom. What the hell was going on?"

"I told you, I don't know. All I know is that it was danger-ous to be with him—and to be away from him. One time he came home with a wound to his calf. You remember. You must have been about nine."

"Sure. He'd been hurt on a hike."

"He'd been shot."

"He told you he'd been shot?"

"No. He said a pick had gone through his leg in an accident on a climb. He'd been treated, but he never went to the doctor for any follow-up visits. When I dressed the wound, I knew he was lying. The entry and exit wounds from a pick would have been neater. This had a small hole on one side and a large tear on the other. I pretended not to notice. If I hadn't helped him, I wasn't sure who would."

Her face was ashen, her pain evident in her eyes. She'd always known how much he loved her, but she'd never known how much he feared for her.

"Cara, we really don't have time for this. Your great-aunt Rachel—"

"Will have to wait. I'm not going."

"I know you don't want to do this—"

"You know I *won't* do it."

Damn. Why did she have to be so much like me? And like her father.

"I don't intend to make the same mistakes that you and Dad did. I have to tell Phillip what's going on. He deserves an explanation."

"You don't have a choice," I insisted.

"You mean like Dad might not have had a choice?"

"Cara…."

She reached for the phone.

"If you make that call, you may be putting Phillip in danger, as well."

That stopped her.

"What are you going to do?" she asked. "If it's not safe for me to be here, it's certainly not safe for you."

"I have a plan."

She nodded. "How long have you had this plan?"

"As long as I've known this day might come."

"It used to include me," she reminded me. "I know you would never have left me with anyone else when I was a child. And I'm not about to let you leave me out now. If we have to do this, we do it together."

"All right then," I agreed. "We leave together."

Cara stood and immediately sat back down. Both of her hands were trembling.

"I think I'm going to be sick." She closed her eyes and swallowed hard.

"You didn't eat, did you?" I asked.

She shook her head. Then she dashed for the bathroom. It was all too much for her system—her father's body turning back up, his colleague James's murder at the airport, no food, no sleep. I could hear her retching through the closed door. After several minutes the toilet flushed and she opened the door. She had to steady herself against the frame. She'd always had a weak stomach.

"I need some time. I can't get into a car like this."

"How long?" I asked.

"A few minutes. Please. Just let me lie down. Then we can go."

She saw me look at my watch. It was already a few minutes after three in the morning. I'd give her half an hour, no more.

"If no one's come for us yet, it's unlikely they'll come tonight," she reasoned.

I didn't like it, but she was probably right. I nodded. If we left soon, surely we'd be fine. I could gather my energy while Cara rested.

I tucked her into her bed, lay down in the dark in my own room and convinced myself we'd be safe for a few more minutes. The dead bolt was on. It was a secure building with a guard station and a fence around it, and my condo was on the fifteenth floor.

The sound of Cara's breathing drifted through the open door. I would have asked her to lie next to me, but she didn't need to know how scared I really was.

My eyes drifted shut, and somehow, despite my best efforts, I fell asleep.

Breath tickled my neck and brought me totally aware, a cold sweat prickling my body. Someone was bending directly over me, checking to see if I was awake, and it wasn't Cara. He had a distinctly masculine scent.

I didn't dare open my eyes. Any movement, even to reach for the gun lying next to me, would be too late. It was probably already too late, but that didn't stop me. My daughter, I prayed, was still asleep in the next room.

In one quick move, I rolled to my back and drew my knees to my chest. I felt my feet connect with something solid as I straightened my legs, shoving with all the force in my body. I heard an *oomph* coincide with a loud thump against the wall, as I grabbed the gun and rolled off the other side of the bed and onto the floor.

INVISIBLE RECRUIT
by Mary Buckham

She'd transitioned from high-society
woman to undercover operative,
but Vaughn Monroe's first
assignment throws her right
back into the jet-set world she
stepped away from. Will she be able
to capture the elusive criminal who
knows a little too much about her...?

**IR-5: Five women,
trained to blend in,
become a powerful
new weapon.**

*Available May 2006
wherever Silhouette
books are sold.*

The Marian priestesses were destroyed long ago, but their daughters live on. The time has come for the heiresses to learn of their legacy, to unite the pieces of a powerful mosaic and bring light to a secret their ancestors died to protect.

The Madonna Key

Follow their quests each month.

Lost Calling by Evelyn Vaughn,
July 2006
Haunted Echoes by Cindy Dees,
August 2006

Dark Revelations by Lorna Tedder,
September 2006

Shadow Lines by Carol Stephenson,
October 2006

Hidden Sanctuary by Sharron McClellan,
November 2006

Veiled Legacy by Jenna Mills,
December 2006

Seventh Key by Evelyn Vaughn,
January 2007

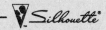

SPECIAL EDITION™

**Bound by fate, a shattered family renews
their ties—and finds a legacy of love.**

Family
BUSINESS

HER
BEST-KEPT
SECRET

by Brenda Harlen

Jenny Anderson had always known
she was adopted. But a fling-turned-serious
with Hanson Media Group attorney
Richard Warren brought her closer than ever
to the truth about her past. In his arms,
would she finally find the love she's
always dreamed of?

Available in May 2006
wherever Silhouette books are sold.

A Boca Babe on a Harley?

Harriet's former life as a Boca Babe—where only
looks, money and a husband count—left her
struggling for freedom. Finally gaining control
of her path, she's leaving that life behind as she
takes off on her Harley. When she drives straight
into a mystery that is connected to her past, will
she be able to stay true to her future?

Dirty Harriet
by Miriam Auerbach

HN40

Available April 2006
TheNextNovel.com